Guardian's Circle: Book 3

Body
and
Soul

J.M. Beal

GOLDEN FLEECE PRESS

Golden Fleece Press
PO Box 1464,
Centreville, VA 20122
www.goldenfleecepress.com

Special discounts are available on quantity purchases by corporations, associations, and others. For details, contact the publisher at the address above.

Epub ISBN 13:   978-1-942195-56-6
Mobi ISBN 13:   978-1-942195-58-0
Print ISBN 13:   978-1-942195-55-9
Pdf ISBN 13:   978-1-942195-57-3

Printed in the United States of America

First Edition

10 9 8 7 6 5 4 3 2 1

DEDICATION

If I didn't know what to say for book two, I'm in real trouble now...

This is the end of our tale (probably. A couple of characters might have an opinion about that, later). It's been a long, bumpy ride and *I* wouldn't be here (never mind the book) without the love and care of some really amazing people.

To Kate and Ashley, who've been my rock in life and in writing. You both keep me going in a million different ways, whether it's reminding me I have skills, or reminding me to stop using punctuation like a German.

To my writing family—all the Refugees past, present, and future. There are no better people to sit around and talk about dinosaur sex and the quixotic nature of the universe with. I love you all.

To all the people who show up in little ways in these books, unnamed. You've made my world brighter and more full and I can't thank you enough.

To my parents, who started this ride but won't finish it, and if I could change that I would.

Spell:

Noun

A ~~fictional~~ collection of words that are used to bring about a magical event.

PROLOGUE

Maysville, Indiana—Fourth Grade.

Jamie sort of hated school. He'd probably hate it all the way, except he did okay enough the teachers didn't bother him about his grades, and Grace was there. Grace hated the part that made her be in the building with all the other kids, which Jamie didn't get but he didn't actually get most things about Grace.

Well, he got the big ones. He was pretty sure if he had to live with her mom and dad he'd be jumpy, too. Mom had that boyfriend last year and he probably owed Grace. He wasn't sure he'd have realized how shitty Mom's new boyfriend was, without being around Grace's parents.

Anyway, he sort of figured Grace was one of those people who're supposed to love school. There were a couple of those in his class. Anna Scott, she was pretty and all the boys really liked her, but she was kind of snobby and liked to prove to all of them she was smarter than they were. He owed Grace for helping him beat her on that spelling test, too. It was fun to see her face. That, and she let him steal a kiss behind the bleachers after that.

Yeah. Grace should be like Anna. All pretty and maybe a little…Aunt Rhoda called it 'proud' when people turned their noses up because they thought they were better than you were. Grace should be proud. And probably moved up into his grade, since he was pretty sure she knew more than the teachers most of the time.

Although that might be part of why she really didn't like school.

That, and the people.

Jamie gets why she's jumpy. Why sometimes he got home and she was sleeping in his tree-house. Why she came over to his house to teach herself how to cook and stuff like that. He didn't so much get why she liked him when she didn't like anybody else.

He had to stop and catch his breath, because he'd started running downtown, about ten blocks ago, and he was still a good solid three blocks from Grace's house and he really, really didn't want to pass out before he got there.

Once he got there he wasn't the only kid around. Every emergency vehicle in town was parked in Grace's yard, and a whole gaggle of kids were whispering about how there was a dead body in the house and they hadn't brought it out yet. Do they think it's the mom or the dad? Everybody knows what they're like, so it'll be one of them.

Jamie recognized old Mrs. Jenkins from next door, and he could tell she didn't know what was going on. She had that look on her face adults got, when they desperately wanted to say everything was okay but they knew it wasn't. Jamie figured she was hoping the ambulance without its lights on was there for an adult.

Jamie hoped that too, which was why he walked right up to the police officer stringing yellow caution tape. Normally he'd be back with the other boys, making up gross stories about dead bodies and all of that. Not this time.

"Kid, get back."

Jamie squared his shoulders and looked the officer dead in the eye. "I'm Grace's friend. I wanna see her."

The cop stopped, looking around him, the same way the fifth-graders at the bus stop looked for an adult sometimes, and cleared his throat. "The girl? You're her friend?"

"Yes." Jamie swallowed. "Grace is okay, right? The guy downtown said it was a woman."

The cop frowned. "Listen, you'll have to wait until we get the body out. I'll ask if you can go in then."

"But Grace is ok?" Jamie pushed.

"She's not hurt." The cop turned, muttering, "not sure that's the same."

Jamie could have pushed about that too, but he got it. He was only ten, and adults never thought kids were listening to them. "I'm gonna sit here on the stairs until you say I can go in," he yelled.

The cop looked at him and huffed, but he left Jamie there. It was only a couple of minutes before the ambulance workers brought the stretcher out. A sheet hung all the way over it, and they weren't in a hurry.

He could tell it was Grace's mom. Her Dad was still out of town until tomorrow, and Grace wasn't that tall. She didn't have boobs either.

The next person to step out was Mr. Willis, watery gaze falling on Jamie. "Jameson Michaels."

Because it's Grace, Jamie keeps himself from taking off for the bushes right then. He doesn't like Willis. Social Workers were all the same. Nancy-do-gooders who thought they knew what was in your best interest, just because your mom worked late and she wasn't around a lot.

"Well. I suppose it's better that someone is here," Willis said softly.

If Willis might let him in to see Grace, Jamie would do what it took to get there. "Mr. Willis, Sir. Is Grace okay?"

"She's…" He stopped. "It is a trying situation. It's probably better if you go home, Jameson. We've contacted Grace's father."

Right. Because that was going to help Grace any. "I'd rather wait and see Grace, Sir."

Willis walked away, shaking his head. Jamie waited and eventually they let him into the house. It smelled funny, and it felt too loud and too quiet all at once, and he didn't really know what to do any better than the adults did.

~*~***~*~

Jamie'd been called out of class before, but it was different this time. He got in trouble, but he wasn't a complete idiot. He knew how to behave around adults, at least enough that they wouldn't get upset with him. Especially when Grace needed him.

"Jameson."

Jamie swallowed. He'd never gotten called out of class by the school counselor before. Another man stood in the hallway, and it took about two seconds for him to remember he was the psychologist they'd assigned to Grace.

Because she hadn't spoken in two weeks.

Five separate adults had explained to Jamie that it was because her mother was dead, and they were doing everything they could to make her better. Which was just stupid. It wasn't like she was a broken doll. Jamie seriously doubted anyone could *make* Grace better. They'd certainly never managed to make her do anything else before.

Also, he had a feeling it was more the spending all night in the house with her mother's dead body—the house that Grace said made noises at night—than the fact her mother was dead.

At least the therapist looked like he was real. Like he'd give Grace a little more time to snap out of this before he tried to take her away.

"We're just concerned, and we'd like to know if she's been speaking with you," the psychiatrist was saying, all soft concerned voice and careful face.

Jamie tried to say Grace was talking to him but apparently he was very, very bad at lying to psychologists.

Jamie didn't care what the guys at school thought, when he raced away, again, just like he had every other day for the last two weeks. He'd been covering for Grace as well as he could. They were running out of time, anyway. She only had about three more days before they were going to insist she go back to school.

He didn't take the time to put his bike down nicely, or knock on the door. Just like every other day he junked it in the yard and raced into the house. Grace's Dad wasn't home this time, which was swell. Jamie wasn't ever sad to miss the bastard, but if the psychologist or the social worker showed up and Grace was home alone that wouldn't make anything better.

The house was creepy now. Since *that*, Grace just laid in her bed most of the time. Stared at the ceiling in the dark room. He knew she still turned the radio on at night, but that was all. She didn't do much during the day. Just like every other day this week, he'd gotten an extra sandwich from lunch—the end of his cooking ability, Grace is the one who actually bothered to learn how to feed herself—and a can of soda.

Sometimes she ate, sometimes she didn't

Jamie opened everything up and sat it next to her on the bedside table, before he flopped on the edge of the bed, dropping his bag on the floor. "School was alright."

Grace blinked, staring at the ceiling.

It wasn't that she was *missing*. He knew she was there. And sometimes if he said something just right he could get a response out of her. She'd almost smile, or she'd blink at him like he'd done something super weird.

But if he did enough of that eventually she rolled over and ignored him.

They just sat there for a few minutes every day, Jamie trying to come up with something surprising enough to actually get through. For the sixth time he thought about calling Aunt Rhoda. He'd told her Grace's mom was dead, and she'd come for the funeral that they hadn't really had.

"The psychiatrist came to see me today. Or psychologist, whatever he is." Jamie stopped, watching to see if she'd answer. "He said he'd come by later. You might not want to be here. He'll have to report it if you're here and your dad isn't."

Still nothing.

"I tried to lie, and say you were talking to me, but he didn't believe me." Jamie glanced at her, still just staring at the ceiling. "You know you can talk to me right? Whatever...I don't care, Grace."

She blinked, but still didn't move, or acknowledge he was there.

"Please?" Jamie's voice cracked, but he ignored that. He didn't like saying please. He wasn't begging for shit. Never said it to anybody other than Grace, and she knew that and... Jamie looked up at her, eyes still locked on the ceiling, and felt something shift. "Fine. You don't want to talk to me, or anybody else you can just..." He stood, grabbing his bag and kicking an empty can out of his way. "You should talk to your best friend, Grace, it's like a rule!"

He turned, and took one step away from the bed when her hand fastened around his wrist.

Jamie froze, head dropping. He hadn't meant to get mad at her. He always felt bad. He knew he wasn't supposed to yell at Grace. If he treated her the same way her parents did she wouldn't want to be around him anymore.

Grace was the only person who liked Jamie because he was Jamie.

He swallowed, about to turn around and let it go. Deal with the fact she wouldn't talk, even to him.

"Don't go," Grace managed, voice cracking in the middle.

Jamie turned, almost afraid to look at her. She looked up at him, half sitting up, eyes wet and large.

"Please don't leave."

Jamie dropped onto his knees, wrapping her tight in a hug, swallowing past the lump in his throat. "You have to talk to me, Grace, it's a rule. A Grace rule. Grace has to talk to Jamie."

"Okay." She nodded, sniffling back her tears and hugging him back just as tight. "Okay."

Aunt Rhoda's—Summer before senior year.

He was seven the year Aunt Rhoda paid a neighbor to put the porch swing in. He was also seven the year Aunt Rhoda showed up two weeks after school was out and packed half his clothes and didn't take no for an answer. Even ten years later Jamie remembers, clearly, listening to his mom and Aunt Rhoda yell at each other. More his mom than Aunt Rhoda. Because it wasn't that Mom would miss him or anything, if he stayed at Rhoda's for the rest of the summer. She just hadn't wanted to admit she couldn't handle him being home from school.

He'd spent two months at Aunt Rhoda's. It'd been uncomfortable for the first week, because he hadn't known Rhoda all that well. She was just Mom's much older sister that only lived like three hours away but they almost never saw her. She sent him cool presents at Christmas, but that didn't make a kid comfortable being in somebody's house.

And then one day she'd taken him to the big state park about half an hour from the house and turned him lose at the river-basin. *I'm not letting you back in this car until you're the sort of muddy a seven-year-old should be* and *the animals stay in the park but if you catch one without hurting it I'll take you for ice-cream when we leave.*

Jamie'd managed three frogs, a small fish, and nearly managed a squirrel before Aunt Rhoda interceded because she was afraid he was going to get rabies.

It was the only summer he stayed for the whole summer, and the only summer he stayed by himself.

He met Grace on the playground that October, and by March he'd talked about her so much, all the times Aunt Rhoda called to check on him, that Rhoda'd insisted on meeting Grace when she came to visit over spring break. She took them to lunch, and Grace was so unnaturally calm even Jamie realized it was weird. Which wasn't much of a stretch. Much as he loved her, Grace was pretty much always weird.

That summer he only spends two weeks at Rhoda's because he didn't want to leave Grace behind and that's conceivably as long as Rhoda can talk Grace's parents into. He'd still probably call that the best summer of his life.

The next year Grace's mother had died and everything had gotten strange, but they'd still done nearly a month at Rhoda's that summer and every summer since.

This was the first summer Jamie'd ever wondered if Grace was going to come. She was sixteen now. Sure, she had a relationship with Aunt Rhoda that had nothing to do with him. Rhoda considered them both family, even if Grace was entirely adopted.

But Grace was angry at him, so he'd sort of thought this would be the year it stopped. It was going to stop soon anyway, because year after next Grace would go to college and make new friends—possibly, he was sure stranger things had happened and he didn't like to think about her being all alone even more than he didn't like to think of her leaving—and they would drift apart and be just like all those other people who talk about the friends they had when they were young they haven't talked to in three years.

Just because he went out and made new friends before she did didn't mean he had anything to feel guilty for. Sure, the guys razzed him about Grace a little and he hadn't said anything about it. But Grace wouldn't have wanted him to anyway. She'd gotten on to him plenty in the past, to stop trying to justify her behavior to other people. And Scott was super nice about letting Jamie borrow his car, which made getting laid a hell of a lot easier.

The thing with the cops was just a mistake, just something that'd happened.

Four months later she could let it go. Any time now.

Grace wasn't giving him the silent treatment, but he was decently sure that was because she couldn't. Rule one. But he was about to make a new rule that said she wasn't allowed to be quietly disapproving, either.

Now wasn't a good time to talk about that though, because Aunt Rhoda didn't know, and he knew damn well *she* wouldn't be quietly disapproving of anything. Aunt Rhoda didn't understand though. They were just having fun, and nobody got hurt. Hell, the electric bill was up to date for the first time in six years.

They'd been at Aunt Rhoda's for two weeks, and they were staying for the whole summer. Grace had a job, three days a week, at the library a couple of blocks away and Jamie was helping the neighbor put shingles on his garage. It was...whatever. This was what everybody else did with their summer, from what he could tell. Normal kids.

He and Grace didn't have much place in that category.

He'd had a girlfriend this year. It hadn't been anything serious, just a bit of fun. She was cute, and as long as he didn't have to listen to her talk for too long they were good. But then she'd gotten all weird and clingy after they had sex, and she'd started saying shit about Grace at school and Jamie'd washed his hands of her. Figured maybe he'd find somebody local while he was at Aunt Rhoda's to mess around with. She couldn't get all strange if he was only around for the summer.

Grace had pointed out there wasn't a time quota on when people could get weird, but he could do whatever he liked.

If he was sleeping with someone else people stopped asking—or at least slowed down with it—if he and Grace were a couple, and why they weren't a couple, and when they were going to start.

She was damn near his sister.

They did spend way too much time together, though.

The screen door opened behind him, and he looked back over his shoulder. Grace had been helping Aunt Rhoda with supper, and Jamie'd gone outside because Aunt Rhoda got strangely territorial when she was cooking and he'd learned to just get out from under foot since he wasn't particularly useful in the kitchen.

"Time for you to escape, too?" He looked back out at the yard, shifting so there was room for her on the step.

Grace clambered down next to him and sighed, wiping a bit of persistent flour off her face. "Something like that."

Jamie laughed, and got it for her. "Smelled good though."

She shrugged.

And then they went quiet. Jamie was used to quiet with Grace, even after she'd started talking again she hadn't had a lot to say. There'd been about two years there where she didn't open her mouth unless she absolutely had to.

But this wasn't quiet because they didn't have anything to say, or quiet because Grace had problems. He was good with those kinds of quiet.

"Whatever it is just..." Jamie huffed. "We've been here for two weeks and you're still holding this against me."

"Holding what against you?" Grace said, voice dry. "I didn't say anything, Jamie."

"Yeah, thanks. Cause that whole silent disapproval thing isn't—"

"I said I wouldn't make your decisions for you, I don't know what else you want me to say," Grace snapped, and rubbed her forehead.

"I told you, we're—"

"Yeah yeah yeah." Grace sighed, fatigued and soft. "Nobody's getting hurt." She looked back over her shoulder. "Aside from how I'm gonna feel when you wind up in jail, do you really want to explain to that to Rhoda?"

"I'm not gonna wind up in jail."

Grace cocked a brow at him. "Is that like the fight club that was 'just for fun,' or the marijuana that was just casual, and can we talk about how much of this shit involves Scott?"

"I don't let Scott say shit about you, you know," Jamie said, clenching his hands into fists. "You just don't get it, this is what normal people do."

Grace looked at him, still and silent for a long moment, before she stood up and walked back in the house.

They finished out the summer, and said goodbye to Aunt Rhoda, and went back to life at home. It was two weeks into the school year when Scott hid his stash of meth in Jamie's bag when he wasn't looking and it was basically just being seventeen and patently not knowing it was there that keeps Jamie out of jail.

He showed up at Grace's door, tail tucked firmly between his legs, and asked about going to college with her. Because Jamie doesn't make good decisions without Grace.

University of Illinois-Urbana Champagne Library—Freshman Year

Grace hummed quietly, elevator music piping into the quiet stacks, one hand wrapped around the side of the ladder as she carefully stacked books back on the high shelves. The low light pooled on the horrible carpeting, metal shelves bright and garish in the background.

Samriel looked around the area, wondering if someone would come trigger the automated lights. Grace didn't have the problem with the dark she'd had, but he knew she still didn't like it. She didn't like having a roommate either. Or sitting through her science classes. The TA from last semester's math class had asked her on a date, but she didn't like him either.

He understood how important college was, in the grand scheme of a human's life, but he'd hoped Grace might *enjoy* it.

She reached up high on the ladder, sliding another book into place, and Samriel tensed. She'd hurt herself on the ladder the previous semester. Fallen off and hurt her elbow. And it wasn't his failure. No one expected Samriel to ensure she was never even mildly injured. He'd been doing something else, Grace someplace quiet and relatively safe. Malek had agreed to keep a mild eye on her, while Samriel was otherwise engaged, but he'd rightfully decided anything that didn't kill her didn't need their involvement.

She came down off the ladder, looking through the books, hair hanging in her face, her humming growing louder for a moment, hefting a large book and leaning down to put it on the low shelf.

He didn't need to be watching her at work. She was safe. She was content. He could have been very nearly *anywhere* else.

The light in the hall clicked on, and he shifted focus quickly.

Jameson loped up the stairs, looking between the stacks until he found her. "I thought you weren't working today?" His voice was low, and it rumbled in the quiet space. Grace had lectured him about keeping a library appropriate tone, frequently.

He'd grown another inch, since Christmas, and his clothes still looked like he was sprouting every time someone stopped looking. He pushed the long hair out of his eyes, and leaned against the shelf next to Grace.

"Because there was all this 'sure, it's fine, I'll help you study for Chem one, Jamie' and I thought that meant you actually helping."

Grace rolled her eyes at him. "Someone called in and they were getting buried. I'm just helping with the shelving. Once I'm done with this cart I'll help you with your Chemistry."

"Because you know I will literally guilt you for the rest of your life, if I don't pass."

She snorted, putting another book on the shelf. "I'm not even a little responsible for your weekend habits."

He stilled for a second, eyes flicking to her.

Samriel clenched his hands, invisible and intangible, just far enough out of phase with them there was no chance anyone could perceive him. Jameson was keeping secrets again. For someone who claimed Grace was the most important person in his universe, Jameson tread lines Samriel didn't appreciate sometimes.

"You did actually remember your book this time, didn't you?" Grace asked, not noticing his strange twitch.

He'd hoped she'd make some new friends in college as well.

Not that Jameson wasn't a better friend than many people would have been. Grace just leaned on him a great deal. Someday he was going to get his own life. A girlfriend who wasn't any more comfortable with his relationship with Grace than the rest of them had been. A job somewhere far away.

"Of course I did." Jameson reached out and tucked her hair behind her ear. "Hey, wanna do Jack's Diner tonight? I have an intense desire for grilled cheese."

She snorted. "Is that what it is?" She gave him a droll look.

"I am wounded, that you think I would ever—"

She laughed softly. "Yeah, alright." She swatted him gently with a book. "Now go find a table so I can finish this, and I'll be there as soon as I'm done."

He snorted, and pushed away from the shelf. "Alright." He stepped away a bit, stopping suddenly. "Seriously, wave an arm at the lights or something. I don't want you to go blind."

Grace made a face at him, and went back shelving books.

Samriel watched her, until she'd finished the cart and started pushing it back to the office. He stood at the edge of the large study room, and waited until she'd slid into a table with Jameson. Until he'd left off flirting with some other woman and paid attention to Grace.

Their heads bent together over a textbook, like so many other times, and Samriel faded away, back to what he should have been doing.

CHAPTER 1

Jamie dumped his plate and fork in the sink, turning the light off. He loved his job, generally. Even liked his students, which was strangely rare in his experience. He was fine with his little off-campus professor housing.

He didn't hate being single enough to rush out and find someone. Whatever Grace said about his standards being too high, he thought they were just fine. As stupidly codependent as he was with Grace, he had every intention of that never happening anywhere else in his life.

So he was fine. Generally.

A little less fine on nights when dinner was baked chicken at nine at night in a dark house.

He could have turned on the lights and the TV and all that, but his day had started somewhere before five, and he had every intention of going to bed *soon*. He grabbed his briefcase from where he'd dumped it on the table, with the mail, and walked it back up by the door. If he didn't do it now he'd be frantically looking for the damn thing in the morning. He snagged the pile of mail, shifting through it quickly before he dumped the bills in their usual pile and chucked the rest. Made sure he'd locked the back door this morning, and turned off the kitchen light.

"Living the life there, Jame," he muttered to the empty room.

And now he was talking to himself.

"I need a dog." Jamie sighed, and hung his jacket up in the closet, making sure he'd pulled his phone out of the pocket. He'd probably wear the professor jacket tomorrow. The one Grace had given him for Christmas that had stupid corduroy patches on the elbows. His freshman students always made cracks about it, but occasionally one of them managed something actually entertaining.

Stranger things had happened.

He closed the closet door, and paused when he heard a scuff on the porch.

They'd had a little trouble with this crop of freshman egging professor housing. So far they'd left him be, but he wasn't holding his breath. He waited for another noise, some tell that he wasn't going to be either calling campus security, or dragging the neighbor's poodle mix back home. Again.

There was another soft scuff, before something thumped hard against the door.

Jamie frowned, stepping toward it. Either someone had just dropped something on his porch and done a runner, or the dog had decided it was moving in. He was two steps from the door, when the knocking started.

It wasn't quiet, polite knocking. "Keep your pants on, I'm—" He hauled the door open, blinking in shock, "right here." His eyes crawled over the form standing on the porch, stopping on the crimson staining all over its side, hidden under a dark jacket. "Samriel."

Strange, pale eyes flickered over him. "Jameson." His jaw twitched. "May I come in?"

"May you...what in the *hell*..."

Samriel started to slide down the door frame, knees going weak, and Jamie reached out and caught him by rote, because the bastard was about to pass out on his porch.

"Have to ask permission, Grace said," Samriel muttered.

He huffed. "Get in here before the neighbors see you bleeding all over the porch." He towed the unresisting form through the door, kicking it shut. "Can't you fix that?"

"Need to sleep," Samriel mumbled, eyes sliding closed. "Just a couple of hours."

Jamie swallowed, settling the long body on his couch, frowning. "Let me call Grace—"

"NO!" Samriel grabbed his arm, almost overbalancing Jamie down on top of him.

Jamie cursed, and caught himself on the back of the couch. "What?"

"Not safe." Samriel swallowed, eyes already starting to slide out of focus. "For Grace. Can't know where I am." His fingers went lax, and he was slipping away again.

"Samriel?"

"Just a couple hours. Don't tell Grace I'm here. She's better off there with Nate and…" he died off then, slipping unconscious.

Jamie looked at his phone, already highlighted on Grace's number. He didn't owe the whatever-he-was a damn thing. Whatever was going on with Samriel wasn't his problem and Grace should know. Grace would want to know.

He sighed, and shoved his phone back in his pocket, going to find his first-aid kit. Because Jamie was a sucker, and whatever he thought of Samriel, he didn't doubt Samriel would do his best to keep Grace safe. Even if that apparently meant crashing at his house while Samriel was on death's door.

He noisily opened the closet door, and then slammed it closed after grabbing his first aid kit. He didn't care if he woke it up. The bastard was bleeding all over his couch, he could deal with Jamie being none too happy to see him. Where did he get off anyway? Just because Jamie was Grace's best friend didn't mean he'd signed on for dealing with Samriel and the stupid other-worldly problems he kept dragging Grace into the middle of.

Jamie stopped in front of the couch, looking down at the pale face and dark lashes.

Fine, that might have been a little unfair. Grace kept insisting it wasn't that 'Sam' was pulling her into anything. According to her the whatever-he-was kept trying to help her, and he genuinely cared about her.

Well, Grace didn't say it like that. The world would end before Grace actually said anyone cared about her, genuine or otherwise. Not unless he'd mentioned it before. Even then normally not.

Jamie grumbled to himself, the entire time he worked the other man out of his jacket, and opened the white dress shirt to expose the giant bloody gash down his side. He winced, and cleaned it as gently and thoroughly as he could. If he'd thought he stood a chance, he'd have made Samriel get up so he could rinse it off.

But he was properly out, and he'd said he needed to sleep. Jamie ignored the huge bruising all over his chest, and checked for other bleeding injuries. There wasn't much else he could do, and he sincerely hoped the bastard wasn't bleeding internally, it probably wouldn't help much to take him to the hospital. Not to mention the questions he'd spend the rest of his *life* trying to answer.

He threw a blanket over the sleeping form and muttered darkly. "I hope you appreciate this, *Sam.*"

Jamie grabbed the other blanket and collapsed in the arm-chair, forcing himself to drop off to sleep.

~*~***~*~

By noon the next day Jamie was about to start climbing the walls. It wasn't that he'd had plans for his Saturday. He hadn't, other than grading and some paperwork Social Services wanted him to file about a case he'd testified on. But it was Saturday, and eventually Grace was going to call, unless something went topsy-turvy in her life—a distinct possibility since Samriel was passed out on his couch in trouble for who knew what.

Jamie wasn't as bad at lying as Grace was. Generally speaking, he was perfectly capable. Even with Grace. He just had to bury the guilt response *really* far down, and ignore it and the attendant ulcers and heart palpitations. And he'd do it, if he had to. He'd done it before, because on any given day there were at least three things going on that it wouldn't help Grace any to know.

He couldn't even say he didn't do it about important things. Pretty much the only time he tried to hide something from Grace it was important: how badly her relationship was going to go, who had gotten their signals crossed and thought they were in love with her, how many times her Dad had gotten in touch with Jamie, trying to find Grace.

Jamie had actually talked to him, much as he'd rather have broken every bone in the bastard's body. Her father had wanted to apologize for the drinking, which was so fucking far from enough they weren't even in the same galaxy. Jamie would tell Grace her Dad was looking for her when he was ready to actually apologize.

No level of alcohol alone made someone *that* horrible.

So he could lie to Grace. Talk about classes and how she was doing and completely and utterly ignore the fact Samriel was on his couch, still steadily oozing blood into his bandages. He'd checked them this morning and they'd looked a hell of a lot better than he'd expected them to, but Samriel was still seriously injured and in trouble. If he lied to Grace and didn't tell her Samriel was there and she got in more trouble...well. He really didn't want to be beating that guilt response down for the rest of his life.

Jamie sighed, and went to get the first-aid supplies. He needed to change the dressings. He hadn't done it that morning because it hadn't been twelve hours yet, and he hadn't wanted to disturb Samriel's rest. But now they were starting to spot through, and that was a good indication he needed to risk waking Samriel up.

He shifted the surprisingly large form around on the couch, and moved the blanket down. He'd left the shirt off last night, because it was basically ruined and he hadn't felt like there was any point to finding a new one yet. He gently peeled the tape back around the bandage, and removed the gauze pad.

Samriel shifted, and Jamie looked up right as his eyes opened, blinking pale-silver instead of their usual blue at him. Samriel shifted, freezing at the sudden pull on his ribs.

"Don't move," Jamie said dryly. "I doubt that feels good."

He swallowed. "It does not." He relaxed—by apparent force of will—and stretched back, holding himself still.

Jamie cleaned the gashes carefully, before pressing a clean bandage to the area and taping it down. Samriel was watching him, still and silent. Which was really freaking uncomfortable, but Jamie ignored him as best he could and finished, patting the wrapping carefully and leaning back. "There."

Samriel blinked at him, swallowing.

"Grace is going to call today—"

"You cannot tell her where I am." Sam gulped, moving tensely. "If you tell her she will come here, and I cannot protect her." He started trying to sit up, muscles tense.

Jamie pushed him back down by the shoulder, huffing. "Goddamn it, stop before you make yourself worse."

He watched, as Samriel started sliding off again, agitated and uneasy, muttering about Grace and keeping her safe. Eventually he stilled, head dropping to the side and muscles relaxing slowly. Jamie stared at him, heart stopping.

He really, really wanted to bitch and throw things, complain about Samriel dropping in on his life and leaving him in a shitty position.

Samriel shifted, and snuffled quietly, dark lashes resting against perfectly toned skin. Bastard was freaking *perfect*. Grace said something about whatever the hell Sam was not looking human, that they made themselves look human. If it was self-defined, just whatever Sam saw himself as, the man had one hell of a tank of self-esteem. Because Jamie knew he was attractive himself, and he'd figured out girls liked him long before he actually found them all that interesting, but he still wouldn't have pictured himself like some ridiculous roman god, all dark hair and perfect cheekbones.

He sighed. Whatever was going on, there was a pretty good chance it wasn't going to be over by Monday morning. He needed to go make sure he could rearrange his schedule next week, even if he was going to stubbornly avoid doing it until he didn't have another choice.

Jamie swallowed, flushing. He should go do that. Now. Because he was starting to feel a little creepy, standing there staring at an unconscious man.

~*~***~*~

"Stop twitching," Jamie ordered, cleaning the nearly completely healed area. In less than forty-eight hours.

"I am—"

"Unless you've got some non-standard joints, there is no way you can do this yourself." Jamie glared at him. "So stop bloody moving and let me finish."

Samriel froze, blinking at him.

"Thank you," Jamie huffed, and finished the bandaging quickly. "There. All finished." Jamie sat back. "Stand up and move around and make sure it stays stuck once you're mobile."

Samriel stood slowly, shifting carefully, nodding. "It will be acceptable until it closes completely tomorrow."

"You're welcome," Jamie muttered, grabbing the used bandages and balling them up in the plastic bag and blowing out a breath.

He studiously ignored Samriel while he cleaned up and put the kit back away. It wasn't just that he didn't like him. Grace had a point, Jamie didn't know him, not the way she did. He didn't really want to, right then. He'd like him to stop pacing around the living room like a stupid, five-o'clock shadow wearing tiger.

Jamie managed to keep his mouth shut for about the time it took him to unload the dishwasher and put the first aid kit away. Samriel was still pacing his living room and staring at the floor like he was trying to make it burst into flames by sheer will.

As it was Samriel, it was probably a legitimate concern.

Jamie liked his carpet, strange desire to not involve the fire department in his life right then aside. He shut the dishwasher with a snap and stood tall, drying his hands. "What part are you having trouble with?"

Samriel glared at him full force, with icy silver-blue eyes and a set jaw. Maybe, if Jamie had been a little less sure about the guy's relationship with Grace, that would have worried him. But he wasn't. He knew no matter how much he annoyed the whatever-he-was, it was never going to degenerate to violence. Probably not even if he threw the first punch.

And, if he were being honest, he'd have had to be a completely different person for the Sam Death Look— patent pending—to faze him. He cocked a brow back, waiting.

"I cannot…move the way I usually do. The instant I try something like that they will find me." Sam turned, staring at the far wall with a dark expression. "Without doing that, I have no way of knowing what the situation at Curt's is."

Jamie walked out of the kitchen, leaning against the stair railing and sighing. "And the problem with asking, like normal people do?"

Samriel turned, huffing at him.

"Not that that's a club I'd put you in, just—"

"The only way to ensure they do not…interfere with Grace is the understanding she does not know where I am." Sam pushed a frustrated hand through his hair. "My contacting her would equally cause a problem with that."

The pacing started again, and despite how badly Jamie wanted to throw something at him, he managed not to. He watched this go for a few more minutes, before he sighed tiredly. "Well, you can't leave them thinking you're dead in a ditch somewhere, or whatever counts for a ditch where you belong, so…"

Sam stopped, looking at the floor, stilling seriously. "I need to know what the actual situation there is. If someone is watching Grace."

"You just said—"

Sam waved him off. "Bazel, or Malek. If someone I *trust* is watching Grace."

Jamie didn't really know who those people were. He'd stopped quizzing Grace for detail answers a while back, if he got them they were usually so ridiculously weird it was hard to handle.

"I could call Nate and lie through my teeth." Jamie bit back a frown. *Why* was he offering to help? He hadn't even thought it, the words had just popped out. He didn't want Grace worrying about Samriel. That was all. Because she would, by now. If he should have checked in with her on Thursday and he still hadn't by Sunday evening she'd be nearly climbing the wall, the way she did that wasn't really climbing the wall and—

"Nate is still at Curt's." Sam looked up at him suddenly, eyes clearing. "Do you have Deacon's number?"

"No." Jamie frowned. He'd met the guy like once, and Grace mentioned him once in a while and she was fond of his girlfriend, from what Jamie could tell.

"555-55—"

"Let me get my phone," Jamie interrupted softly, moving to find it in the kitchen, against the counter. He grabbed his phone and pulled up the dialer. "Okay."

"555-555-3353."

Jamie dialed the number, and listened to the ring tone, wondering how in the hell he was going to talk his way around this one. Clearly he was going to have to do the talking at first, until they were sure of some things.

"Hello?"

He thought he recognized the voice, so at least he probably had the right person. "Hey, Deke." He swallowed. "It's Jamie."

There was a long, slightly dead pause, followed by a dark curse. "You know when Nate said you were a scarily efficient stalker, I sort of thought he was joking."

He winced, not commenting on that.

"Can I do something for you?"

Jamie swallowed, and decided to skirt as close to the truth as he could. "I hope so. I talked to Grace earlier and she's…tense? And also lying to me again, I think. And I could call Nate and pester him to tell me the truth but I think she's pretty likely to notice that I've done that. You're not at Curt's, are you?"

"No." There was a quiet pause. "Willy and I are still at the shop."

"Cool." In for a penny, in for a pound. "What about…um…what's his name. Willy's Dad?"

"Grace told you about that." Deke didn't sound too surprised though. "No. He's at Curt's. Just until…"

When he didn't seem willing to keep going, Jamie let it go. "Alright. What about the other guy? Merric or—"

"Malek."

"That's the one," Jamie said, glancing up at Sam, hanging on their conversation.

"He's…not at the moment. He's a bit busy."

Jamie sighed. "Alright. Thanks man. I'm just trying to gauge how bad things are."

"Sure."

Jamie made a face at Samriel, because now that he was done with his fact-finding mission he didn't have the first freaking clue how to get off the phone. "So…"

Deke cleared his throat. "No problem."

Jamie was about to find his way to a 'goodbye' when he heard another cough.

"Hey Jamie?"

"Yeah?"

"You're not a very good liar, but I'm gonna let that go," Deke said softly. "If you answer one question for me I won't even tell Nate you called."

Jamie swallowed. "What's your question?"

"Are you in trouble?"

That was a million-dollar question. And the honest answer was probably 'yes' at some point. But right now? "No. No, I'm good."

"Right." Deke sighed. "That changes, you've got my number now."

"I do. Thanks. Bye."

"Bye."

Jamie hung the phone up and blew out a breath. "You people are entirely too nice for anybody's good."

Sam frowned at him, shoulders tense and stance off. "What did he say?"

"You didn't hear it?" Jamie cocked his head to the side.

Sam flushed. "I have dialed back as far as I am able, to heal and not leave a trace. I am not human in that I will not age, and normal human injuries will not kill me. My…senses are not as acute as they should be."

"Alright." Jamie swallowed. "Deke says he and Willy are at the shop, and Willy's Dad is hanging out at Curt's until the other guy comes back. Probably from trying to figure out where you've gone."

Sam thought about it for a ridiculously long time though. Jamie was hovering over Grace's contact on his phone by the time he nodded his head. "Yes. I will at least tell Grace I am alive."

Jamie hit the contact, and nearly threw the phone at Samriel. He wasn't touching that with a ten-foot pole. He'd done every 'failed to check-in' conversation with Grace he ever wanted to.

CHAPTER 2

Jamie didn't just sit there and stare at Samriel on the phone. He sort of wanted to. There was something vaguely surreal about Grace chewing out someone other than him. They'd lived in their own little bubble for so many years, he was still adjusting to the concept that there were other people on the planet that were allowed to intrude on her life.

It wasn't a bad thing. He was good with Curt, and the others. And Nate was a fucking miracle, he wasn't about to look that in the face. Pretty much the only person he had a problem with was Samriel, and maybe he was being a stubborn ass, but he was allowed.

"No." Sam shifted, shoulders tight. "Grace, I…" He huffed. "I did not. I took no less care with myself than I ever do…"

Jamie snorted. The giant hole in the bastard's ribs might have something else to say about that.

"No. No, I can…" Sam stopped again, rubbing the back of his neck. "I understand. I could not tell them without putting all of you in danger. This was a risk, but it was the smallest one available."

Jamie settled on the stairs, watching the whatever-he-was pace back and forth across the area in front of him. He didn't feel for Sam, he'd brought the uncomfortable on himself. Did Jamie maybe understand how Sam felt right then, being lectured by Grace and not really having anything to say back to it? Absolutely. And it was usually about thirty times worse because when Grace was upset she just sounded disappointed. He'd pissed her off badly enough to make her *angry* twice since he was eight, and neither of those were times he'd ever voluntarily repeat. But there'd been plenty of quiet, almost cold disappointment when he'd crossed a line somewhere or screwed up some other way. She always forgave him, and usually more quickly than he deserved, but he'd felt them all keenly.

"No." Samriel's jaw clenched, and Jamie wondered if it would help any to tell him not to argue. "No, I do not need to…." He stopped, face almost paling, and pulled the phone away from his ear, hitting the speaker. "There."

"Hey, darlin'." Jamie pushed a hand through his hair. "Sorry."

"You don't have anything to be sorry for," Grace huffed. "Thanks for helping."

Jamie snorted. "Bastard bled all over my porch." He glanced up at Samriel, cocking a brow at him. "I wasn't about to turf him."

"Sam," Grace started.

"I am—"

"Fine. Yeah, you said that one like sixteen times and I believe it a little less every time, right now." Grace blew out a tired, tinny breath. "So…Jamie…I know you're probably busy but if Sam leaves there pretty much at all or gets anywhere near the rest of us they're going to find him in about two seconds flat. Which would be…bad. Also, Bazel says he's not strong enough to protect himself if they do find him or—"

"So keep him here."

"Please?" Grace replied easily. "And obviously you can call from your phone whenever. That's fine."

"Sure." Jamie nodded. "I'll tape him to a chair or sit on him, whatever, until you tell me he's allowed to leave."

Samriel frowned, face dark and less than pleased.

"Sam, bite it." Grace paused, talking to someone else for a minute. "Alright. I'm…going. Both of you behave yourselves and I'll call you as soon as I know anything else."

"Sure." Jamie smiled wryly. "Bye, sunshine."

"Sam, say goodbye," Grace said, voice tense.

Samriel deflated suddenly, all the fight going out of his form. "Goodbye, Grace. I…"

"Yeah," Grace sighed. "Me too."

The line went dead, and Jamie took his phone back from Samriel's lax fingers. That was a marvelously *fun* conversation. He glanced at the clock and bit back a curse. Nine o'clock and he was already more than ready for bed. Tomorrow was going to be fun.

There were a few hundred things buzzing around in his brain, things he could say to Samriel. He wasn't sure that he had any real issue with making things harder for Sam. Whatever was going on—it had to be something big, Grace had almost sounded worried—he imagined Sam had brought at least a little of it on himself.

But he didn't know that, and no matter how little he liked the guy it was late and he was still pale and almost green so clearly he was going to have to swallow his crap and be an adult here.

He turned back from plugging the phone in and Sam was already settling himself back onto the couch, eyes sliding shut.

"That was fast."

"Should stop tomorrow," he mumbled. "Emotional…expenditure makes it worse."

He was asleep before Jamie could offer to let him use the guest bed, or even really make out what he was talking about.

Jamie wandered through the house, making sure everything was locked up. He stopped for just a second in front of Sam. Bastard *still* wasn't wearing a shirt, and he'd just dropped back on the couch and gone to sleep without even pulling the blanket up past his waist.

Which was his own goddamn problem. Jamie was *not* tucking him in.

He spun on his heel and walked to the stairs. He had classes in the morning, and he was going to have to either go grocery shopping or figure out something for them to eat for dinner tomorrow—he had stuff in the house for breakfast and lunch—and…

Jamie hung his head forward, and turned around and walked back to the couch, spreading the blanket up to Samriel's shoulders, grumbling at himself the entire way. He could say he was doing it for Grace, but that excuse was starting to get a little thin.

Mostly, he was just a sucker.

~*~***~*~

He didn't know if Samriel understood Jamie'd freaking tucked him in the night before. He was tense and off in the morning. Moving gingerly. He had actually managed to change his bandages himself, even if they weren't quite as neat as they would have been if he'd waited for Jamie.

"You have work today," Sam said, looking him over as he walked down the stairs.

He couldn't deal with this before coffee. Just nope. He had remembered Sam needed a shirt today, at least. He tossed the old t-shirt at him and headed for the coffee machine. He couldn't look at *that*, and deal with half the universe pilling up behind him before he'd even had caffeine.

Just no. No no no.

Sam stood awkwardly in the living room, tugging the shirt down over himself and *not looking at Jamie*. His eyes turned all powder blue and sparkly when he blushed.

Jamie nearly gave up on swallowing the first cup of coffee and considered just eating the little pod full of grounds. That might get the caffeine into his blood stream faster, at least. Might get him through this day without him doing something elementally stupid. Either professionally or personally.

Hate sex sounded like a fine idea in principle, but he didn't like his life messy, if it was avoidable, and he wasn't entirely sure Samriel was even capable of sex.

Not that he was thinking about it.

Jamie swallowed half a cup of coffee straight out of the machine—thankfully it didn't come out boiling—and ignored the other man watching him with curious interest. "Yes. I have classes today." He glanced at the clock. "I need to leave in about thirty-seconds. Just…don't leave today because I promise whatever Grace does to me if I lose you, it'll be nothing compared to what she does to you." He took another deep pull.

Sam nodded, not answering that.

"I'll be back around six, as soon as I'm done with classes. You should be able to find everything." He finished his coffee and dumped the cup in the sink. He'd grab another in the department lounge once he was on campus.

"Of course." Sam started to fold his arms over his chest, and then stopped, face tensing.

"Yeah, I wouldn't do that if I were you." Jamie grabbed his jacket and his bag. "Don't burn the house down."

He stepped out on the porch and nodded goodbye, pulling the door closed. He had one foot off the porch before he stopped. He was being ridiculous. Sam was *thousands* of years old—he didn't know exactly how old— there was no reason to be worried about him sitting in the house by himself all day.

Jamie had told him he could find the things he needed. He didn't need someone to hold his hand all day. He'd be fine.

He forced himself to walk to the car, one foot in front of the other. He was being ridiculous and stupid. Jamie lectured himself sternly, dropping his bag in the back of the car and hoping in the front seat. He glanced at the house once, as he started the car.

Everything looked normal. Sam wasn't even watching him out the window. Everything would be fine.

Jamie put the car in gear and headed for Campus. He'd even managed to stop lecturing himself by the time he got the parking structure and pulled into one of the instructor parking spaces. He'd looked up the university policy on taking a leave of absence for personal reasons last night, because if he couldn't get his life under control in a couple of days he was probably going to have to do that.

On the plus side, he knew for a fact they were more understanding when you weren't stiffing an entire semester, and he wasn't. There was only a month until the end of term, and his classes weren't heavy; an upper level that was nearly self-study and two undergrad classes, neither of which were intro. He knew of at least one adjunct who could have followed the rest of his syllabus for those and done a fine job.

Of course, this would be the day he managed to run into the department dean five minutes after he got on campus. Before he'd even made it to the building.

"Jay." Howard smiled at Jamie, shaking his hand heartily. "You're looking well this morning."

Jamie snorted. "You're being kind, Howard. I've only had one cup of coffee and I'm haggard."

Howard laughed softly. "I would never say that to you." He frowned. "You do look a little…" He cleared his throat. "Everything all right?"

Jamie smiled wryly. "I'm having a personal issue." He shrugged, deciding to be as honest as he could be. "And I'm sincerely hoping I can get it wrapped up this week without interfering with anything. If I can't, I may need to talk to you about taking a sabbatical."

Howard sighed. "How sad. Well, first, refresh me on what you're teaching this semester."

"Understanding Social Patterns 312, Family Dichotomies 215, and Advanced Special Topics 527," Jamie answered. "Anderson could handle Understanding

Social Patterns, might even be good for him to get a dry run before next year." Jamie was good at twisting things to work for him, even if it wasn't a skill he employed at lot.

Howard smiled wryly. "I imagine the same with Family Dichotomies. And 527 is nearly self-study. Is there any reason you couldn't still deal with that?"

"Not that I can think of." Jamie tugged on his ear, thinking. "I may need to be out of town for a couple of weeks, but I shouldn't be away from the phone or email."

Howard stopped in front of the building. "Well I hope it works out for the better, but if it doesn't let me know and we'll start that ball rolling." He clapped Jamie on the shoulder. "Always better to have said something early, so it's not a surprise to anyone."

Jamie nodded, smiling. "I'll make sure and get all my grading done. Hopefully that'll tempt fate my direction and make it not be an issue."

Howard laughed softly. "I imagine. It's not something drastic?"

"Grace." Jamie smiled wryly. He could say that, because Howard had met Grace. She'd been his date to the last two faculty black-tie affairs. "She's having some life complications, and the world would end before she'd ask me for help, but…" He shrugged.

"Family is important," Howard nodded. "Even the one you pick yourself."

Jamie said goodbye, and headed for his office. Working in the Sociology department, most of the staff was pretty understanding of your crappy family history. And however contemporary the University policy on sexuality was, the Sociology department had a warm, accepting reputation that accepted all cultures, races, and sexual orientations equally. On paper anyway.

That was probably unfair. His hang-ups as being 'out' as a bi-sexual were entirely his, and had nothing to do with the rest of the world.

Mostly he just didn't like the concept of being forced to share his personal information with anyone he didn't have to. When it came up, he was honest about it. He was entirely too old to be lying to anyone. Howard knew he was bi-sexual, and generally his students figured it out by the time they got around to talking about sexuality and culture—that whole not hiding thing—and he'd yet to turn down a request the Queer Alliance had made of him.

He wasn't a 'shout from a megaphone' kind of person. More power to the people who were.

He fully accepted he might have felt differently about that if he'd been forced into the closet—or forced into secrecy, he wouldn't have called himself 'in the closet' ever. If he'd realized he pitched for both teams when they were still living in the small town they'd been born in and he'd had to hide…

Jamie couldn't even finish that in his head. He remembered what he was like as a teenager perfectly well. It wouldn't have ended well, but 'hiding' wouldn't have been the way he handled that. And assuming he hadn't been stupid enough to wind up with AIDS or fuck only knew what else, Grace probably would have killed him for putting them both through that.

~*~***~*~

Jamie was swiftly entering the danger zone of becoming one of *those* professors. The ones that bitched about how much more studious people were during their university days and turned their noses up at the new generations. He'd had a couple of those in his university days and he didn't remember any of them fondly.

He drew the freaking line at being thrown up on. By a junior no less. What part of the unwritten college rule about underage drinking had they missed? You got all your alcohol poisoning fun-times out of the way your freshman year. You damn skippy didn't start drinking on Sunday night, and you didn't show up to class hung over and half-dead either. On a Monday. Seriously. If Jamie hadn't had a clean shirt stashed in his office he might have failed the kid.

Jamie shifted the bags in his hands and climbed up the stairs in front of the house. He wasn't late, at least. Not that it would have mattered if he was. Samriel could wait. He'd brought food, and a movie. The movie was because there was absolutely no way he was spending the night sitting in the quiet house with Samriel, just staring at the walls.

He also balked at the concept of going to bed at freaking nine-thirty again. He was so not old enough for that. Thirty-three was way the crap too young to start cashing in on life. He wasn't thinking about how close he was to doing just that, pushing through the door and kicking his shoes off as he went. He dropped his brief-case next to the coats and shrugged off his jacket, one arm at a time.

"I brought dinner." Jamie dropped his jacket on the rack, and turned around. "I don't know how you feel about baked chicken, but it's about all I'm capable of cooking."

Jamie froze, looking around the mostly dark room. It was just because he'd expected Samriel to be moving that he'd missed him. Sprawled out across the floor of the living room, one arm caught underneath him and legs splayed where he'd fallen.

"Fuck."

Jamie rushed the food and things into the dining room table, dropping them on the empty surface. He moved back to Sam and checked for a pulse, not that he had the first clue what it was supposed to feel like.

There was one though, so that was a plus. Samriel's chest was moving, breath coming in soft, slow pants. Jamie pulled Sam's arm out from underneath him, and shook him. "Samriel."

No response. Maybe his eyelids flickered a bit, but that was all.

"Samriel!" Jamie tried a harder voice, a little more boss.

Still nothing.

He shifted Samriel around and carefully got his hands hooked under the other man's armpits, hauling him toward the couch as carefully as he could. "Holy crap you're heavier than you look." He tugged again, trying not to wrench him around too badly. He didn't know what shape Samriel's side was in, since he hadn't seen it that morning.

Clearly he should have insisted, because *something* was wrong.

He finally managed to get Samriel onto the couch, ignoring the noises he was making trying to lift the bastard. "Seriously. I'm not in this bad a shape. How much do you weigh?" he muttered to himself, dropping Samriel's legs on the couch.

Jamie stood, and pushed a hand through his hair. "Sam." He clapped in front of his face—not that he really *wanted* to startle him awake—but it still didn't work. He grabbed Samriel's uninjured side and shook vigorously.

That at least got him a couple of tensed muscles and a pair of ice-blue eyes.

They started to slide shut again, and Jamie nearly kicked him. "No, stay with me."

But it was too late. Still, if he was alive enough to open his eyes that was good. Jamie went to grab his phone, because about the only option he had was calling Grace to see if she thought they should be heading to the hospital. He thought no, because the guy wasn't freaking human and that was likely to raise a couple of red-flags somewhere.

He grabbed a glass of water out of the kitchen, because that had always been Aunt Rhoda's answer to anything, health-wise. More water. Nobody liked to be dehydrated. He filled the glass in the sink, watching the drips where he'd missed the glass skate past his upturned coffee-cup and into the drain.

Jamie blinked, heart stopping in his chest. "You are *kidding* me." He slammed the water off, and opened the fridge.

Bastard hadn't touched anything. The kitchen was exactly the way Jamie left it the night before. He swallowed his instinctive desire to scream at him— thousands of years old and couldn't freaking remember to feed himself—and took the glass of water back over to the couch.

It was his upholstery, if he wanted to throw water in someone's face he was allowed.

CHAPTER 3

Sam opened his eyes slowly, disoriented in the dark room for a long moment. When had it gotten dark? He'd been sitting in the living room and his stomach had hurt suddenly. More than his side, and then he'd—

Jamie moved, and Sam jumped, startled.

"Oh, look who's awake again," Jamie said darkly, dropping down onto the coffee table in front of him.

Sam started to sit up. His side must have—

"Don't move," Jamie groused.

Large, warm hands fastened on his shoulders and pushed him back on the couch. His head spun, and *hurt.*

"You are so lucky I didn't call Grace." Jamie handed him a glass, half-full of water.

"What?" His voice croaked, and he tried to swallow.

"Drink first."

Sam would have argued, but clearly Jamie seemed to have some idea what was going on. Much as the other man clearly didn't like him—Grace kept saying he'd get over it in time, but Sam wasn't quite sure about that—he trusted Jamie not to poison anything.

He wasn't so sure that wouldn't work right now.

He swallowed the water slowly, because his form didn't always appreciate human food. But it was apparently fine with the water. He handed the empty glass back to Jamie, and was about to ask some sort of question as to...

Well, the list was rather long, actually. When had the other man returned? How had he lost track of so much time?

Jamie refilled the glass and handed it back to him. "I don't know how old you are, but the fact that I apparently needed to tell you to *eat* is more than a little disturbing."

Sam blinked, swallowing.

"Yeah." Jamie grimaced, face dark. "I poured about two glasses of juice down you before you woke up at all. Drink that."

He automatically drained the glass before he'd even thought about it. Before he'd considered what he was doing. His brain was slow, and sluggish, like nothing wanted to work right, and that shouldn't have been. He wasn't actually tied to this form.

Jamie plucked the glass out of his hand and filled it again. "One last time, and if you look a little less dead I'll get you some food."

Sam frowned. "I shouldn't—"

"Yeah, well." He huffed, shoulders tense. "You do. And if you make me call Grace because you're not eating and I found you passed out on the floor I'm putting *all that* on you because my day's been more than a little ridiculous as it stands."

Sam wanted to say he was sorry about that, but he got the distinct impression it wouldn't have been welcomed.

Once he'd finished the water, and been glared at to stay put until Jamie came back with a plate, Sam almost felt reasonable again. His body had stopped screaming at him from every conceivable place, that seemed to help a bit.

Jamie handed him a plate, piled with noodles and meatballs. "Eat slow. Your stomach might have an issue if it's seriously empty, even after the water."

He nodded, flushing, and started eating. The food actually tasted interesting. He'd noticed already his physical systems seemed to be more acute like this. He supposed the amount of power he was generally shoehorning into a physical form when he manifested over-rode all that. His side certainly hurt a great deal more than it had before, and he kept unconsciously favoring it.

"I'm going to check that tonight."

Sam froze.

"Because I had to tug your ass off the floor," Jamie grumbled. "And clearly you're not going to tell me if it's a problem."

Sam frowned at him. "I have never had to pull this far back before. I wasn't aware I actually needed to feed myself like this."

Jamie cocked his head to the side, green eyes strange and curious. "Don't you normally feed yourself?"

"No."

"Even…whatever you're supposed to eat?"

Sam cocked a brow at him. "What would you imagine that would be? Maeleket are essentially energy beings. We do not eat."

Jamie snorted. "Well, that sort of makes my case for me. I'm guessing you don't exactly bleed, either."

Sam gingerly pressed a hand to the gash on his side, swallowing. "It does not feel pleasant."

"Yeah, well, I don't want to think about how much it probably pulled when you bandaged it yourself this morning," Jamie said, gesturing with his fork before he went back to his own food.

It had been a little tender, but it wasn't anything Sam couldn't handle. "Still. I do not—"

Jamie looked up at him, face set. "I will call Grace. I've got no masculine scruples about siccing her on you."

Sam frowned.

"She asked me to keep you in once piece until you're better," he said seriously. "If one of us is going to get in trouble for failing that, it's going to be you."

Put like that, Sam didn't have much choice.

~*~***~*~

He was forcing himself into that same mind-set the next morning. Jamie had come down the stairs early, and proceeded to outline everything he wanted Sam to do during the day.

"Don't answer the door," Jamie said without stopping to look at him.

He was still doing it. They weren't orders. Jamie was just covering the bare minimum. Sam could have explained that now that he understood how fragile his manifested body was going to be, he could work with that and he'd be fine.

"Neither of us need the headache of my trying to explain who you are to my neighbors. The landline shouldn't actually ring; aside from the fact no one has the number except Grace, I keep the phone turned off."

He'd seen Curt get like this with Nate occasionally. From what he could tell Nate had long ago perfected the art of nodding and letting Curt run out of steam on his own, rather than trying to assert his independence or capability.

It probably didn't help that he'd fallen asleep about five seconds after he'd finished eating the night before. He'd known he was gravely injured, but he was ready for the trouble staying cognizant to go away. That was rather difficult to work around, obviously.

Theoretically it would today. But he didn't for a moment believe it would help him any with Jamie to mention that.

"Don't mess with the windows either." Jamie stopped, actually glancing at him. "I wouldn't put it past my neighbors to be nosy, so just…stay away from the windows and don't draw attention to yourself."

Sam was hardly likely to do that, but he didn't say anything. Just nodded and waited for Jamie to reach the end of his lecture. Or realize he was on the verge of being late for his classes.

"I'll be back by six-thirty, and I'll bring something for dinner, unless you happen to know how to actually cook?"

Sam swallowed. "No." He could feed himself for lunch. He'd watched Nate forage enough to know what was easily edible inside a refrigerator that wouldn't take any work from him.

"Alright." Jamie nodded, and handed him a cell phone. "Clearly you know everyone's cell number so I didn't bother programming anybody in there but me. Do you know how to work it?"

"Yes." Sam said, huffing. "I do."

Jamie grabbed his briefcase. "Call me if you feel not-normal or—"

"If I feel unusually ill or out of sorts suddenly I will call." Or he'd call Grace, and make sure he wasn't forgetting something simple.

Jamie paused at the door, arresting just for a moment.

Sam waited for another question, or more orders. For something. Jameson was hesitating, like he was concerned. But given how little the man cared for him, that seemed unlikely.

After a moment he shook his head, said a quiet goodbye, and disappeared out the door.

Sam looked at the room around him and the phone in his hand. It would be irresponsible to call Grace just to ask what he was supposed to *do* with himself for the next nine hours. He had so little experience being alone in the human realm it was laughable. Granted, he'd followed Grace for all those years, just trailing along behind her, but he hadn't had the option of doing anything in her universe. Not to mention he'd been actively watching her all that time.

Even if she wasn't doing anything, she was still a stimulus in his environment. More than normal even. Grace didn't make sense always *now*, that he could actually ask her to explain things or clarify if she did or said something that lost him. When that hadn't been an option she'd made even less sense.

Jamie's house was much nicer than the ones either Jamie or Grace had lived in when they were children. He wondered around in the kitchen, checking the placement of all the pots and pans in case he felt like using them during the day. Opened the refrigerator and checked the contents for easily edible foods he was sure were safe. He was fine, Jamie had a vast array of lunch-meat. Most of it was actually on the correct side of the expiration date.

He frowned at the packages that weren't, and finally decided to throw them away. He had the distinct impression Jamie wasn't going to appreciate that, but when they'd been in college Jamie had eaten some past-expiration ham and been so deathly ill Grace had nearly missed a final trying to care for him. He knew for a fact Jamie hadn't eaten ham again for nearly a year and a half.

Clearly he hadn't learned his lesson yet.

And in theory his form wouldn't have any trouble with expired lunch-meat, but after yesterday Sam wasn't in any rush to check that. If he was capable of being made ill by human weaknesses, this would be the time that happened. He'd rather not have to go crawling to Malek, hoping the other Maeleket could heal him, for something as stupid as food-poisoning.

He wandered back into the living room, looking around at his strange nest of blankets and things. Nate always assumed when Sam was around and they weren't with him that just sat in a chair and did nothing all day, waiting for them to come back.

He could have done that. He was perfectly capable of just letting time pass.

That didn't mean he wanted to do that. He certainly didn't want to do that for days and days while he waited for things to be safe enough he could contact the others in a more real manner. He looked at the television, and then glanced at the remote.

Curt didn't even really own a television. Grace usually had one, because she was fond of movies, but she didn't just watch TV. She didn't hate it, or preach against it. She just didn't find it very interesting.

Sam reached out carefully and lifted the remote. He was spending so much more time now, around humans and interacting with the human world. It wouldn't hurt to do a little reconnaissance. To see what the not-Grace portion of humanity was watching.

He pressed the power button, and flipped through the channels until he found a panel of women, discussing something called extreme couponing, with attendant oohs and aahs from the audience.

He honestly didn't understand most of it. They moved on to other topics after a moment—those were a bit more interesting than extreme couponing, he wasn't sure how buying more of something you didn't need was saving money—and eventually had a heart-felt, obviously scripted interview with a movie actor. Sam recognized him, he'd been in some dinosaur movie when Grace was young, and she'd been exceedingly attached to it.

After the panel of women was a panel of men that made even less sense to him. He decided trying to hold that information was just clutter and let it go. He was about to give up and turn the television off when it started grand, serious music and showed him an exterior view of a strange looking space-ship he couldn't imagine ever actually working.

Three episodes later he did remember to get up and find himself something to eat.

~*~***~*~

The Captain of the ship was entirely too understanding with his crew. If they were consistently going to get so wrapped up in their private lives that they put everyone else at risk clearly they should not have been allowed such leniency.

The andriod's impossible crush on the blond woman had nearly resulted in the death of three junior crew members in the last two episodes. Not to mention the captain himself rushing into dangerous situations without properly considering all outcomes.

As a being technically made out of 'pure energy'—he wasn't, but Sam was granting himself a bit of leniency because he was relatively sure a Maeleket was actually the closest physics would allow to an 'energy being'—he would not have suddenly, miraculously known how to over-take a spaceship, nor did he think it would have jumped right into that level of manipulation of the humans.

Though given what his own kind had done with humanity once they'd started interacting with them, the writers might have had a point with that.

Sam heard the scratch of a key in the lock, and looked up in shock. It was six-thirty already. He snapped a hand out and turned off the television, just as Jamie stepped through the door.

Jamie rose a brow at him, and clicked on the entry-way light.

Sam stood, clearing his throat. It was age and superior self-control that kept him from blurting out a host of excuses as to why he'd gotten sucked into the television.

Jamie flicked a glance at the television, and then turned to hang his jacket up.

Sam forced himself to move, taking the bag of food containers so Jamie could put his things in their normal places. He took the little cartons into the kitchen and sat them out on the table, before grabbing plates and utensils.

Jamie came in behind him, dropping a stack of papers on the counter and rolling his sleeves up, huffing out a small breath. "I hope you like Chinese food. I tried to get normal stuff."

He wasn't sure what constituted normal, for Chinese food. Asian peoples ate a wide variety of things he knew westerners found unpalatable. He'd spent enough time around Jamie to understand he was generally less picky than other men of his age and cultural experience. He had swallowed a live fish once, at the behest of some of the other children in their science class.

He didn't ask if Jamie remembered that. Sam doubted he'd forgotten. Grace hadn't spoken to him for a week.

Apparently what Jamie had meant by 'normal' was vegetables and beef or chicken, everything mild and somewhat easy.

"I wasn't sure what your stomach could handle so I tried to take it easy," Jamie offered, flushing. "Do you care if I turn the radio on?"

Sam shook his head. It wasn't as if they were going to make dinner conversation. Not more than the occasional word. Apparently. Listening to the radio would be less awkward than sitting in total silence while they ate.

He'd shared more than a few meals, since things had worked so he was allowed to actually be involved in Grace's life. Even Chinese food. It was a particular favorite of Curt's, and on his last birthday Sam had helped Nate practically kidnap the other man for lunch in the next town that had an actual Chinese food restaurant. He hadn't minded doing it. Curt had been more than a little touched they'd gone to all the trouble. Because it was his birthday and they cared about him.

Sam was coming to terms with that. Curt wasn't…it wasn't that he didn't trust the older man or anything like that. He just pushed Grace sometimes. He toed the line of having issue with her strangeness and Sam was protective of exactly who Grace was, strangeness and all.

"Did you check in with Grace today?" Jamie asked, after ten minutes of quiet, steady munching.

Sam shook his head in the negative.

"I sent her a text on my way home, just to ask if everything was still alright. She said it was." Jamie poked at his food, picking the peas out of the fried-rice.

Sam withheld a wince at the sudden clanging in his head. It was growing steadily, and had been for a few moments. He swallowed his bite of food, and took a drink of water, wondering if that would make it dissipate.

It didn't.

"I imagine she would have called one of us if there was a problem." Sam winced, resisting the urge to rub at his head. He didn't want another lecture like the one this morning, and a head-ache—uncomfortable and distracting as it was—wasn't going to kill him. "Most likely you, right now."

Jamie snorted. "Thanks for that. I want to play telephone right now because she can't just call you."

Sam clenched his jaw, a new wave of pain running across his head.

Jamie stood then, taking his plate to the sink, and starting to box up the food. He did pause, to see if Sam wanted more, but he didn't seem like he wanted to talk. Given the way his head was behaving right then, Sam was fine with that.

Or at least he was until he could just barely hear Jamie muttering to himself as he put their dishes away and came back for the rest of the food. He scowled at Sam, grabbing the last container, and opened his mouth on some comment about how Sam had messed up, he was sure.

"I didn't like you much either, once," Sam spat darkly.

Jamie froze, hand clenching on the container almost enough to crush it, muscles standing in stark contrast on his arms. He stared at Sam, hard, for a ridiculous tense moment before he walked heavily over to the counter and rifled around ominously.

Sam swallowed, and gave up and rubbed his forehead. He hadn't meant to ever say anything like that.

Jamie walked back over, tense and menacing, and Sam reminded himself that Jamie had grown out of his tendency to be violently angry early. Even when backed into a corner. That wasn't the most helpful thought, given the fact the man had actually *had* a tendency to be violently angry and Sam was never entirely sure how well that was buried with anyone other than Grace.

He slapped his palm on the table, before Sam, leaving two small pills next to his mostly full glass of water. Sam watched him grab his jacket and thump up the stairs loudly, turning off the hall light before his bedroom door shut smartly.

He stared at the pills, wondering if it was the Chinese food making his human stomach flip-flop around, or something else entirely.

CHAPTER 4

Sam glanced up at the tread of feet on the stairs, and quickly finished at the stove. He was clinging to the idea that his difficulty sleeping yesterday had been a combination of watching television all day—he wouldn't be doing that again—and being over the last of his serious physical issues and not anything else.

But given the fact he'd woken and launched into attempting to make Jamie breakfast the ice under his feet was a bit thin.

Sam didn't know how to cook. Not really. But given the time he'd spent following Grace around, and Grace generally speaking knew her way around a kitchen, he'd picked up a couple of things. He could reheat soup, or whatever else happened to just need a couple of moments in the microwave or a pan.

He could make Toad in the Hole.

That wasn't apology food. Grace only cooked Toad in the Hole when she really felt like it, and Sam couldn't remember a single time she'd done it because she'd felt compelled to apologize to Jamie for anything. But he also couldn't remember her having a lot of instances where she'd needed to apologize to him in any case.

Sam vividly remembered the way she'd learned. She'd been thirteen, just months after he found her, and one morning she'd just pulled out the eggs and started cooking. It hadn't gone well, really. It'd taken her nearly an entire dozen eggs to get it down—she'd thrown the rejects out to the neighbor's dog—and she'd been patient and calm the entire time. By about the sixth egg he'd stopped being terrified she was going to burn herself—Sam hadn't had any understanding of when it was okay to let a child cook by themselves—and started wondering how long she was going to keep trying.

Until she'd gotten it, apparently.

Jamie at fourteen hadn't been interested in eggs, but he'd eaten every scrap Grace gave him without a single word. By the time they were in college he'd apparently started to like it.

Jamie stepped off the last stair and his nose twitched as he sniffed, frowning. "Did you..."

Sam tried not to flush—it didn't work well, he really didn't have control of his physical form enough to manage that sort of thing—and slid it onto a plate. "Go ahead and sit."

Jamie swallowed. "Did you make me toad in the hole?"

He shifted, turning and holding the plate tightly. He wasn't good at apologies. "It's the only thing I know how to make."

Jamie cocked a brow at him. "Did you make some for yourself too?"

Sam nodded. After the lecture about eating and all that he certainly wouldn't have neglected that. He moved to the table, placing the serving dish he'd filled with eggs and toast on the table between their places. There was juice, and sausage as well.

"I thought you said you couldn't cook." Jamie looked at the table, frowning slightly. "Not that I'm surprised you can make 'Grace breakfast' but..."

Sam swallowed. "It's all I can make." He sat down carefully. "It's an apology. I should not have..."

Jamie frowned at him, eyes darkening.

"I was in pain and obviously I do not handle that particularly well."

Jamie sat down and dug into the food, and they ate steadily. He said something quiet and complementary about the cooking but didn't seem much easier, and Sam accepted that hadn't been enough of an apology and he was going to have to explain himself.

The issue was going to be doing that without making things worse.

He was running out of time, because Jamie was nearly done with his food and once that had happened it would only be a matter of time before he gathered his things and left for the day.

"I'll try to be back by—"

"It wasn't—" Sam stopped, biting his tongue, because they'd both spoken at the same time.

Jamie swallowed, wiping his face. "It wasn't…?"

He cleared his throat, forcing the words out. "You were young and…learning I guess." He flushed. "Sometimes you did things that worried me."

Sam watched as Jamie shifted around in his chair, and turned the silverware over in his hands a few times, searching for the right words. Jamie wasn't throwing anything in Sam's face despite how bad a job he'd done of expressing himself, so he could give the man time to find the words he wanted.

"Past tense?" Jamie managed finally. "Not anymore?"

"No." Sam shook his head suddenly, heart thumping distractingly. "Not for years."

Jamie nodded, gathering his breakfast dishes up slowly. "Rule number two?"

He swallowed, nodding carefully. "Grace isn't the only one with problems. I know."

"I suspect you do," Jamie muttered uneasily.

He'd been around for all the 'Grace Rules' obviously. Well, technically Rule #1—Grace had to talk to Jamie, even if she didn't want to—happened before he came along. #2 happened shortly after Grace learned to cook toad in the hole. #3—Jamie can't lie to Grace, even if he thinks it's for her own good—came about a year later. #4—Jamie is under no obligation to explain the human race, even if he wants to try—happened the year Jamie graduated high school and involved a jealous girlfriend

Grace never even met. #5—Jamie is allowed to remind Grace, at will, that she is a large part of his life by his choice and he is not 'stuck' with her—came after the fight their sophomore year in college when they didn't speak for a full three weeks. Sam missed the beginning of that, and they don't talk about it, so he actually doesn't know what it was about.

Sam took his dish in, and started loading the dishwasher. It was better than following Jamie around like some sort of waif. He hadn't realized that was a pattern until Nate had gotten on him, for following the rest of them around the way he used to follow Grace. Generally, Sam didn't worry about it. Because the person he followed most still was Grace, and she didn't seem to care.

He'd already done something wrong with Jamie. It wouldn't help any to follow the man around the house until he was leaving for work.

Sam repeated that in his head until he'd finished with the dishes and wiped down the counters. He looked up, freezing at Jamie staring at him over the kitchen island, watching him carefully.

Jamie cleared his throat, rubbing the back of his neck. "There's a guest-room upstairs. You're obviously going to be here for a while, you don't have to keep sleeping on the couch." He grabbed his keys and things off the counter, and shrugged. "It's all set up. I left the door open."

Sam nodded, and waited for the list of instructions that had prefaced Jamie's leaving for work the day before.

But they didn't come. Jamie said a quiet goodbye and let himself out of the house, leaving Sam standing alone in the kitchen, with another day to fill.

~*~***~*~

He'd contemplated the television for a grand total of eight seconds.

Yesterday hadn't gone well, and he had no desire to run the risk of that sort of headache again. Not only had it been vastly unpleasant, and led to him saying stupid things to Jamie, he'd been twitchy half the night and had a difficult time getting the sleep his form needed when he was injured.

There was a cookbook in the kitchen, and after this morning's luck with the toad in the hole he did briefly think about trying to cook something. Not that he would have launched into anything new and expected that to feed them for supper. There was too much risk there. Too much likely-hood it wouldn't work and then they'd be trying to fend for something else to eat.

But he could try to make himself something for lunch. Something simple possibly.

That lasted through a careful perusal of Jamie's one and only cookbook. It wasn't so much that Sam wasn't capable of understanding the instructions, or even of completing the steps. Jamie lacked even the most rudimentary of ingredients for anything he could find. If he weren't so cut off from his abilities he could have just made them.

But that wasn't an option.

He wondered back into the living room, and he was about to sacrifice himself to the television when he noticed the bookshelf built into the opposite wall. It wasn't anything like the bookshelves around Grace. There were little slots left open for statues and things, and open space. Grace didn't own a bookshelf that didn't have at least twelve more books than it could physically hold crammed onto it. It was worse now, being at Curt's, because she'd been randomly adding all variety of 'hunting' books and lore books to her regular run of fiction and history and whatever else caught her fancy.

Jamie's was mostly a run of strange paperbacks with half-naked women on the covers, but there was one book on the second shelf he recognized. It was a large, leather-bound edition of *War and Peace* Grace had given him for his twenty-first birthday.

Sam knew it was a classic, and of a time in human history he actually hadn't been around for much of. Or he'd been around, but he'd been a little preoccupied to be paying much attention to the wider human condition at the time.

He pulled the large, heavy tome down from the shelf and settled into his nest on the couch.

The true superiority of books over television became apparent when it was time for him to eat lunch. The book went with him to the kitchen, and to the dining room table while he ate. He did contemplate putting it down after lunch. If he was going to use the guestroom upstairs then he did need to at least look at it, and he should do that before Jamie returned.

But it was barely two in the afternoon, and he had another four hours and Pierre had just decided he should assassinate Napoleon, which given his handling of everything else, Sam couldn't see him completing without some difficulty.

His phone is nearly itching in his pocket. He hadn't spoken to Grace in *days* and it did genuinely bother him. New to the 'human condition' or not, calling Grace to make her explain this would qualify as a rather giant excuse, and it would put her in danger. He wasn't going to do it, even if it was somewhat randomly running through his head.

It wasn't all that unusual for Sam to be a little at loose ends about humanity. Before Sam had been assigned Grace's family, he'd worked with a Hebrew family. He'd had them for nearly four hundred years. Particularly, at that time, it hadn't been at all unusual for a Nephete family to still belong to a wider human religion. Even if Sam had known if there actually was any sort of human god—he didn't, but that didn't really mean anything either way—it would have been very seriously against his purpose as a Warder to say anything about that.

Some Warders had the sort of personality they could deal with the more religious families without there being issues. Sam wasn't one of them. He'd managed it for his five-hundred year term, and then he'd asked to be assigned someone different. Someone who was possibly willing to listen to him when he suggested they not do things.

At the time, the only open line had been Grace's. They'd lived in the area modernly known as Russia. Vasili had been young, and newly in charge of the family. His father hadn't had a Warder, but that was a stubborn resistance to the fact nearly everyone on the planet assumed they were three steps away from being dark. Vasili had worn his dark reputation like a badge for most of his life, but he'd never even contemplated actual darkness, and he'd taken Sam's council seriously.

That was so long ago there was surprisingly very little of human behavior he could correlate. Some of that might have been his general distance from the humans at the time. He'd been dedicated to Vasili, and even if he hadn't been attached to him, he'd worked well with him.

Vasili's great-granddaughter had been the closest Sam had ever felt to failing. Not because Mariska wasn't a good soul, or because she was particularly interested in power for power's sake, or in control. Because she'd had an over-enthusiastic sense—inherited from her grandfather—of her own internal compass, and a ridiculous faith in humanity that tried to lead her astray.

Grace was the first person he'd seen in the family in nearly a millennia that held that internal compass. He'd recognized it nearly the first week he'd seen her. That had been Vasili's leading characteristic, and it'd given Sam hope that there was something left in the family worth preserving.

He'd been uneasy though, because Vasili hadn't had the world stacked against him the way Grace had. Vasili had the love and devotion of a large family, and the respect of people who knew him.

Grace had had Jamie, a father she couldn't even look in the eye, and Jamie's Aunt Rhoda. It wasn't much to anchor a personality on.

She had more now, and as dangerous as life was she handled it well. He had to remind himself of that often, but it was starting to sink in. He did wonder sometimes if she would have been more like Mariska, if she'd had a more stable childhood. He would have dealt with the extra work, if it meant she was happier.

Sam blinked at the words before him, realizing he'd slipped off into his memories rather than reading. He'd been doing that more recently, not just since he found himself backed into a human form. Since he'd been spending actual time with Grace and not just following her around, silent and invisible. He shook the thoughts off and immersed himself back in the narrative world of early nineteenth century Russia.

The click of a key in the lock shocked him out of the continuing saga of Peter and his ever-present, ill-advised quest to assassinate Napoleon, and Sam was blinking at the clock as Jamie let himself into the house.

He looked down at the book in his lap, confused, before blinking owlishly at Jamie.

Jamie stopped inside the door, and snorted softly. He put his things away and held up a bag of food from yet another take-away place.

Sam swallowed and tried not to wince has his side pulled when he shifted, looking down to check the page-number of where he was in the book.

"You know it might hurt less if you stopped doing things for eight hours straight," Jamie offered, as he kicked his shoes off.

Sam blinked at him, brain still fuzzy and disconnected. It wasn't a pleasant feeling. "If Natasha is in love with Andrew why does she consider eloping with Alexi? And the other girl, Mary, if she cares for her promised why is she being so inconsistent when he is actually about? Also, Peter could not manage to finish off

Dolokhov, how does he think he's going to assassinate the Emperor Napoleon?"

He blinked at Sam, and snorted suddenly. "That's…" He cleared his throat. "Right. I'm not trying to explain Russian lit on an empty stomach." He headed for the kitchen. "Come eat, and I'll try to boil it down to something other than 'they're all being idiots' for you."

~*~***~*~

Jamie wasn't fond of *War and Peace*. He didn't like the portrayal of the female characters as empty and infatuated with nothing but men and babies. He didn't like the way the people who were self-sacrificing to a fault and pious were the only one's portrayed with any actual internal goodness. He didn't like the over-simplification of the politics between Russia and Napoleonic France.

Sam knew better than to ask why he thought it should have started in the middle.

And after the explanation of the people and a certain level of the politics he managed to absorb with his meal—pizza today, he was going to find some way to inject a suggestion that Jamie procure groceries any minute now—he sort of understood why. He could absolutely tally a ten-year-old Jamie who'd sat down and read it cover to cover because someone told him he couldn't, that he wasn't smart enough. Jamie had a level of rebellion in his soul that Sam admired, but it was probably to the best of everyone it had never bled off on Grace.

Sam had been around for their teen years. He'd seen Jamie get talked into less than ideal situations by that. And he'd chaperoned enough First's—Grace was his one-hundred and forty-seventh—he understood that was a general part of human nature. That didn't mean he appreciated having to deal with it. Particularly the sixty or so times there hadn't been anyone else to guide them, just him.

From the distant understanding of that Sam had, he could still tell Jamie had come out the other end of it better than anyone would have realistically expected early on. He was smart, and talented—Jamie was much better with people than his solitary life-style would lead one to believe—and capable.

"So…" Sam frowned. "Grace giving you *War and Peace* for a gift…"

Jamie smiled wryly. "She wasn't just being a pain, though she does that sometimes too, I'm sure you've noticed."

Sam flushed, shrugging. "I think she did once. I didn't catch on and Nate suggested she shouldn't." He looked down at his food, poking at his left-over crust. "She does it to him once in a while."

He nodded. "Anyway, I was genuinely proud for a long time that I'd managed that." He nodded to the book, sitting across from them on the table. "I got over that around college. But twenty-one wasn't the easiest year, I'm sure you recall."

Twenty-one had been particularly difficult. There'd been the argument with Grace, and Sam had witnessed a decent amount of…issue over Jamie's sexuality no one but Jamie seemed to have had a problem with.

Well, Sam seemed to recall the girlfriend at the time had had a problem with it.

"I do." Sam said, clearing his throat, when he realized Jamie was waiting for him to answer.

Jamie snorted darkly. "Anyway, she wanted to remind me of something I should actually be proud of. It was that or the college essay that actually got me in. *War and Peace* didn't require breaking into anything."

He didn't know exactly what Jamie's college entrance essay had been about. He'd obviously never read it. He could have, easily. It wasn't as if getting into the college offices would have been difficult. Whatever lines Sam had trouble with, regarding Grace, he hadn't had too much trouble finding them in regard to Jamie. Jamie wasn't his responsibility, outside of the things he did that impacted Grace. Those couldn't have been the only things Jamie would have had to be proud of, but at that moment Sam wasn't coming up with anything else.

Other than Grace.

"Anyway." Jamie sighed, standing from the table and grabbing his plate and the empty salad bowl. "That's enough about *me* for one night."

Sam watched him step away from the table, muttering quietly enough Sam actually couldn't hear him, and heading for the kitchen.

"Why don't you like me?"

Sam instantly wanted to call the words back, turning back to the table and closing his eyes.

CHAPTER 5

Jamie stood frozen in his kitchen, fingers wrapped around his used plate, and watched Samriel's ears turn steadily redder. Was that even supposed to happen? If the body was just mass called into effect around whatever the Maeleket actually was, did he have blood normally? True, he had a pulse but Jamie had sort of expected that to be a screen. To just be his way of hiding what he really was in case anyone happened to be looking closely enough to notice. Though the whole bleeding all over his porch probably meant there was something physical going on Jamie just didn't understand.

"I apologize," Sam rambled. "I shouldn't have..."

Right. He'd asked a question. Jamie swallowed. "Do you really have to ask?" He set the plates down carefully. It wasn't that he was going to throw them. Jamie had grown out of throwing a temper tantrum a damn long time ago.

But maybe this was good. Maybe they should get this out in the open, because clearly he was stuck with Samriel in his life to some level. The bastard was immortal. He was going to outlive Jamie, and he wasn't going to walk away from Grace any time soon. Neither was Jamie.

"I have no concept what I could have—"

"All those years." Jamie didn't wait for him to finish. Maybe it was rude, and maybe he knew better, but right then he didn't actually care. "And yeah, Nate gets it too, I know he does. And Curt." Jamie grabbed the edge of the counter just clinging to something. Something solid under his fingers that reminded him they were there and they were all—theoretically—fine. "But they weren't there for it. They didn't have to take care of her, or convince her to talk again, or fucking stick around for a night so she'd actually *sleep*."

Sam blinked at him, confused and blank. And maybe that was the part that bothered him more than anything.

"Just because she was physically fine didn't mean *anything*." Jamie forced himself to swallow, and breathe. "Maybe you couldn't talk to her yourself, but she was goddamn nine, you should have done something."

Sam swallowed, and opened his mouth. But nothing came out. He closed it again after a moment and let out a soft huff. "I…" He frowned. "If I had ever thought Grace was unstable enough to need intervention I would have…thought of something."

Jamie stared at him hard, blood thumping unsteadily in his ears. Because not talking for three weeks after her mother died wasn't unstable enough. Not sleeping, and learning to dead-bolt her bedroom at ten, and—

"And if I had found her at nine, I would have…taken her away, which I fully realize you would not appreciate."

Jamie stopped, breathing through the noise in his head and trying to focus. "If?" He frowned. "You said you found her when her mom died."

"No." Sam shook his head slowly. "I realized she was still alive when she was nine. She…created a wave the night her mother died." He cocked a brow. "It took me the better part of four years. I had to track her through the human records. It's nearly a miracle I managed to find her at all."

Jamie leaned back, shocked. "Four years?"

Sam nodded. "Just before her thirteenth birthday." He swallowed. "By then the blockage she'd created in her head was so cemented I was afraid to tread to close to it in any way, and she was too old to be trained in any case so…" He flushed. "The council made me watch her for a year to ensure she wasn't... Even untrained she was obviously going to have some power and they were concerned she'd be dangerous." Sam rubbed the back of his neck. "It was...hard." He looked at Jamie then, eyes serious and honest. "But certainly by the end of the summer if she'd been unduly struggling I'd have stepped in."

He didn't have an answer for that. At least nothing that amounted to more than annoyed arm-flailing. Thirteen and on hadn't been grand, but it wasn't the four years that'd come before. But he still should have done something, and Jamie was going to come up with a way to express that.

But his phone started ringing, Grace's special ring-tone echoing through the kitchen.

Sam stood up suddenly, completely and totally focused on Jamie's phone as he answered it.

"Grace has your number, I doubt she'd be calling me if there was a problem." Jamie said, answering the phone. "Hey, Sugar."

"Hey." Grace sighed, sounding tired and worn. "Tell Sam everything's fine."

"She says everything's fine," Jamie said, putting another dish in the sink. "And if he believes that I have some land to sell him."

Sam frowned at him, and he could hear Grace snort over the phone.

"It's..." Grace sighed. "Whatever. How are you two doing?"

"We're good." Jamie forced himself to answer as normally as he could. What was he supposed to say? *Sam's weird and I don't know how to deal with him, and I think I hurt his feelings, and he's kind of an ass when he's in pain and I don't want to get to know him so come retrieve your...thing.*

Aside from what Grace would probably say if any of that left his mouth, he didn't have any intention of cashing in his man card. He wasn't going to whine at her about how little sense Sam made.

"He hasn't burned the house down yet, and he seems to have figured out how to feed himself."

Grace sighed tiredly. "And how are you?"

"I'm—"

"If you lie to me I can't help," she prompted, before he'd even finished it.

"I'm alright." Jamie smiled wryly, rubbing his forehead. "It's been a long couple of days and I'm tired and..." He stopped there, about to say something he didn't want to. "I'm just tired."

"Alright." Grace sighed again. "Don't tell me," she teased.

"Grace..."

"It's fine. You're allowed to think over things on your own for a while before we start arguing over whether or not you have to spill to me."

"Thanks." Jamie smiled. "How's Nate and everybody? And what's his name, Sam's replacement."

Sam glared at him, eyes dark.

"Oops, I just annoyed Sam."

"Tell Sam he's not a replacement." Grace muttered, voice tight. "My shadow was better at it."

Jamie cocked a brow at Sam. "She says her shadow was better at it."

Sam flushed, obviously pleased, but he still looked uneasy.

"We'll get by," she said softly. "Anyway, unless you'd like to start sharing..."

"No." Jamie rubbed his forehead. Because this was one of those random things he probably needed to figure out for himself. Whatever his problems with Sam were, he wasn't going to land them in Grace's lap. Especially when she wasn't there. "No. Not yet."

"Alright." Grace blew out a tired breath. "Do you mind handing Sam the phone?"

"Nope. Night, Love." Jamie handed the phone to Samriel, and started gathering the dishes. It was late. They'd spent a lot of time over steadily cooling pizza discussing melodramatic Russians. He was going to pretend that, and the crop of freshmen grading he'd discussed today, was why he was tired and ready for bed. Not because he was going to have to reevaluate his Sam position.

"No," Sam muttered. "We are fine." He closed his eyes, sighing. "I realize I am not any better at lying to you than he is." He looked up at Jamie, and swallowed. "I am not trying to use the Grace rules, but we are both of us adults. We can deal on our own. How are *you*?" He frowned.

Jamie paused, because given the way things were right then it was entirely possible Sam would get a wildly different response to that out of Grace than he'd have gotten. He didn't feel left out by that. He understood he didn't exist in the same reality Grace did anymore. Most of the time he was even alright with that. Nate would usually tell him what he needed to know, and Nate would have taken a nest of fire-ants to the face for Grace so he could obviously be trusted to keep her as safe as anyone reasonably could.

"That would be bad. Are they..." Samriel paused, frowning. "Malek...no, I'm not saying you should. However...whatever is happening inside his head, it is unfair of him to expect you to... No, I know it's not." He huffed. "Grace. I am older than you are by a large enough number of years you consistently do not like me to remind you of it. I understand life is not fair, or that no part of this situation is fair, but you sound genuinely frustrated with Bazel which is unlike you. Even if there is nothing I can do, I would like an honest answer."

Jamie watched him frown and tense a bit, at whatever answer he'd gotten.

"Promise me if he...if you feel..." He almost smiled, relaxing slightly. "Yes. That works, promise that."

She did apparently, and Samriel said his goodbye's and hung the phone up.

He glanced at Jamie, and handed the phone over. "She said she was as well as could be expected, and if he aggravates her to the point she begins contemplating anything unusually stupid she will call."

Jamie snorted, nodding, and tucked the phone away.

~*~***~*~

They hadn't talked any more before bed.

Mostly because Jamie was a giant coward about certain things, and he'd needed a little time to figure out where up was, after the revelations. Which had made the morning as cripplingly awkward as one would expect. Jamie would have tried to fix it before he left for work, but it hadn't felt right. He was thirty-three. Old enough to realize how badly this conversation was going to go if he tried to have it before he was ready.

So he'd gone to work and spent the day mentally wrangling freshmen and university politics. He didn't feel better. But walking through the door and finding Samriel nowhere to be found, he'd have been one heck of a liar to pretend he didn't have a moment of panic there. Like the other man had gotten tired of waiting for him to start the conversation and just left.

Of course he hadn't. All the chances Jamie kept giving Samriel because he meant so much to Grace, he'd never thought that only went one way. He dropped his things in the kitchen and looked out into the sun-dappled back yard.

Given the way Sam seemed to start doing something and then not stop for hours, Jamie sincerely hoped he hadn't been laying out in the sun in the back yard all day. His baby-sitting duties stopped well and truly before abject-stupidity-sunburn treatment. There was baked chicken still in the oven on a timer though, and he seriously doubted that had just happened a couple of minutes ago.

Jamie was glad for his tiny back yard. It was one of the few on the block fenced in. The previous tenant had needed a way to keep his dog handy so by dent of window placement and fencing Jamie's yard was completely and utterly private.

Sam was sprawled out on his back, looking up at the sky over his head. Jamie watched his absolute absorption with the clouds, the way his head moved with them, neck arching once in a while, attempting to follow one over his head.

There's a thing in my back yard, possibly older than all of recorded human history, watching the clouds.

Jamie watched for a moment longer, before he walked out into the yard and carefully sat down next to him. He realized how old Samriel was. That he wasn't human and normal wasn't actually a thing and all that. But he'd been treating him like *Sam* for days. Like the kind of strange, backward guy who meant a lot to the person who meant a lot to him. Because everybody else in existence who cared about Grace got a lot of leeway out of him, Sam shouldn't have been any different.

Sam glanced at him, steady blue-silver eyes, before going back to his cloud-watching. "I can't call Grace and ask why finding out…that created a roadblock." Sam frowned. "Well. I could, but I arguably shouldn't be calling her at all right now, and that would be an abuse of the option."

Jamie relaxed back in the grass, watching the puffy clouds float over-head. "Is that how that works? Grace makes sense of the humans for you?"

Sam shrugged, un-insulted.

Jamie hadn't meant it as an insult, hadn't even meant it as a dig. More that he wasn't always sure he was alright with people leaning on Grace. Not that it was for him to be alright with. Grace was perfectly capable of telling people to back off her.

He just tended to think she wouldn't do that, with people she really cared about.

"I…"

Sam looked at him, waiting patiently.

"When I thought you'd been there and just not intervening I was angry." Jamie sighed, shifting. "But…I don't know. I guess I was a little thrown by how much it bothered me that she was really alone."

Samriel looked back up at the sky, deep in thought, and Jamie wasn't exactly waiting for the next bit of conversation with baited breath. He wasn't running away, but that didn't make him exactly ecstatic for the prospect.

Sam cleared his throat. "But she wasn't." He flicked a glance to the side. "She had you."

"I was eleven. I wasn't that much help."

"More than you imagine," Sam offered softly. "Certainly from what I saw."

That was the clincher, wasn't it? That they'd both spent all these years with Grace. All that time, Jamie there actively, doing everything he possibly could to try and keep her together. It hadn't been great for either of them, he was sure. He didn't have Samriel's abilities, and Sam hadn't had the option to actually communicate.

It was a marker of how screwed up they all were he didn't think either of them would have wanted to trade. He certainly wouldn't have.

There had been rocky moments, sure. Things he and Grace still didn't talk about. What was he supposed to do about that? *So Grace, it's been ages and I never actually asked. Why'd you basically stop talking for six months after your Mom died?* He wasn't sure he was old enough yet to handle the answer to that one. He'd certainly heard all the theories, over the years. He liked them right where they were, as theories. Theories were just hypotheticals, and he could ignore those. Ignoring worked for them. It was their thing.

Sam huffed suddenly. "I have been lying here for three point two hours. In what way do humans believe that random collections of vapor in the atmosphere contain shapes?"

"Imagination." Jamie smiled wryly. He wasn't going to ask if Sam had an imagination. Right back to treading that line, about how unusual to make the other man feel. "See, that one looks like a dragon riding a crop duster," he offered, pointing to a random cloud.

He could nearly hear the gears in Sam's head turning, he was trying so hard to visualize it. For two solid minutes as the cloud gently puffed over their heads, brows growing together and face darkening.

Jamie broke, laughing, and shoved his shoulder gently. "I'm joking Sam. At best that one looks like a smooshed marshmallow."

Sam blinked at him, shocked. "You were teasing me."

He was not analyzing what that strange mix of awe and affection in Sam's voice did to him. "Don't...whatever you are have a sense of humor?"

"Maeleket." Sam offered. "We do not, necessarily." He frowned. "Or I do not. I am learning." He shot Jamie a dark look. "Nate does not derive as much joy from teasing me as he does Curt. He claims I make him feel guilty because I don't get it."

Jamie watched him, pegs slotting to place in his head. "You do. You have to, if you've spent all that time with Grace."

Sam smiled, mischievous and dark. "No comment."

Jamie laughed, leaning back in the grass and just relaxing. It'd been a while since he'd done that, actually. "That's sort of priceless."

Sam snorted. "Grace insists eventually he will realize I am doing it, and probably declare us open season."

"Still probably worth it," Jamie agreed, nodding.

~*~***~*~

The up-swing to he and Sam making some sort of hash of their issues with each other was that things had gotten much less awkward since then. They'd relaxed in the grass, staring at the clouds for a while, and when it was done they'd talked about Jamie's classes and colleagues over dinner. Jamie had gone to work the next morning and come back to the house still in one piece and Sam reading one of his old fantasy novels, the house smelling like roasted pork chops.

He'd been subdued for most of the evening, but Jamie had an eerie feeling Sam was missing Grace. He'd caught him idly swiping at the screen on the phone Jamie had given him four or five times, like he desperately wanted to call, but it wasn't safe. A few days on, Jamie was starting to feel a little... He felt bad, much as he wanted to pretend that wasn't it. Sam was kind of a dick sometimes, and he got himself into trouble— presumably, Jamie still didn't have the slightest idea why Sam was hiding out in his house—but he obviously cared deeply about his friends.

He understood some of that. Right now he and Grace were in a place where they were okay with only talking every couple of days. But that waxed and waned. There were times they were a little more codependent than that. Where Jamie felt twitchy and wrong unless he talked to Grace every day, and saw her as much as they could manage on the weekends.

Jamie was fervently hoping Nate and Grace had a little more time to figure out their relationship before they hit one of those again. Because right now Nate didn't feel threatened by him, and maybe he never would, but maybe was no kind of guarantee.

Sam cooked again, so even if Jamie was inclined to whinge about being the one to do the dishes, tonight wouldn't be the night he did it. He'd lived with Grace for long enough in their collective lives, he knew how to manage roommates. Not well, because the only person he'd ever managed to room with, with any level of success, was Grace.

He glanced up as Sam came down the stairs, having changed his shirt. Jamie wasn't sure why, but he didn't feel like asking.

"I will need to wash things soon." He didn't look like he was over the moon about having to do that.

"Do you know how to work the washer?"

"Not with any confidence," Sam answered wryly.

Jamie wasn't sure if it was contact or the fact they'd ironed their problems out, but he'd started to notice there was this ridiculous undercurrent of wry humor in nearly everything Sam said. It wasn't overt, or probably even noticeable to most people. He imagined Grace would have picked up on it, at least the self-deprecating 'whatever I look like I'm not human' part of it.

Stuck in the same house for six days, and they'd managed to bury the hatchet. Grace was going to be insufferable.

Assuming things weren't so busy she failed to notice.

Which wasn't really a better place to be. Jamie was pretty firmly in the camp where he didn't want Grace's life being so complicated she started missing things like that. Particularly about him and Sam.

His phone chirped, and he glanced at it.

Grace: Development. Don't over-react.

Jamie snorted, shaking his head. "Sam?"

"Yes."

He jumped, looking up at the other man standing directly across the kitchen bar from him. He'd thought he was somewhere else.

"Grace says someone is coming." He turned the water off, drying his hands.

Sam frowned. "What?"

"Well, she said 'don't over-react' which means the same thing." Jamie shrugged.

Sam swallowed, his shoulders tensing and his entire posture changing. He was tense and foreboding all the sudden, not the guy Jamie'd been sharing space with these last couple of days. "She did not say who?"

"She didn't." Jamie rubbed the back of his neck. "I'm sure she had a reason."

There was a stuttered sort of flash, and suddenly there was another guy standing in Jamie's house. "Obviously we are still attempting to ensure your safety," the new guy groused, arms crossed over his impressively large chest.

"Malek." Sam swallowed, face flushing.

So this was the one Jamie hadn't ever actually heard anything about. Jamie looked him over, still standing giant and imposing at the edge of the kitchen.

He was *big*. Sam wasn't exactly a small guy—or he hadn't manifested as a small guy, whatever. Malek was a good six inches taller than Sam. Sam was bloody as tall as Jamie and honestly Jamie could probably count on one hand the number of people he'd known in his life who were taller than he was.

It wasn't just the height either. Malek was broad shouldered and heavily muscled. He sort of looked like one of those Greek statues of Zeus come to life, complete with the lightning-bolt eyes. He had presence too, something about his existence in the house making the air practically crackle. Jamie couldn't imagine what that was like to be around, if you were supposed to notice shit like that.

He wasn't. Much as his life had suddenly taken a sudden and occasionally destressing sharp left into *Strange, population 312*, Jamie was human. Staring at a thing in his house that definitely wasn't no matter how attractive it made itself.

"Samriel." The new guy's face pinched slightly. "Aside from looking distressingly close to human, you look well."

"I am fine."

Malek cocked a brow at that, and Jamie had to agree with that particular assessment. Aside from how not-fine Sam had been just a couple of days ago, he didn't even sound like he knew how to say the word.

"Jameson has been...hospitable," Sam managed uneasily, tripping over the words.

"Wow, thanks," Jamie breathed out. He probably shouldn't. He'd been having to constantly remind himself lately that Sam wasn't human, and the new guy didn't take any reminding. He wondered if that was a first meeting thing, because now that he thought about it Sam hadn't seemed all that human the first time Jamie had met him.

Or that might have been the situation. Grace had nearly fried her own brain, and he knew Sam well enough now to know how uneasy that would have made him.

No telling how much damage Jamie'd done with the not liking him thing.

But there wasn't anything he could do about that now, and if they were about to pop of to the great wide yonder without him he could at least try and keep things civil.

Sam flushed like a twelve-year old who'd just stuck his foot in his mouth, looking away. Malek laughed deep and kind, and hauled Sam into a hug. "Grace is quite attached to you, given the fact she's started to snap at me several times in the last few days. I'm sure Jamie has treated you well for no other reason than that."

Sam frowned. "She has been..."

"Entirely my fault." Malek smiled forbearingly. "She has been tense and concerned about the both of you, and I have not been particularly careful with that. I was rather more concerned with making sure we could fix this without putting you at undue risk."

Sam flushed.

"You can explain in a moment." Malek sighed. "While I would very much like an explanation," he paused, voice fatherly and strict. "I'd rather not leave the rest of them at Curt's alone." Malek nodded. "I am here, I will mask your presence. Shift back and we are returning to Curt's."

Sam nodded, and looked at Jamie, swallowing. "Thank you for your help."

"Don't thank him yet," Malek said dryly. "He's coming with us." He paused, looking Jamie over. He wasn't particularly subtle about it. Clearly he was measuring him up. But his eyes were still clear and frosty-green, so Jamie had passed. "Unless of course you would prefer not to."

"No, I'm coming." He dropped the dish-towel he'd forgotten he was still holding, and nodded once. "Let me lock up and grab some clothes."

It was tempting to hide around the corner on the stairs, and see what they did when he wasn't right there. If Malek or Sam said anything when they were alone.

He didn't. Jamie'd learned at a young age not to eavesdrop, you only heard things you didn't want to. So he raced up his stairs as quickly as reasonably possible, ignored Sam's open door—it wasn't Sam's, it was the guest room because Sam was leaving and why in the name of all things fluffy did that bother him?

Jamie only needed about twenty seconds to pack his things. He wasn't quite paranoid enough to keep a bag waiting at all times, because if he did and Grace found out about it she got upset with him and his fatalistic tendencies. Which didn't so much matter when things were bad. If he thought there was any realistic possibility he was going to need to go fast he kept things packed.

He pulled the duffel out from under his bed, checking the bag of toiletries he kept in it. He grabbed clothes, and the discreet knife he'd bought off a motorcycle-gang member the year Grace turned sixteen. It wasn't the nicest blade, and he certainly could have bought one legally that was better.

It signified something. The person Jamie should have been, as opposed to who he was. The gutter rat that settled his problems with a blade or his fists who'd never have survived his teens without something to strive for, held against the respectable professor who spent his summers helping troubled kids.

Jamie wrapped his hand around the pommel, feeling the strange weight in his palm and the tension in his muscles. It wasn't a pretty thing. Cardboard vinyl sheath, black electrical tape wrapped over the handle, old tarnished metal glinting in the over-head light.

It was a marker of how screwed up he was, that he understood how unhealthy it was that everything he ever did was for Grace.

He just didn't care.

He blew out a breath and dropped the knife back in the bag, zipping it carefully closed. He turned the light off and walked slowly down the stairs. If Malek and Sam had moved, they didn't look like it. Sam was waiting for him, posture intentionally loose and easy. There was a tension around his eyes that made it a lie.

Malek watched Sam's tense shoulders and stiff spine carefully.

Jamie was good at reading people. He could have blamed it on the job, on being a ridiculously overqualified social worker. But right there in his main room, Sam tense and quiet, Malek watching him like a concerned father, that wasn't the social worker. That wasn't textbooks and adult experience. Anybody who pretended a person could learn that as an adult was lying.

So. This is awkward.

Jamie cleared his throat and held his bag out for Sam. He didn't ask if Sam had locked the doors, or moved from the spot he was standing in. He hadn't. He just dropped his bag into Sam's outstretched hand, and moved to lock the doors and turn off everything but the hallway light.

He cast around for something to say. The silence had officially gotten a little long in the tooth. Grace was better at that than he was. In that she wasn't, she just seemed to barrel out with whatever she thought needed to be said and didn't really think about it. Painfully embarrassing and uncomfortable as that could be, he did occasionally miss it.

"Are you prepared?" Malek asked, kind and almost careful.

Jamie nodded. "I'm assuming you don't want to use my car, but I don't know…"

Malek smiled reassuringly—which was really freaking creepy, Jamie could do without the kindness and understanding actually—and shifted. "It is a relatively simple thing. I will take your arm, and then we will be at Curt's."

Jamie only had about thirty questions—was it likely to go wrong, would he see little blinky lights, did anyone ever get motion sickness—but they weren't helpful, and the answers didn't actually matter so he held his arm out to take his bag back from Sam, fingers snagging the handle as Malek's hand landed on his other arm.

CHAPTER 6

Sam didn't let go of the bag, and when Jamie felt anything again it was Sam who had his arm instantly wrapped around his side to hold him on his feet. "Jamie?"

He had to blink for a minute, because aside from the fact he'd just been nowhere for who the fuck knew how long, Sam sounded worried and uneasy.

Malek frowned, face pinching. "Bother. It didn't occur to me you might be unusually sensitive."

Grace was suddenly right there, hand wrapped around his wrist, eyes giant and concerned. "Alright?"

Jamie forced himself to swallow, nodding. "Creeped out, but fine."

Sam hadn't let go of him yet, which meant he was rather at a disadvantage when Grace grabbed him and tried to squeeze the life out of him. Sam loosened his hold on Jamie, shortly before they fell over, and patted Grace on the shoulder carefully, eyes wide and imploring.

"You're the one who let her think you were dead," Jamie said, straightening carefully. "Don't look at me."

Nate laughed, clapping him on the shoulder. "Sure you're okay?"

"Fine." Jamie rolled his shoulders. "You ever done that?"

"Nope." Nate bit the word off. "Looking at your face I don't think I want to."

Jamie looked around, taking in the press of people into the small kitchen. He and Nate, Grace and Sam, Curt, Malek, Deke and presumably Willy—she was the only woman in the room other than Grace, so it wasn't much of a long shot—and a sour faced Greek reject with his arms folded over his chest and body posture a cross black-belt would have been proud of.

Nate followed his gaze and huffed softly. "Yeah. It's been..." He cleared his throat and slapped Jamie on the shoulder. "Hey, you're in one piece and Sam's in one piece and we're all here so—"

"What happened?" the new guy in the back practically barked, Curt and Nate both glaring at him.

Malek sighed. "Bazel, give Grace a moment to assure herself he is still in one piece, I doubt she'll let him skirt around answering."

Almost on cue Grace pulled back and slugged Sam in the shoulder. "I'll be careful Grace, I know what I'm doing."

Sam half-heartedly flinched back. "I did not say—"

"Sam." Jamie rubbed his forehead. "Shut-up while you're ahead."

Malek laughed softly, and Nate and Deke both snorted.

Grace grabbed Jamie in a quick hug, kissing his cheek.

Jamie squeezed her, nearly lifting her off her feet. "If you thank me I'm going to make faces at you."

She smiled, easy and light, nodding. "I know. You wouldn't turn someone away if they needed you."

He was never as sure of that as Grace was, but on the plus side he'd spent so much of his life trying to be worth her friendship it was sort of second-nature anymore. Absolutely anyone who was friends with Grace that turned up bleeding on his door-step he was going to do whatever he could for.

Not to mention, he sort of...liked Sam.

Christ his life was a mess.

"Perhaps Samriel would be kind enough to tell us what happened now," Bazel grated.

Sam glared at him, arms crossing over his chest. "I did my duty, as decided—"

"The decision," Bazel said coldly, "was that you would go and speak with Tanik and the other, lower members of the council and possibly some other Warders as those are contacts the rest of us do not have, and that you would endeavor not to—"

"Bazel," Malek chastised, looking for all the world like he didn't want to be playing mediator right then. He turned to Sam, face easing. "What went wrong?"

Sam folded his arms over his chest. "I went to Tanik's hart, but before he returned Helin found me. It took very little time to realize he had gone dark." He glared at Bazel, hackles up. "We fought, I bested him easily."

Malek nodded sadly. "I've found his...body."

That was a strange place for a connotation, and Jamie was absolutely not going to ask why. Ever. Mostly because he felt like someone had just walked over his grave.

Sam paled, looking at Malek imploringly. "I did not kill him. I would not have, because dead he could not answer questions."

Malek relaxed, obviously relieved. "Indeed. Which is why they did, obviously. Did you see who it was?"

"No." Sam swallowed. "But to have managed to appropriately shield themselves from me." He shrugged.

"It had to be a council member." Bazel swallowed.

"It did." Sam nodded. "I got away, but I was...badly injured. I thought it best if I went somewhere off radar."

"Of course," Bazel muttered. "Much better to let us think you were dead."

"As opposed to actually being dead, yes," Grace snapped.

Jamie watched, intrigued, as Nate reached out and fastened his hand on Grace's shoulder. It was subtle. He wasn't trying to shush her—which Jamie would have had issue with no matter how much he liked Nate—just remind her the rest of them were there.

"Was he working with this Tanik?" Curt piped up.

Sam shrugged.

Malek sighed. "Do you remember anything about the attack?"

Sam cast back, eyes distant as he thought through it.

"Anything at all." Malek prompted, patient and easy. "A sound, or a voice. A smell."

Sam blinked. "I smelled metal. Not…it was…harsher than one would expect. More…refined than elemental."

Malek blinked, clearly putting something together in his mind. "We need to know if Tanik is involved in this." He looked at Sam and Bazel. "I will go look for him, I will not be quiet about it, we don't really have a better choice."

He paused for a second, like he was giving one of the others a chance to raise an objection, or make another suggestion. Sam nodded, and Bazel just watched them all with the same dark face.

Malek nodded. "Very well. He will come here, I am sure. I would suggest placing some sort of protection on Jameson," he smiled easily. "The rest of you will be fine. Keep watch," he said to Sam and Bazel, before reaching out and doing something that enveloped Sam in bright white light, and left him clearly all back to good.

Then he disappeared.

Grace sighed, and tugged on Jamie's arm. "Come on. I've got a medallion you can use."

He let her drag him out of the kitchen, Sam tracking them with his eyes, Nate and Grace communicating non-verbally.

"It's a little strange, that you have a language now that doesn't involve me."

Grace blinked back at him, leading him into what he was guessing used to be the living room. He'd never actually been in Curt's house. It looked about like he'd imagined, stacked to the ceiling with books and papers, odd bits of crap squirreled away in the corners. "You don't sound upset by that."

Jamie snorted. "You know I'm not."

Grace flashed him a smile, and riffled around in a desk drawer, careful of all the other junk on it. "I know it looks like a giant fire-hazard, but Curt starts to get twitchy if

I reorganize too much." She glanced around. "Used to be worse, actually." She made a sound of pleasure, and stood up with a giant metal disk in her hand, almost the size of a tennis ball, holding it out to him.

"What changed?"

She smiled wryly, shrugging. "Sam. Said it was a fire-hazard and Curt and I could tame it some, or he'd do it."

Jamie snorted, lips curling into an unsurprised smile, while he settled the heavy disk over his neck. "So how much use is this against a rogue...whatever Sam and the other guys are."

"Maeleket," Grace said easily. "Not much against them, but they tend to leave the human's alone. It's a...cultural thing. Sort of." Her brow pinched. "Sam doesn't talk about it much, and Malek might but he's actually not around all that much."

"And Bazel?"

Grace's nose wrinkled. "Is Bazel. He's Willy's dad, and I'm sure he answers questions for her. I don't really know him."

"You don't sound upset by that."

She stopped riffling through papers, looking up at him. He could see the exact moment it clicked for her, that she was talking to him again and not any of the other people rattling around in her life. It was like all the tension just flowed out of her shoulders. They were back to where they'd always been. Him and Grace. Whatever else happened in the world, or with them, they always had that.

It'd taken him *years* to understand that no matter where they went or what happened, what their lives became or who they loved that was never going to change. Grace had been his best friend since the day they met and she'd be his best friend until the day he died—past it, if there was some sort of after-life out there—and vice versa.

They hadn't, either of them, had much of a steadying influence when they were kids. Other than Aunt

Rhoda—she'd done about as much as she could, in regard to informal adoption—it'd always just been the two of them.

Grace shifted, sitting on the edge of the desk, shoulders shrugging. "He's...strange? Nate thinks he's just worried about Sam."

"And you don't?"

"I don't know." She smoothed her hair down. "Nate's better at that stuff than I am, generally. He figures Sam and Bazel have been friends for a long time, like..."

"*Long time*," Jamie input.

"Yeah." Grace nodded. "So I don't know. He's been kind of a giant pain in the ass these last few days and it could just be that he's worried. And he was being kinda shitty there, which I suppose could just be worry." Her face clouded. "We've been friends for a long time, and we're generally not shitty to each other even when we're worried, are we?"

"No." Jamie leaned forward and kissed her on the forehead, pulling her into a tight hug, smiling. "But I don't think we're any kind of indicative of what other people do."

"Point." Grace sighed, arms wrapped around his shoulders. "I missed you, in case I didn't get a chance to say."

"You didn't, but I guessed. Ditto."

She laughed, and settled the large metal disk under his shirt. "Don't take that off, for right now. I'll see if Deke and I can work up something a little less conspicuous, but that'll probably be tomorrow at best." She frowned. "Which is assuming you're sticking around."

"I am."

Grace looked him in the eyes, serious and sure. "No chance I can talk you into going back to your own life?"

"No." Jamie shook his head, smiling wryly.

Her eyes narrowed, and she cocked her head at him. "Jameson Nathaniel, are you trying to pass a rule two off as a rule five?"

He couldn't help his blush, or ducking his head and rubbing the back of his neck, even though it was a giant freaking tell. "Not really *trying*."

Grace just cocked a brow at him, waiting.

"Your life is obviously being a bit rocky right now, and I'm *here*, so…"

"And the part that's a rule two?"

"There's not…I'm…" Jamie flushed, and closed his eyes and took a deep breath because Grace wasn't going to drop it unless he explained, or double-invoked rule two which he didn't really want to do. "Being stuck in a house together made us work some things out." He swallowed. "Us as in Sam and I."

Grace blinked, brain making connections at about a million miles an hour and he knew for a fact at least three or four of those were going to be way the hell too close to the truth for him—however incompatible they were, Sam was fucking gorgeous and Grace obviously already liked him and on the list of 'Traits for Jamie's perfect Guy/Girl' those weren't maybe the top, but they were pretty high.

"So you—"

"I DON'T CARE HOW RIGHT YOU THOUGHT YOU WERE!"

Grace froze, blinking in shock, and Jamie barely had time to grab her by the elbow before she was heading back for the kitchen. Given he didn't immediately recognize the voice, and there was screaming, he was going to guess it was Bazel.

Wonderful.

CHAPTER 7

Sam clenched his hands at his sides. He knew it was a human sign of anger, but he didn't really care. The pulse thundering in his ears was new, but not distracting enough to pull him back from the words coming out of his mouth. "I was as careful as I could have been."

He and Bazel had history. Generally speaking it was history Sam didn't exactly understand. Bazel had already been on the council when Sam came into being, and he'd spent his first years at the Council coming to terms with the fact Bazel actually paid attention to him. Long before he should have. It wasn't as if in all that time they'd never disagreed. There had been several times—the decision to leave Aziel with his family absolutely—when they'd had different views on something.

But they'd always worked through it, and Sam was decently sure Bazel had never been on the verge of screaming at him. "It was imperative—"

"I DON'T CARE HOW RIGHT YOU THOUGHT YOU WERE!"

"Would it have been better if I'd led them here, when I couldn't help protect Grace or—"

"You have a duty!" Bazel slammed his hands on the table. "Your ridiculous attachment to Grace makes you—"

Sam didn't realize he'd stepped forward. He'd heard humans for ages complain that they were so angry everything devolved into a red haze and they didn't recognize their actions. He hadn't precisely thought they were lying, he'd just never thought it applied to him. Right until he felt himself slam against Jamie.

"I understand you're upset," Jamie said softly, hand fastened around Sam's wrist, still full in his space. "You two arguing to the point you forget what you're saying probably isn't a grand idea right now."

Sam blinked, world phasing back in around him. Grace had her hand on his shoulder, and Willy had grabbed Bazel. Bazel looked like he was perfectly willing to send the humans off somewhere else and finish their argument. Jamie—who hadn't even *liked* him a couple of days ago—had just leapt right in, like there was absolutely no chance Sam was going to forget who he was fighting with and hit Jamie instead.

Or maybe it'd just been instinctual, the sort of human Jamie was.

He was still there, muscles were bunched and ready, but he wasn't unduly tense. Something in Sam's mind whispered that whatever tension there might have been was because Bazel was behind him and Jamie'd only just met him.

He swallowed, forcing himself to relax. Their current issue aside, Bazel was something to him in a way very few others of his kind were. He didn't want Jamie, or anyone else, to form an unfairly negative opinion of the other Maeleket.

Jamie let go of him slowly, realizing he was calm again. "Just…go to separate corners as much as you can and finish this later when we don't need you both to keep everybody else safe."

Curt elbowed Grace softly. "Should bring him around more often, boy talks sense."

Sam couldn't focus and it was that, that convinced him Jamie was right and he needed to go. Or one of them needed to go.

"Fine," Bazel huffed, and turned to leave.

"No." Sam swallowed, focused on the quiet humor in Jamie's face, the way he was still just standing there. "No.

I am not fully recovered. I will stay on the wards." He flicked a glance at Nate, waiting for him to catch on.

"Got it." Nate tugged Grace back just a step. "Take as long as you need, we'll holler."

"Take your cell phone," Grace insisted. "And don't go far."

Sam stopped, halfway to the door, and looked at Grace carefully. Theoretically she would be fine in the house. Bazel was capable of taking care of her, and Nate was there. Deke rather needed Grace in one piece as well, even if he hadn't exactly come to terms with why that was yet. Grace reached out blindly, fingers wrapping around Jamie's wrist despite being pulled tight against Nate.

Sam nodded once and stepped out into the cold, steel-gray night.

~*~***~*~

He'd thought, when he walked out of the house, that he would work on Grace's surprise.

Sam was very careful to never call it a house, or a home, or anything else. The only thing he ever referred to it as was Grace's Surprise or 'the project.' He paid very little attention to what he was saying when he was alone with Grace, but he still would have remembered not to say anything to her. He didn't know why he wasn't ready to call it a house yet.

Much as he hated to admit it, he'd rather lost control of his lines with Grace. He didn't care what that did with his standing with the council, or what the rest of the Maeleket thought of that. They didn't know Grace. They hadn't watched her over all those years, been there all the times she'd gotten up and dusted herself off and kept moving.

He pressed his palm to the finished corner, feeling the wards reach out and recognize him. They were spectacular, given they were still unfinished. Deacon would need to access his entire store of magic to finish them completely, and that would require telling Grace, so they'd finished the wards as much as possible and left the rest for when the actual house was finished. It was laying groundwork, just like Deacon and Nate had done for the plumbing and the electricity.

They calmed him though. Whispered through his mind and said 'home' and 'welcome.' Unfinished or not, they were still keyed. Keyed specifically to Grace and Nate, and built to recognize and protect the people they cared about. He knew Grace could feel the pull from the house, despite the ridiculous amount of effort they'd put into dampening it.

Not just so the warding wouldn't give the secret away. There was a point when you protected something so stringently it became a target.

Sam choked out a half-chuckle and dropped his forehead against the wall in front of him. The irony— situational, not literal—in that wasn't lost on him. Assuming Bazel hadn't been just pulling arguments out of thin air, that was his problem as well. Bazel felt like not only was Sam neglecting his duty to the council to be with Grace, to protect her and keep her safe and happy, but he was putting her in danger doing it.

His stomach squirmed and fell at the thought. He had a worryingly instinctual response to Grace being in danger. Worrying, because he wasn't supposed to *have* instincts. Instincts suggested genetic knowledge, suggested a bloodline and a...before. Maeleket didn't have that. They didn't have parents, or families.

He looked up at the side of the structure before him, hand still pressed against the ward point. They didn't have houses either. They didn't want them. True connections, emotional connections were a waste of time. Humans needed society, they banded together to protect each other from danger. From darkness and predators. From winter and starvation.

Before the invention of the Council there had been no Maeleket society.

Not that Sam remembered that. Sam had come into being shortly after the council was brought about. He'd been young, for a race that didn't really mark time, when he became a Watcher. Not long after he'd become a Warder. The only purpose he'd had in his very long life was the Council. Was their dedication to correcting the mistakes other less scrupulous Maeleket had wrought on the human realm.

He'd long ago stopped internally trying to twist his dedication to Grace into that. Grace was Grace. A law unto her own in more ways than just Sam.

A footstep sounded on the path, and his power spiked as he turned.

Jamie stepped around the trees, looking up at the half-finished structure, cheeks already pink from the walk from Curt's. His breath clouded before his face, and he shoved his hands deep in the pockets of his borrowed jacket.

The cold was coming on fast, and Sam found himself instinctively measuring whether or not the leather jacket Jamie had borrowed from Nate fit him well enough to keep him warm. It was a little short in the arms, and he doubted it would zip over Jamie's chest, but the other man didn't seem uncomfortable.

"You aren't supposed to be here," Sam said, finding his voice.

Jamie walked forward, looking it over, before pushing a hand against the wall. Sam knew Jamie couldn't feel the wards, but they'd definitely felt him, reached for him so strongly and instinctively they nearly tugged Sam a step closer.

"Nate told me," Jamie said, smiling at him absently. He was tracing his hands over the edges of the windows, eyes almost reverently tracing the interior spaces. "He's building her a house," Jamie whispered in awe, voice low and warm.

"He is."

Jamie took his hand off finally, shoving his hands back in his pockets. "And you and Deke are helping."

Sam swallowed. "With the protections mostly."

"Protections?"

"Magical warding." He followed, drawn as Jamie walked over to sit on the picnic table. "Spellwork attached at the pre-built level is stronger than things added once a building is finished. The lay-work was Deacon's idea."

"And your contribution?"

Sam almost flushed. "Keying it specifically to draw energy from and exert energy for the people that Grace and Nate care the most for."

Jamie cocked his head to the side. "Why?"

"If they have children." Sam swallowed. "Keying it specifically to them means that however that group grows and changes, it changes with them."

He smiled, eyes warm. "The human heart is boundless."

They waited quietly in the night, until the snow started softly falling and the air grew colder. Until Sam started to actively pay attention to Jamie's body temperature because he had to be growing cold.

Jamie laughed, scratching his nose with his shoulder. "I was going to ask if you were cold, but that's probably a stupid question."

Sam felt his lips curl into a smile. "Malek healed me so I am no longer wrapped into something approaching a human form. I am still manifested. It would be a rather large signal if I didn't notice the ambient temperature."

"Point."

They'd fallen silent again, and Sam finally gave in and sat on the picnic table as well.

"Do you want to talk about it?"

Sam blinked at Jamie, lost.

"The yelling at a guy I'm pretty sure you like." Jamie frowned. "Or more his yelling at you. Despite about throwing a punch, you weren't yelling. Do you yell?"

He swallowed, parsing through the rattled list of questions. "I...I do not know." Sam's brow furrowed. "Not really. When they took you." He flushed, flicking a glance at Jamie. "I rose my voice at Grace."

Jamie cocked a brow, waiting.

"She was determined to go after you and I didn't want her to." Sam rushed on. "Not that I wasn't dedicated to helping you or anything of the sort. It was a trap and he wanted Grace specifically. And he'd placed a spell on her that meant I couldn't trace her." He sighed. "Which was probably a side effect of ensuring Deacon could not find you through Grace, since he didn't know about me at the time."

Jamie started laughing, dropping his head down and resting his elbows on his knees.

Not that Sam didn't like the sound of Jamie's laughter. He just didn't understand what he'd done to illicit it. He looked up at Sam eventually, eyes strangely bright in the dark night. "What?"

Jamie shook his head, pushing his hair back from his face. "You're how old and you've never raised your voice before you were around for Grace being stupidly protective of me?"

Sam looked down, eyes focusing on the ground at his feet, the gentle energy given off by the life struggling to survive in the cold ground giving him something to focus on. "I understand I am overly committed to Grace."

Jamie choked out a laugh. "I've got no stones to throw about that, and you know it."

Sam blinked at him.

"Come on, Sam." Jamie sighed. "You were around for years." He shrugged. "I've turned 'overly committed to Grace' into my life's quest. Keep it to yourself, but I understand exactly how unhealthy that is."

Sam frowned. "But?"

"That doesn't mean it's a mistake." Jamie smiled wryly. "You know just as well as I do what I'd have been, without Grace."

"I would not think you would be so open about that."

Jamie sighed. "I can't not be. I have to own that, otherwise I'm slipping back into..." He stopped, and smiled sadly at Sam. "Having shitty role-models as a kid isn't an excuse for being a shitty person as an adult."

Sam swallowed, recognizing the words instantly. "Your aunt is a very opinionated person."

Jamie laughed, shaking his head. "You're just as terrified of her as the rest of us are, admit it."

He flushed. "I am not afraid of her."

Jamie cocked a brow at him, just waiting.

"My desire to not know her opinion of my life does not equal fear." Sam shifted. "I believe Grace would agree with me, that is self-preservation."

"Probably. We haven't told her about any of this, you know? And for the record, in case you managed to miss it, Grace is even worse at lying to Rhoda than she is at lying to me."

Sam frowned. "Would you tell her?" Grace had initially tried to keep things from Jamie. Not because she'd thought he wouldn't believe her, but because she hadn't wanted to burden him with it. And Sam supposed he'd just assumed Jamie would do the same with his Aunt.

Never mind the fact Jamie's mother still existed in the world, not that they spoke more than rarely on Christmas.

"Not if I don't have to." Jamie frowned. "We've gotten off topic, was that intentional?"

Sam blinked. "No." He looked back at the house. "I have known Bazel for...a long time."

"Thank you, I'd rather not know the actual year marker," Jamie muttered.

He almost smiled. "It is possible he really is simply upset with me because I could be putting Grace in danger." Just having to say that out loud threatened to choke his voice off. Made his throat strange and thick in a way he didn't really know how to deal with.

Jamie reached up and wrapped a warm large hand over Sam's shoulder, just squeezing.

"He could also feasibly be upset with me simply because my duty to the council became…"

"Threadbare?" Jamie offered softly. "From what Grace said that wasn't all about her. At least not directly."

Sam let out a humorless laugh. "They handed an idiot the family I'd looked after for *millennia* and he drove them into the ground in less than three generations."

"And now you're afraid to walk away from Grace for more than a day because something might happen to her too?"

Sam frowned at Jamie, huffing. "It does. Frequently."

"You have a point." Jamie wiped his hands on his thighs. "Listen, I'm just going to throw this out there." He glanced at Sam. "I don't know all the politics and…whatever else. Because I still don't actually know what you are. That's a little me not being comfortable asking, and a little having bigger things to worry about." He sighed. "I don't understand why there's so much connotation floating around about you getting attached. I can't imagine actually caring about the people you're supposed to protect and shepherd being a bad thing, but like I said, I don't really know."

Jamie watched Sam for a long moment. "Grace likes you, honestly and completely, I think you understand how rare that is in a way these other people don't. And for a minute we're going to pretend you're human and I'm just going to give you advice like you are." He paused, drawing a deep breath. "You didn't want Grace to go running into a trap looking for me, but you didn't stop her. Maybe that was because she didn't let you, but I don't believe it's just that. Just because your lines are getting a little blurry, that doesn't mean your instincts aren't good. There are going to be things you can't protect her from, any more than I can, or Nate can."

Sam frowned.

"Sam. I've pushed it off for *years* but at some point her Dad's going to come waltzing up the driveway." Jamie looked at him, eyes dark and serious.

"Then why haven't you told her?"

"Because it wouldn't help any." Jamie pushed a hand through his hair. "I might, if she ever actually acknowledged his existence, but Grace deals with the things she can. If she won't talk about it I don't make her." He wrapped his hands tight around the edge of the picnic table. "And because he makes me angry enough, I start losing where my lines are." He closed his eyes, blowing out a breath. "The point I'm trying to make here is that it's a crap situation and you're a little out to sea but you're *trying*." Jamie forced a smile. "And I think the other guy is too, and it's hard to watch your friend do things you think might be mistakes and not at least try to stop them."

Sam swallowed, trying to take all of that in. He'd given up on finding a box for Jamie. Whatever they'd been a few days ago, before Sam appeared at his door trying to bleed to death, they were friends now. Obviously, because Jamie was entirely the sort of man to try and make anyone feel better.

He wouldn't sit out in the snow and cold so Sam could have a mild panic incident for anyone. "We should go back." Sam glanced back toward the house. "Grace will worry about you."

Jamie stood, stretching, and watched him. "It's not me she's worried about."

Sam flushed.

"But it's officially a little past comfortable out here. Inside sounds good."

~*~***~*~

Sam sat in Curt's kitchen and tried to feel the vibration in the wards. They should have calmed him. They recognized Grace just as readily as the others did, and he could feel them just as well.

91

He knew why it didn't work. The wards there weren't Grace's. They accepted Grace, and Grace had helped re-strengthen them a couple of times, since she'd more or less moved in with Curt. They weren't built for her. Weren't expressly chosen to connect in the way that would latch onto Grace the best.

Because they'd been wrong, actually. Now that the block was out of Grace's head, she was perfectly capable of a rather startling, scary amount of craft. Frequently Deacon barely managed to finish explaining something to her, and she'd managed it.

She knew how to do things now. Knew how to manage temporary warding, and protections, and any of a hundred things. Sam knew he could ask her to do that. He doubted he'd even need to finish the request and she would. Because he'd never said the feel of her energy comforted him but he seriously doubted she didn't know.

A beer bottle dropped down on the table to his left, and Sam blinked as Nate settled into the seat next to him.

"You're freaking me out here, Sam."

He blinked at Nate, looking around because he hadn't heard Nate walk into the room and that wasn't good. They were alone, the house quiet and still.

"Grace and Jamie are looking at some books, because if he's sticking around even short term she's going to make sure he can protect himself." Nate forced a smile. "Curt went to do something. I didn't really ask. Deke was helping Grace with Jamie, and Willy's with her Dad."

Sam nodded. "Curt didn't leave?"

"No." Nate snorted. "So."

"I am...freaking you out." Sam frowned. "Why?"

Nate pulled a long draught from his bottle, and wiped his mouth. "Because you disappeared for a couple of days—and even if it was the right thing to do, you know you scared the shit out of us—and now you're back but you look..."

Sam cocked a brow at him.

"I don't know man. You look lost."

He knew Nate hadn't started that sentence expecting it to end there. They were a strange crew. Sam with no instincts, Jamie denying his with everything he had, and Nate who just jumped into his feet first and trusted them to keep him on the right track. Sam didn't begrudge him that. He could see, from outside—or as outside as he could get—that the concept of falling in love with Grace might have scared Nate away, if he'd thought it through first.

The fact Nate kept finding the ground under his feet, kept finding the right way through the snarl of strange that was inside Grace's head was its own sort of miracle.

That didn't mean Sam knew what he was talking about right then.

Well, he understood the concept of lost. Because after six thousand years, the fact still remained he'd never found himself backed into a corner, facing down an unknown number of foes that consisted of his own kind. He'd never been *here* before, so of course he was lost.

"Is this a you and Jamie thing, or a 'the world is falling apart around us' thing?" Nate took another sip and dropped his elbows onto the table, leaning forward. "I only ask because I'm not sure Grace would notice and if it's the first I'm not sure you want Jamie rattling around in your head trying to help."

"Me and..." Sam frowned. "In what way to you mean a 'me and Jamie' thing?"

Nate blinked at him, cocking a brow high. "In the way that before last week you two couldn't stand to be in the same room together? In the way Jamie went all tense and quiet any time your name came up and you got this stupid furrow between your eyes any time his came up and now neither of those things happen? In the way he jumped in your space when you'd forgotten the rest of us were here and not only didn't you throw a punch—which I never counted much of a risk anyway—you didn't even push him off."

Sam watched Nate for a long moment, aware the other man was going to wait patiently until he got some sort of answer, and Sam was going to give it to him. However long he'd been following Grace around and everything else, Nate was actually his first true human friend. It was Nate that looked at him and asked for an explanation. Nate who accepted he had his own issues first, and still tried to help.

Nate who arbitrarily decided to shorten his name, and then invested it with so much emotion Sam couldn't help but adopt it.

"There was a...a misunderstanding."

Nate frowned. "About Grace?"

Sam nodded. "Jameson thought I'd found Grace right away, and just...hung back because she was physically well and I wasn't supposed to interfere."

"Shit." Nate took another long gulp. "I can see where he'd be pretty ticked about that." He peeled at the label, glancing up at Sam. "You don't know what happened, do you?"

"No." Sam frowned. As Jamie had said, Grace didn't talk about things. Sam knew how things had been from the age of thirteen. Not before then. He could guess, at a lot of it. "Do you?"

Nate rubbed the back of his neck. "I know her Dad said something...um...something he shouldn't have after her Mom died."

Sam blinked. "Did she say what?"

"No." Nate choked out a laugh, shaking his head. "No. Just putting the pieces together." He forced a smile. "It's not like I'm gonna ask."

Sam frowned, wondering how many people in her life had assumed Grace didn't want to talk. "One of us might need to, eventually."

Nate sighed, rubbing his forehead. "I don't know. I sort of think if Grace wanted to talk about it she wouldn't need an opening. And with anybody else I'd say keeping themselves that tightly wrapped wouldn't be a good thing. But that's just the way Grace works."

Sam smiled wryly, nodding.

"And that was an awesome attempt at a change of topic. Much as you and Jamie both have problems with this, the universe doesn't revolve around Grace." Nate smiled at him, eyes warm. "And I'm the one that's in love with her."

He winced, flushing.

"I promise not to freak out and start second guessing everything that comes out of your mouth if you tell me you don't know what you're doing."

"How could it possibly help to say that out loud?"

Nate watched him for a long moment, before he pushed out a huff. "I'm not good at this man. Curt, or Deke; shit, anybody but Grace is generally better at emotions than I am, whatever that says."

Sam blinked at him.

"I'm good with fear." Nate gave him a wry smile. "Plenty of practice with that. I've never found it all that helpful to pretend I'm not afraid, that just gives it extra places to squirrel in. I'll give you an observation, between knowing you for however long it's been now, and spending the last week in this house with Bazel?"

He nodded for Nate to continue, because whatever he was or wasn't admitting he valued Nate's opinion.

"You guys suck at fear. Every time Grace is in trouble you damn near fall apart for the first five minutes, and forget what you are and aren't supposed to do. He's been goddamn chewing on the walls like a gun-shy hound on the Fourth of July. And maybe that's because it's not something you deal with a lot, or…hell, I don't know. Is that it?"

Sam smiled sadly, shaking his head. "Probably. We aren't accustomed to physical danger for ourselves, absolutely."

"Sure, and then you wrap worrying about Grace and the rest of us into that. And he's got to worry about Deke and Willy, with the added fun that she's probably a bit of a target anyway, no matter how understanding Malek's been about her."

Sam shifted his shoulders, trying to roll some of the tension out of the muscles. It was a bit overwhelming, hearing it all laid out. "I know nothing."

Nate watched him, waiting.

"I do not know who was pulling the strings with the one who tried to remove me from the equation. I do not know what this is about, or how many of my kind are involved. Finding others to fight against that will be difficult, even with Malek."

"And there's a limit to how helpful the rest of us will be," Nate finished for him.

"Absolutely not." Sam swallowed. "Grace has all but convinced me we were wrong about the concept of miracles, and you and Curt both have been known to manage your way around the impossible. I've no clue what Willow is actually capable of, pushed into a corner, and you're cementing your bonds more and more all the time." He flushed. "That doesn't make me happy about dragging you into a problem that shouldn't be yours to shoulder."

"But *you're* ours," Nate said, frowning. "So of course it is."

Sam flushed, looking away.

"Dude, did I just make you blush?"

Sam rubbed his face with his palms. "Remind me why I tolerate you?"

Nate clapped him on the shoulder. "Because Grace loves me."

Sam looked up at him, feeling his face heat again because clearly he needed to fix that. The universe wasn't resembling the sort of place right then that you could leave someone unsure of where they stood with you. "I…I am vastly appreciative of the fact she's found someone. That is not why I am fond of you." He pushed on, despite the fact clearly neither he nor Nate were comfortable with the conversation. "You are one of the best men I've ever known and I am lucky to know you."

It was Nate's turn to blush, and rub the back of his neck. "Thanks." He forced a smile. "I know you don't just like me because of Grace, but it's nice to know…that."

Curt stepped into the doorway then, and froze solid. "Should I go?"

"No." They both answered at the same time, and then laughed.

Curt looked between them and rolled his eyes. "You boys come up with any plans?"

Sam huffed. "I am—"

"I know how much older you are," Curt stopped him. "You sit in my kitchen making each other uncomfortable with *emotions* and constantly teasing each other like you're twelve, I'm gonna call you boy."

"All the shit you give me about repression and you say 'emotions' like it's a four-letter word," Nate muttered.

Curt made a face. "I'll admit lately you've been a little less likely to bury your emotions underneath six miles of whiskey."

Sam frowned, cocking his head to the side. He'd never seen Nate drink all that much. He knew a lot of the other hunters around them drank a fair amount. Sam had never actually *met* Nate's mother, but she'd been skirted around in conversation plenty.

Nate clearly guessed what he was thinking though, because he answered Sam's question before he found it. "It took me like five minutes around Grace to realize it was going to make her uncomfortable if I tried drowning my problems in a bottle." He flushed. "And before anything else she was making my job a hell of a lot easier."

Deke wandered back in then, fiddling with some sort of amulet. "How screwy is it that it hasn't even been a full year yet since you two met?"

Nate glared at Deke, huffing. "What color was it you just finished painting your bedroom?"

Deke flushed. "Fuck you."

"Sorry, I'm taken." Nate smiled into his beer-bottle.

"Yeah well," Deke sighed, finishing what he was doing and dropping down at the table. "We all know Grace is a saint."

Willy came in then, dropping onto the last chair, making a face at their looks. "Sorry, the best friend bickering is..." she paused. "Are they seriously always like that?" she asked Nate.

"Yes," both Sam and Nate answered.

Willy snorted. "Dad's watching them like they're a ping-pong match."

Nate leaned back, clearly listening. "It's about a book, isn't it?"

Deke blinked at him. "How can you tell?"

"There's no..." Sam wrinkled his nose. "They don't either of them precisely yell, but it gets much less quiet when they're actually arguing. Now they're just discussing stridently."

"What are they talking about?" Nate asked, looking at Willy.

Willy flinched. "Apparently she didn't think to mention there's a decently large chance of blowback with most of the craft she's been doing lately." She flicked a guilty glance at Deke. "And then somehow Jamie figured out that people you care about can lessen that and—"

"And she didn't ask and he's rightfully upset about that," Curt finished knowledgably.

"You know it's not that simple," Nate said darkly.

Curt turned, leaning against the counter, huffing. "If that was you in there would that matter?"

"On which end?" Deke muttered.

Nate sighed. "Listen, it's—"

Sam felt the ripple rocket through the wards, when another Maeleket crossed them, and it was blind fear that had him out of his chair and out of the kitchen, because it wasn't in there with him which left Grace and Jamie.

CHAPTER 8

Sam didn't drop his guard just because he recognized the Maeleket standing across from Bazel. Or because Jamie had apparently had the sense of mind to pull Grace back behind the desk and leave Bazel between them and Tanik.

Tanik turned, gold eyes scraping over Sam's form the same way they always did. Maybe if it'd been a Maeleket that Sam actually trusted he'd have felt better about the sudden appearance. Or if it'd been someone else's place he'd been waiting in when Helin attacked him. As far as he knew he and Tanik did not actually have issue.

"Samriel." His lip curled. "Apparently the rumors of your demise were premature."

Other than the fact they didn't like each other.

"You do not sound thankful for that," Bazel practically growled.

Tanik looked back at him, nearly rolling his eyes. "I must say Bazel, I'm surprised. We've all aligned ourselves to Samriel and his pet humans. I would have expected better from you." He glanced at Willy then, lip curling. "But possibly not."

"Why are you here," Sam tried to interrupt, because however he generally felt about Tanik, Sam didn't have to watch it happen to know Bazel wasn't going to handle someone casting aspersions on Willow well.

Tanik huffed at him, dark-skinned brow pulling in annoyance. "Your...presence was all over my hart."

"But you were surprised he wasn't dead," Bazel grumbled, hands curling into fists.

"I didn't know it was his until I was here," Tanik countered coldly. "Does the rest of the council know how far off track you've gone Bazel? I would be interested, because there was a meeting yesterday. I seem to remember those being a rather important part of your *duty*." He sneered. "They would be interested, to know I found you here *playing* with Samriel."

Sam jumped between them, ignoring the crackle of Tanik's energy behind his back, it was only defensive, because Tanik had realized Bazel was about to rip his head off. He ignored the strange warmth in his chest, because Jamie was still back behind Bazel with Grace, with clearly no intention of getting between Bazel and Tanik.

"Let me go," Bazel growled lowly, eyes practically crackling power at him. "Samriel—"

"He is attempting to aggravate you into a misstep," Sam tried to keep his voice level and emotionless, hoping it would help Bazel get control again. "You are a respected Council member, you cannot simply—"

Tanik made a soft clucking noise. "How sad, you've reached the point the *ehachi* is reminding you of your duties."

Sam had been called worse in his time. He was good at his job and he had gained the respect of most of the council. That didn't mean it hadn't been an up-hill struggle most of the way. He was relatively sure he'd been called worse in front of Bazel.

He had to use his power, had to lock himself into the floor to keep Bazel from pushing past him. His eyes were white, and if Sam were human just touching Bazel's skin would have burned him.

"Samriel, I will move past you if you make me," Bazel said darkly.

Sam withheld the desire to shake him. "You *cannot* harm him."

"Do listen to Samriel." Tanik chuckled darkly. "As you always have. He is definitely right this time. You could do nothing to me."

"Shut up," Sam said over his shoulder. "Unless you are less intelligent than I thought." He fairly obviously hadn't meant that as Bazel wasn't capable of hurting Tanik. He meant it in regard to the fact Bazel ripping the other Maeleket into pieces without proof of his wrongdoing would severely compromise Bazel's position on the council. Might even be enough to get him labeled as Crossed.

He looked at Bazel and tried to think through, find some way to get him calmed. Sam could practically feel Bazel's anger thrumming under his skin. It was terrifying. Sam had spent his entire life with the quiet understanding he felt things in ways the rest of the Maeleket didn't.

He'd never been anywhere near this. Maeleket didn't get like this. They didn't grow angry and forget where they were or what they were doing. Tanik was going to assume that still applied to Bazel, that this was entirely a show of dominance.

The most out of control Sam had ever been he'd stopped when Jamie touched him. If that was a sign of trust…he couldn't think that. He couldn't deal with the concept that Bazel didn't trust him, couldn't even toe near it. From his earliest memories Bazel had been something to him. Granted, Maeleket were not better at friendship than they were at general connection, but Bazel had always felt like his friend. Sam had never understood if that was because he was different to the rest of them and Bazel was humoring him, or if perhaps they were both different.

But he'd long since decided he didn't really care. Since the day he joined the council he'd trusted Bazel with everything he had. Sam needed that to be reciprocated, because he wasn't entirely sure where it left him, if it wasn't.

"It's rather interesting, Tanik, the language you choose," Malek's voice echoed in the room, an abrupt flash of light heralding his sudden arrival.

Sam wanted to let go, step back and be done, but Bazel hadn't changed. He was exactly as tense and harsh as he'd been since Tanik showed up.

"Malek." Tanik swallowed, and shifted back from all of them.

Whatever they all considered the point of the council, of the bands they held together by, all of them understood instinctively they were nothing against Malek. He'd crossed the divide first, subsisted along-side humans for longer than any of them really knew. On the whole Sam guessed it had to be less than fifty-thousand years, but how much less was entirely unknown. Malek smiled benignly on them, and let the council make decisions, and existed in the shadows because he *chose* to.

"You should be careful with yourself," Malek husked. "Someone chose to use your hart to lay a trap for Samriel." Malek narrowed eerily blank-gold eyes at him. "I would be very disappointed to find you were actually involved with that."

"No, Malek." Tanik paled ashen. "I would never interfere with your favor."

Malek nodded, expression easing into a strangely creepy smile. "Good. Off you go then, we have things to discuss." He waved negligently. "Oh, and do not mention this to the council."

Sam tightened his hold on Bazel, because he'd felt the sudden tension in his muscles as Tanik left. "What are you doing?"

"What am I doing?" Bazel looked at him through dark, stone still eyes. "I am *trying* to protect you. Your precious—"

"Leave Grace out of this," Sam interrupted him, voice dark.

"Why? That's what this is about!" Bazel pushed him off suddenly, releasing just carefully enough it didn't hurt either of them. Though it did light up the house-wards suddenly. "You chose to tip the balance! You took the Rus line, when no one else would, and you made them something powerful! You made it possible for her to trap Aziel, and you refused to assign to another family when they—"

"And who left Aziel vulnerable to a scared girl locking him into a serving that wasn't even supposed to be possible!" Sam shouted back. "I wasn't the one who abandoned Mary, and I wasn't the one who failed to properly ensure the line was broken before we walked away! And I never asked you for protection, it is not your right!"

"I am your brother! Of course it is my right," Bazel shouted, pushing him.

"Bazel!" Malek's strident voice actually shook the house, before everything just...stopped.

Bazel backed off instantly, looking horrified, realizing he'd crossed a line.

"What?" Sam looked between them.

Malek rubbed his forehead, sighing. "Bazel, go calm yourself."

"I did not—"

"Go." Malek brooked no argument. "He should hear it from me and you need to calm yourself."

With a bare nod, Bazel disappeared.

Nate cleared his throat, shooting a strangely charged look at Grace. "We should...you probably want to talk and..."

Sam jumped, feeling Grace's hand on his arm.

"Are you alright?"

"I...he..." Sam didn't realize he'd grabbed Grace's wrist until he felt her hand fasten on his forearm, squeezing slightly, comfortingly.

Malek shifted uneasily, and Sam watched him flick a glance around the room. It wasn't helping him any that the other Maeleket was uncomfortable.

"How?"

Because, at the end of it all, that was the more pressing question. Unless there was something rather serious he hadn't been told—well, that was obviously a foregone conclusion. Maeleket didn't have children, not that were actually Maeleket.

"It is a rather telling explanation. I have no issue answering in front of them, but you might—"

"No." Sam interrupted. He needed a steadying influence. Needed something to make him feel more grounded. All he could compute right then was betrayal.

Malek smiled sadly, nodding. "Very well. How is Bazel your brother?"

"Are we not—"

"You are Maeleket." Malek snorted. "Technically, more than any of them. You are mine."

Sam swallowed. "Yours?"

Malek sighed, and shifted to lean against the desk. "A very long time ago, after some of the other Maeleket had joined me, and the humans were beginning to change their concept of their creation, I decided to see if it was possible to…create." He shrugged. "It's probably for the best that others went a bit wrong with their fondness for experimentation before I got there."

He blinked. "You…created Bazel. From what?"

"Nothing." Malek frowned. "Well, obviously not nothing. I owe you an explanation, but that is something I keep to myself."

High-handed and annoying as that was, Sam could understand the danger inherent in that sort of knowledge, so he let it go.

"Anyway. I created Bazel to see if I could. And rather made a mess out of it actually."

"What?" Sam asked.

"He was a *child* Samriel. I think, having watched humans for as long now he would be classed as a toddler," Malek explained. "I hid him, until I could help him make himself look like the rest of you. Eventually he grew into that, but it took a very long time."

"And…me?"

"I waited, because given the fact Bazel actually needed a father, I wasn't sure how well I'd done. But then he grew into something marvelous and I thought…" He sighed. "It was a risk, but I thought it was possible. That I could skip the part where you were a child. And I was right, you were just as you are now."

"Why didn't you tell me?"

"Because you were, on the surface, just like the rest of them." Malek smiled sadly. "The knowledge would have been a burden to you."

"In the beginning," Grace said, voice low. "But for…however long, there was never a point it might have helped to know?"

"No." Malek shook his head. "And I understand I've given you a different burden. You have *always* felt things differently from the rest of them. You want connections, in a way no one but your brother ever has." Malek shrugged. "I gave him that as well as I could, but I didn't do near as well as you have. And neither he nor I can give you what you need." He nodded to Grace. "It's taken you millennia to find someone who can offer you that."

"So I am not Maeleket."

"Of course you are." Malek frowned. "You are my son, and Bazel's brother. You are unique, because you have a family in a way none of the rest of them ever will, but you are still Maeleket. You still have powers the way the rest of them do, they work the same way."

Sam frowned. "But they do not. I can wrap myself into a human form better than—"

"Samriel." Malek sighed. "You have skills. You can control your form exceptionally well, but in honesty your brother is better at it than you are. You are both capable of understanding motivation better than any of the rest of our kind." He shrugged. "You are both better at understanding emotion, at using imagination."

"Is that why Bazel's been so…" Grace died off, obviously incapable of finding a good descriptor for the other Maeleket's behavior.

"It is." Malek nodded. "I'm afraid I could not offer him much comfort. I feel your presence, Samriel, the same way you feel mine or his. And I could still feel it, weakened and strange though it was. But I could not…I did not tell him that."

"Why?"

"Because if I was wrong." Malek swallowed. "The fact remains you did rather scare us." Malek held a hand up. "I am not implying you should have done anything different. Whatever is going on right now, we must do everything we can to fix this, to keep them from becoming something dark and twisted." Malek carefully reached out and grabbed Sam's shoulder. "But he thought you were dead, and no amount of talking could convince him that wasn't true."

Sam swallowed.

"I imagine it's not helping that he's less than pleased with me because he feels we should have had this conversation quite a long time ago."

Grace was still touching him, still trying to ground him in the only way she knew how, and Sam rather desperately wanted to fall into that.

"Now, I understand you might want to continue discussing this, but I need to go make sure Tanik doesn't know anything he's keeping from us." Malek watched him carefully. "Can you focus well enough I can leave you here?"

Sam nodded. "Where is Bazel?"

"Upstairs," Malek answered. "He didn't go far. He's still about, but I would give you both a little time before you try speaking."

"I will."

He nearly fell over when Malek hugged him suddenly, tight and serious. "I have long wanted to call you Son, Samriel. Believe me, I have never held my tongue for shame."

Malek left then, and a still silence cloaked the room.

Eventually Willow cleared her throat. "I'll go upstairs and check on Dad." She started to walk past Sam and then stopped and hugged him suddenly, before going quickly from the room before he could say anything, or return the embrace.

The rest of them filtered off then, and until Sam felt the pressure on his arm shift he'd thought he was completely alone. The sawing sound of breathing made it into his mind first, and it took him a moment to realize it was his own. A moment longer to assimilate the feel of the hard floor under him, legs crunched up under him where he'd folded onto the ground.

Grace's arms were wrapped tightly around him, her forehead pressed to the back of his neck, holding him tight and solid. Sam's hand was clutched in her shirt, so tightly he could see the bones in his knuckles, could feel how close he was to completely straining the material, but he couldn't stop. He didn't dare actually touch her, wouldn't trust himself not to harm her by accident.

His entire life, and they'd never told him. He was an experiment, another broken thing they weren't supposed to do that was—

"No." Grace sniffled, squeezing him tightly enough it should have hurt. "No."

Sam swallowed. He'd said that aloud then. "I…"

"There is *nothing* wrong with you." Grace buried her face in his shoulder, and he couldn't imagine how her leg muscles were handling the strain.

It was that, the thought of causing Grace pain, that sent him sprawling on the floor in such a way she didn't have to crouch over him. Until they were splayed out on the floor, Grace still touching him. He could feel the energy she put off. It pushed against his senses like it always did. So much like what her line had always been, but with different notes. Different highs and lows, like a song that vibrated in your bones, that you'd known forever but someone had just subtly changed the key.

Malek was right, something about Grace made him feel more connected than nearly anything else.

Sam squeezed her carefully, swallowing. He didn't have to say anything, didn't need to thank her, or explain what was going through his head. He stood carefully, hauling them both to their feet, and tried to smooth out the wrinkles he'd put in Grace's shirt.

"It's alright." Grace grabbed his hand, stopping him.

Sam swallowed, looking at her. "If I was going to be related to someone I wish it'd been you."

She swallowed, tears in her eyes, and pulled him into a tight hug. "But you are related to me."

He closed his eyes, blowing out a steady breath.

"We're...us." Grace sniffled. "Nothing changes that."

He smiled sadly, nodding.

~*~***~*~

It had been nearly a day, with no real answers. Sam wasn't precisely avoiding the rest of them, but he had spent a rather large amount of his time, alone, in the 'library' Curt kept squirreled into a corner of the basement. It was the furthest in the house he could get away from Bazel, from the feeling of his presence leaking through the house.

Sam didn't begrudge him being there. He couldn't. Whatever was happening around them was serious enough he didn't want to be solely responsible for keeping Grace and the rest of them safe. He certainly didn't want to be responsible for Willow.

His niece.

That part he was still actually having a bit of trouble with.

Sam didn't have the human escape of sitting in the basement, in the only chair, staring at the spine of the books and forgetting what time it was. Of not knowing whether the sun was up or down, or how long it was until the next meal. He couldn't get that far away, here. He could hear them moving upstairs and he wouldn't have had to exert any energy at all to know everything they said. It was actually requiring a lot of effort to do the opposite.

Sam wasn't licking his wounds. He wasn't necessarily upset with either Bazel or Malek now. He just...What was he supposed to say? Six thousand years old, and he didn't have any sort of experience for sudden family members. Grace had been as helpful as she could be—a quiet presence and support whenever he needed it. She seemed to feel it, before he was anywhere near looking for her, or asking for her, she'd just shown up.

Nate had found him this morning and offered him a cup of coffee that they both knew he wasn't going to drink. It was the gesture. Nate's way of saying that he understood things were...wrong right now, but he was there if Sam needed anything.

Jamie had perched at the top of the stairs earlier, but he'd gone off to do something else and left Sam to his own thoughts. Sam watched the dust-particles dance in the still room, undisturbed by anything he'd done, clogging up the shaft of light under the old-fashioned fixture.

"There's something strangely disturbing about the fact I can tell you're still here, even when I can't see you," Jamie said, suddenly at the bottom of the stairs.

Sam blinked, turning to look at him.

"And there you are." Jamie moved, coming over to slide down on the floor, in front of the book-case, legs stretched out in front of him.

"I can get you a chair," Sam offered, voice low.

Jamie cocked a brow at him. "Or I could grab the one by the desk, if I felt like I wanted one."

He bit back a frown, and tried to think of something to say, because arguably Jamie wanted something. He wouldn't have just come looking for him. "Did you need something?"

Jamie snorted. "I thought possibly you'd like some company, since you've been down here more or less all day."

Sam frowned. "I am doing my duty, if you have—"

"You're licking your wounds in the basement to avoid your brother, who's hiding upstairs," Jamie snapped, before he even finished. "And I get that, and it's…whatever." Jamie flushed. "I get it. You don't have to pretend."

Sam shifted, leaning forward in the seat. "Grace—"

Jamie rolled his eyes at him. "Sam, Nate and I are both here. If there was a problem we'd have told you."

He frowned, nose wrinkling. "Even now?"

"You're not twelve." He shifted, curling one leg under him and pulling his knee up. "The instant your panicking starts bothering Grace we'll tell you."

"Thank you."

"Sure." Jamie shrugged. "Do you want to talk about it?"

Sam pushed a hand through his hair. "Nothing has changed."

"Really?"

He glanced up, flushing. "He is my…brother. And my…differences make sense now, after a fashion." He frowned. "But if his concern is just because he is my brother, I do not understand."

"I do."

Sam blinked.

"Listen, Grace and I grew up together, for all I'm a little older. In all that time, all our strange bits and problems, it has *always* been my job to take care of her." Jamie forced a smile. "But if you asked her she'd say it wasn't."

He huffed. "But you leave Grace to her own decisions."

"I do." Jamie nodded, pushing a hand through his hair. "But not because I necessarily want to. If I started trying to make her decisions for her, or clinging to tightly—

again—there would be fallout and I know that." Jamie shrugged. "I've had more than twenty years to work out how to keep her close enough to keep an eye on her without pushing her away. And I know that doesn't seem like long to you—"

"But in your life-cycle it is long."

"It is." Jamie dropped his head back against the shelf gently. "I'm just saying, it's obvious he cares about you, and he sees you as his brother. I've had more than twenty years and I still have a tendency to twitch when Grace gets in more trouble than her norm."

"He didn't stop," Sam said softly. "If I'd let go even a bit he'd have—"

"Made a mistake?" Jamie frowned. "And that's somehow your fault?"

Sam looked at the floor, words chasing around in his brain.

"Come on, Sam." Jamie kicked him softly, getting his attention. "I'm not a mind-reader. I can't help if you don't tell me."

"But you want to help?"

Jamie huffed at him. "We're friends, aren't we?"

"Yes."

"Well." Jamie cocked a brow at him. "Tell me what you're thinking. Why is it your fault he lost control?"

Sam looked back toward the stairs, because he couldn't look at Jamie while he said the words. "I stopped for you. I…lost my temper. For probably the first time in my life, but you were there and I stopped."

"Because you were afraid you were going to hurt me?"

"I would never harm you," Sam said, glancing at him with a frown.

"I know." Jamie smiled wryly. "Not that it even really occurred to me."

"Why did you do it?"

"I imagine the same reason you did." Jamie cocked a brow at him. "You were going to regret that."

Sam forced himself to swallow, drew a deep breath and tried to push a little further away from his...human form. He needed a little distance right then, because it kept having emotional responses and they were *distracting*. "What if I stopped because I trusted you?"

"Alright." He nodded. "But that doesn't exactly follow that he doesn't trust you just because he didn't."

Sam blinked.

"Maybe he was more angry than you were." Jamie cocked a brow. "Maybe you were actually in danger and I wasn't." He shrugged. "Maybe there was an asshole poking at you still and he wasn't feeling like letting it go?"

"Tanik is never quiet about his opinion of me."

"Yeah, well." Jamie rubbed his forehead. "You weren't where I was, so I'll tell you I was possibly a little concerned Grace was going to chuck something at the bastard's head once he started talking."

Sam choked, almost laughing.

"And I don't think she actually understood what he was calling you any more than I did."

"She didn't."

Jamie nodded. "When I stopped you Bazel shut up." He smiled wryly. "Also, you were angry at him, not me. And not really angry, just—"

"Annoyed with his mouth," Sam finished, borrowing an expression from Curt.

"That." Jamie nodded. "And I'm kind of giving you shit for hiding down here, but I get why. Just don't spin it out too long. You'll have to talk to him eventually."

"Even if I don't know what to say?"

"Even then." Jamie pushed himself to his feet, stretching. "Are you coming up for dinner?"

Sam blinked at him. "I don't need to eat."

Jamie cocked a brow at him. "Would it kill you to sit down with us and fake it?"

CHAPTER 9

Jamie knew, from some things Grace had said over the last few months, that she and Sam weren't always on the same page. They disagreed and had to talk things out, loudly. Sometimes Grace wanted to do things, and Sam wasn't okay with them.

He'd—apparently wrongly—assumed that Sam was learning to let the early part of the argument go.

His gut said right then was one of those times there was no other option. New to most of this situation or not, Jamie could tell there was absolutely no way Grace is going to stay at Curt's while Nate went off on a job. Hell, it was decently telling Nate wasn't trying to leave her there. Not that he thought Nate ever tried that, but if he was going to start it would be that kind of time.

Jamie was all sorts of happy about the fact nobody—not even Sam—was saying the boys should go off and do this, leave the girls locked up safe with Curt. But whatever the job was, it wasn't a one-person job, and it wasn't something Deke and Willy were equal to. In the universe the rest of them exist in that pretty much left Grace and Nate.

If he thought he could do it without getting his head bitten off he might explain some of that to Sam.

Sam was having kind of a shit week, and he wasn't thinking clearly and there was no way in hell Jamie was going to just jump into that. He'd absolutely give the guy any sort of advice he could possibly need, when they were alone. He'd even offer advice unsolicited, which he tried not to do because there was no part of a sociology degree that meant people wanted you to ride in on your white charger and fix their lives.

Sam and Grace had been arguing each other around in circles for nearly half an hour. Jamie could tell it was a marker of how much Grace cared about Sam, that she was still talking to him and she hadn't just packed up and left already.

"You cannot do this! I—"

Nate let out a shrill whistle, stopping all of them in their tracks and making Curt curse darkly under his breath about the noise. It was so shrill, and serious even Sam stopped and stared at him. Nate forced a smile. "Why don't you come with us, rather than burning a bridge?"

Sam huffed, arms folding over his chest.

"Give us ten minutes to get packed," Jamie said easily.

Sam whipped around, eyes dark and brows drawn together, and Grace opened her mouth.

"Grace Hope Cleary, if you start in on the same thing Sam was just saying to you at me—"

Grace huffed. "Jesus Christ, Jamie, you don't have to middle name me." She flushed. "Fine. Fine with me."

"Hope?" Nate muttered, looking like he was going to break out laughing.

Grace glared at him. "What's your middle name again?"

Curt laughed, turning to gather some food for them to take. "Jamie, you might want to pack extra layers. If they're wrong and it's some sort of water nymph they can affect the local weather."

He left, upstairs to pack what few possessions he'd brought with him again, aware Sam was following on his heels. Mercifully he didn't badger Jamie, just followed him around silently, randomly popping things Jamie might need into existence as he was packing.

He'd bet his left arm Sam wasn't done.

If he wanted to be Jamie's own personal thunder-cloud that was his own problem.

He could have kept Sam in the house, packed slower and talked to Curt a little about what they were going after, and suffered through some sort of ridiculous level of strange with Willy and Deke. It would have kept Sam away from Grace and Nate.

He was right to consider it, because the instant they were out by the Charger, Sam started again.

"This is ill-advised."

"We heard you the first eight times," Nate muttered. "Jamie, can you finish loading the rounds into those clips so Grace can pack the bow?"

"Sure." Jamie grabbed a large capacity clip and started steadily feeding bullets into it.

"You do not actually know what this is, and if Malek calls while the job is in progress I cannot actually be in two places at once." Sam crossed his arms over his chest.

"Then you'll go do whatever Malek needs and we'll finish the job," Grace said reasonably.

Jamie could have told her reasonable wasn't going to work.

"There is no guarantee you will not get into trouble."

"There's never any guarantee of that," Grace huffed. "And seriously, Sam? How many times have I managed to wind up hip deep in…whatever without even trying?" She checked the spring on the cross-bow, loading a canister of bolts as well. "At least when we're chasing something I'm reasonably prepared."

"In the midst of some sort of larger issue is not a good time to go chasing after more trouble!"

Nate rolled his eyes, shooting Jamie a dark look, and throwing the extra bags in the trunk. "That all your stuff?"

"Yep." Jamie nodded, loading the last clip into the ammo bag, and handing it over. "And that's all of those."

Nate nodded. "I'll go tell Curt and the others we're going."

Grace dropped the last thing in the trunk, slamming it shut, and turned to clean up the tornado of mess they'd left at the work-station Nate generally used. Jamie could tell it was the same place he worked on vehicles, because there was an odd mix of tools out that suddenly made sense when you figured someone was either working on a car or cleaning a gun.

Or working on a gun. He could see at least two places where the small cross-bow that was somehow Grace's job had been repaired.

"I don't want you to do this," Sam stated flatly.

"I have to." Grace locked the work-table finally and dropping the key into the glove-box of the Charger.

"You do not—"

"I do." Grace sighed, standing up and shoving her hands deep in her pockets. "Sam. This is what we do. And yeah, right now it's pretty damn inconvenient." She shrugged. "Most of the time it's pretty damn inconvenient. Hell, half the time one job doesn't wait for the other to be finished and we're balancing whether we should send someone else or try and rush through and get there."

Nate came back out of the house, cooler full of food slung over one shoulder. "You'd think we were going on vacation, the amount of food he packed."

Nate dropped the cooler in the front, and slid into the car, checking something on the map he kept tucked under the visor.

"Grace, I cannot—"

"Sam!" Jamie winced, backing off. He hadn't meant to bark at him.

Sam glared at him, opening his mouth.

"Get in the car, because after all that freak-out I'm not leaving you here."

Jamie could see the argument, the tension in Sam's shoulders and the gear up to start in on Jamie now.

Jamie cocked a brow at him, and pulled open the passenger door, scooting the seat up so they could slide into the back. "If you make me get in first I'm not above taking up more than my fair share of the seat out of spite."

Sam glared, shoulders tense and movements choppy, and crawled into the car, settling in behind Nate and glaring at the windshield.

Jamie blew out a breath, sharing a look with Grace. *How do you manage this?*

Grace snorted. "You're the one signing up for it voluntarily," she muttered as he climbed in.

He wasn't sure if she meant the hunting, or the Sam.

~*~***~*~

It was a little over ten hours from Curt's to Pine Bluffs, Wyoming.

Sam gave up on being a quiet ball of radiating disapproval by the second hour, but it was still a long, tense drive. Jamie had never in his life been good at car trips and even teaching Sam how to play random card games that popped into his head didn't take ten hours.

He probably slept six of it, which he would absolutely regret about the time he should be going to bed.

Pine Bluffs was on the edge of Nebraska, just into Wyoming, and it was further west than he'd ever been in his life. It looked about like what he'd expected. Wide scrubby grassland with bluffs off in the distance. He assumed the spindly, sick looking pine trees were the reason for the name, they were about the only ones in town. There wasn't a lot of anything else, actually. A rodeo, the general run of schools—only one of each, because it was a tiny town of less than two-thousand people. It was the sort of place that wouldn't even have a school, if there was anywhere nearby to bus the kids to instead.

The hotel was a little ratty and run down, like about eight million others that used to spring up everywhere there was a highway. Back in the days when people really traveled and there wasn't a chain hotel every six feet.

They'd passed a Howard Johnston or something like that three hours ago. They were well out of chain territory.

Nate sauntered out of the lobby, keys in hand, stupid goofy smile on his face.

Grace laughed softly. "Either he managed to get connected rooms, or it's one of those themed rooms."

Jamie snorted, stretching out as well as he could in the back. "Make his day, does it?"

"Almost as much as the ones with Magic fingers," Grace said, yawning.

Sam wrinkled his nose. "That might be more information than I need."

Grace threw a wrapper at him, as Nate opened the door.

"Last two connected rooms they had!" He tossed a key back to them. "There's some rodeo event this weekend."

Grace pulled a face. "Do we have a cover story, or are we winging it?"

Nate grinned at her, starting the engine. "It's your favorite."

Grace dropped her head back and groaned. "What kind of reporter am I this week?"

"Country Music Times."

Jamie swallowed his instinctual comment to that. There were about two things in life Grace disliked as much as she disliked country music.

"I hate you a little right now," Grace muttered.

"If I let you have first crack at the shower will that make up for it?"

"Probably not. I get first crack at the shower, and you have to go find food." She looked at Nate. "And if we have to go to the rodeo you're on library duty for like a year."

Nate stopped in front of a couple of dark rooms, in the mostly empty parking lot. He leaned over and kissed Grace on the temple. "I'm not gonna make you go to the rodeo if I don't have to, sugar."

"Uh huh." Grace popped the door open, moving to the back to grab some of their stuff. "I'll enjoy being the one who goes shopping while you do the library work then."

Jamie stood, stretching his back and trying to force his muscles to loosen. "Jesus."

Grace thumped him on the side, smiling. "Still moving there, sunshine?"

He hugged her suddenly, dropping his head on her crown. "Watch it, little-bit. I'm not above making you go to the rodeo just to watch you twitch."

Grace cocked a brow at him. "If you drag me to the rodeo so help me god I will get the boat song stuck in your head until the *end of time.*"

Jamie shut his mouth and held his hands up. "No Celine Dion required."

Nate opened the door to their room, letting out a cackle. "Hah. Called it."

Grace whimpered, pressing her face to Jamie's shoulder. "It's orange."

Jamie leaned his head in, laughing softly. He wasn't sure 'orange' covered it. He was about to say something about that, when Sam swung the other door open and actually let out a strangled noise.

He looked into the strangely accented explosion of teal, with the rose pink bathroom furnishings clearly visible from the door, and the painted velvet masterpiece of...a ship? He was guessing it was supposed to be a schooner, but the sails were wrong.

There were tassels on *everything.*

Nate snorted, shaking his head. "Could be worse."

Jamie cocked a brow at him, wondering how that might be.

"At least there aren't mirrors on every available surface and strangely unidentifiable stains." He shrugged. "Rooms are decently clean, too."

Jamie huffed. "Would this be a good time to say something about the life on the road you've dumped my best friend into?"

"Jamie." Grace's voice was dark and huffy, like she'd had enough of their over-protective instincts for one day.

"He was joking," Nate called through the open door, slapping him on the shoulder. "There's a diner up the block a little." He cocked a brow. "I'm going to get food before it closes. You coming with me, or is Sam?"

"Probably me." Jamie dropped his bag on one of the narrow beds. "Unless you think Sam's going to get himself in trouble?"

Nate shrugged. "Does it matter if he does? We're here now. They can look after themselves for a bit."

Jamie bowed to Nate and his understanding of the Sam/Grace dynamic. Nate had spent the last several months watching them learn to navigate this. Jamie'd heard a little about it, but not much. Grace hadn't talked about Sam much, because Jamie hadn't been okay with him.

He felt more than a little guilty about that now, but there wasn't much he could do about it.

The diner was about as non-descript as everything else in town, but it smelled like the food would be decent. Jamie wasn't sure if they were ordering food for Sam because he might actually eat it, or just to keep up appearances, but he wasn't going to ask in the middle of a semi-crowded room in the middle of a town that was so small it made where they grew up look big.

Jamie remembered life in a small town. Part of that was probably indelibly bleached onto his character. Don't make waves, don't be different, don't be loud. Skate under the radar and survive to get out. It's the general non-humor of his life that it was harder for him to do than it was for Grace.

But Grace and her disconnect from the rest of humanity was another of those things they don't talk about. That hadn't changed any just because she'd made a few more connections. The list of people Grace cared about was still sort of ridiculously small. It was really just luck the instinctual leap from that never became relevant. He was pretty damn happy 'sociopathy' wasn't a thing anymore—wasn't a valid diagnosis anymore. That didn't make him any more inclined to try and get Grace a diagnosis of anything. He had vividly unhappy memories of his college psych professors looking at people like they were lab experiments.

They got back to the hotel in decently short time, but Grace was already out of the shower. She and Sam had stretched out across the bed in her and Nate's room, heads at opposite ends staring at the ceiling.

Nate snorted, setting his part of the food down. "I half-expected you to be asleep by the time we got back."

Grace stretched, sighing. "I'm hungry."

She pulled herself from the bed, and Jamie blinked when she stopped to watch him for a second. Took entirely too long to find the thread of the conversation they weren't actually having.

Wanted to be awake incase you had second thoughts, he can practically hear her say in his head.

And he's got no answer for that but to hand her her food, and drop into the chair next to the table. *I'm good.*

Grace settled in Indian style on the bed, and poked at her food for a second. "Did anybody at the diner know anything?"

"I didn't ask." Nate dropped down next to her, stealing a pickle out of her box. He wrinkled his nose. "Probably could have, Jamie was there and he's decently observant."

"Not today," Jamie offered, snorting. "I don't have the car stamina you two have."

Grace smiled, private and dark, and Jamie threw a napkin at her.

"Get your head out of the gutter."

She snorted. "You got where it was without my saying anything."

"We went through puberty together," Jamie pushed a piece of wilted lettuce off to the side of his own box. "So

I'm pretty inured to the fact you have the internal monologue of a twelve-year old boy."

Nate nudged her with his shoulder. "Knew we worked for a reason."

Grace rolled her eyes at him.

"That, and your willingness to pretend the words coming out of my mouth are the ones I mean," he finished wryly.

Sam settled in next to Jamie, and peaked at the food they'd gotten him. Like he was thinking about it. But no one was expecting him to eat, and obviously he wasn't going to right then. "I was not aware that was a problem you had."

Nate cocked a brow at Sam. "When was the last time we had a conversation that wasn't about hunting?"

Sam frowned. "We talk about Grace."

Jamie laughed softly, watching the way Nate turned red and buried his face against Grace's shoulder. "Dude, pretty much everybody thinks they're bad a small-talk. At least anybody with any emotional depth."

"So." Nate took a bite of his food. "We'll figure out what's going on tomorrow."

"Curt sounded like the coroner was pretty far out of his depth," Grace offered, finishing her food. "That might be a good place to start." She shrugged. "Might need to split up though. Four of us wandering into the Coroner's office might be a little much."

"Sure." Nate nodded. "You and Sam take the coroner's office? Jamie and I can go check in at the newspaper, see if we can find anything out?"

Grace frowned, nose wrinkling. "Yeah. Jamie'd probably be better at talking his way into the Coroner's office without telling them anything though."

He finished his food, and dumped his container. "Yeah, if you want me to pull the 'health and human-services' bit, let me know." He yawned. "I'm going to bed, despite the ridiculous amount of time I slept in the car." He moved forward, and kissed Grace on the temple.

"Night."

He clapped Nate on the shoulder, and worked his way into the room he was 'sharing' with Sam, and grabbed his stuff. Washed his face and brushed his teeth. Changed his clothes. He paused for a second, opening the door to the bathroom. Sam was stretched out on the bed closest to the door, staring up at the ceiling, the connecting door to Grace and Nate closed.

There was something ridiculously wrong about Sam lying on top of the covers, all clean clothes and unrumpled perfection. Nothing at all like the guy he'd had sleeping on his couch for a couple of days. That Sam had looked...

Well, he hadn't actually looked human. But he'd looked a hell of a lot more approachable.

~*~***~*~

"Hey, you're not upset that I stuck you with me, are you?" Nate said without preamble, sliding into the car in front of the diner, on their way to the local newspaper office.

"No." He frowned, cocking his head. "Was there a reason for it?"

"No offence, but you don't do this? Grace knows what she's doing, but if I'm going to leave her with somebody other than me..."

"Sam has some chance of realizing when shit's about to go bad?" Jamie offered.

"Something like that." Nate sighed. "Also, figured this way we've got somebody with a college education going both directions."

Jamie laughed, shaking his head. "You think the coroner would ask what my Doctorates was in, if I showed up and said I had one?"

Nate winced. "Probably not." He flicked a glance at him. "So...I'm just gonna say this, cause I'm not as good at the non-spoken shit as you and Grace are."

"Okay." He blinked, turning to look at Nate. "Dude, whatever's on your mind..." He shrugged. "The non-verbal thing is because it's Grace and at this point we've basically been living in each other's pockets emotionally since were babies."

Nate snorted, nodding. "She's not telling you that she's sort of terrified you're going to get wrapped up in this and quit your job."

Jamie choked out a shocked, sharp laugh. "Because your life is so exciting?"

"Yeah, that's exactly why."

Jamie winced. Pithy and distancing was sort of his default setting. He'd learned not to do it with Grace a long time ago, but that didn't mean it didn't slip out with other people. Who it probably shouldn't have. And it was Nate, who was going to get a sort of ridiculous amount of play out of him because Grace was settled and *happy* in a way he hadn't ever thought was going to happen.

"Because it's me, and her," Jamie said softly, honestly.

"That." Nate rubbed the back of his neck. "It sounds sort of stupid for me to say that this isn't the life she wants for you. Cause I pretty seriously doubt it's the life you want for her."

"It's a life." He flicked a glance at Nate. "It's a little more mortal peril than I'd rather have her deal with, but I'd be a pretty ridiculous liar if I said I wanted her to go back to hiding out in her little house in Indiana with no social life at all."

"She was happy there," Nate pointed out.

"Grace doesn't do happy." He huffed. "She does content. It's not the same thing."

Jamie was so wrapped up in thinking about all the years he'd been around Grace while she was just *there*, it takes a while for the stony silence on the other side of the car to break through.

"Shit."

Nate opened his mouth, to say something about how it was okay probably.

"Sorry. I forget sometimes that there's more baggage with us than there is with the rest of you." Jamie rubbed his forehead. "I wasn't talking about now. I don't think you actually want me to tell you…anything."

Nate frowned.

"It's sappy, and I'll say it if you say you want to hear it." Jamie frowned. "Or you keep acting like you need to."

He stopped the car outside the newspaper office, shaking his head. "No, I get the point."

"No," Jamie huffed. "You really don't. Grace is happy, and I can't…" He swallowed. "I'm not quitting my job to be part of this because A—I freaking hate car trips, B—I despise small towns, Grace got out of that a little more unscathed than I did, and C—" He paused, catching Nate's eye. "She doesn't need me to. We're *long* past the point in life where I'm going to be stupidly clingy about the fact she's growing without me."

Nate flushed. "Al…alright."

Jamie rolled his eyes at him, as they got out of the car. "Dude, you're building her a secret house. We're *fine*."

They stopped on the pavement in front of the newspaper office, and Jamie could see Nate focus completely on the job at hand.

"So do we have some sort of cover story for this, or are we just asking questions?"

Nate shrugged. "Newspapers work better if you play it by ear."

He shoved his hands in his pockets. "I'll follow your lead."

The office was cleaner than you'd have expected. On some level Jamie had wanted it to be like his brain said newspaper offices used to be. All big drafting tables, and orange carpet with little offices off to the side and bits of paper everywhere and a kind older woman who still called herself a 'secretary' sitting at the front. An old press in the basement and one of those glass coke-bottle machines sitting in the corner.

"So you'd be the boys in town with the girl from CMT magazine, would you?" The guy behind the counter was exactly what he'd expected though. Looking them over with narrow eyes and dark annoyance.

"We are." Nate leaned against the counter, irreverent charm flowing easily. Like he was always like that and the old man behind the counter wasn't going to bother him at all.

"So what can I do for CMT Magazine?"

The 'so you'll get out of my sight' was left unsaid, Nate didn't mind that either.

"Well, *she* needs a Rodeo Schedule. I'd love to hear about this homeless guy they found outside town a couple of days ago."

The guy grabbed a rodeo schedule, sighing. "Heard about that, did you?" He slid the schedule across the table. "What would that have to do with her article?"

"Nothing." Nate shrugged. "I'm trying to convince her to write a book about all the strange stuff that happens out in the country." He looked wide-eyed and honestly young. "We were in Arizona last month, and somebody found one of those giant rat things with a human finger in its stomach, but there was nobody missing a finger."

"Giant rat thing?" Someone else in the office said, confused.

"A cucuburra, I think that's what they're called."

Jamie snorted. "Capybara? Kookaburra is an Australian bird."

"That's it." He waved at Jamie, shaking his head. "Which was kinda strange anyway because they aren't supposed to live there, right?" He shook it off. "Anyway, when we see stuff I always ask around 'cause I figure she's going to wind up accidentally gathering information and eventually I'll get her to write it."

"And because you're twelve," Jamie offered, joking easily.

The guy in the back laughed softly, coming forward to the bar. He was closer to their age, and exactly the kind of person Jamie would have wrapped around his little finger in high school. Not that he'd done that. The fact Grace was so inwardly weird had knocked him out of that sort of behavior before it'd even started. At least in the general, "just for kicks" sense.

"David Welling." He shook Nate's hand, and Jamie's. "Frank's the sort who gets uptight about having strangers in town."

"Sure." Nate shrugged. "We get that a lot."

David nodded. "It's pretty strange though, just so you know."

Nate grinned. "The stranger the better."

Jamie's a thirty-four-year-old college professor, and at least half of graduate-school he paid for as a part-time social worker. He's got better than decent facial control, so he can hold the easy, uncomplicated expression on his face through the kid's description of the old hobo they found on the edge of the town, thoroughly stripped of all his blood with one small mark on him.

He refused to imagine what it'd taken to teach Nate to hold onto the lackadaisical, easy expression he's wearing through that.

"Well that's officially creepy," Jamie muttered, once they were out on the street again.

Nate snorted. "A little." He pulled out his phone, and called Grace on speaker. "Hey, anything?"

Grace sighed. "Coroner's running himself in circles trying to figure out what he was cut with, that left that little surface damage but still hit an artery. And I promise the sheriff's going to be convinced he was moved and all the blood is somewhere else. You?"

"Newspaper office didn't know who he was, so he's probably not a local hobo."

"Hitchhiker?" Grace offered. "Equally likely it's someone in town for the rodeo or—"

"So help me God Grace, if you say 'just passing through' and make us chase this damn thing across six counties I will never let you forget it."

Grace laughed softly. "Yeah yeah, one time." She sighed. "Meet us back at the hotel?"

~*~***~*~

Grace had pictures of the body, which was a little creepy. Almost as creepy as the fact once they put their heads together it takes her and Nate about three seconds to figure out what the thing is. Which shouldn't bother him. He knows they're both good at this. Grace is a freaking sponge, when it comes to things she reads and hears, and if Nate weren't ace at this stuff he'd be dead already.

It was still a little uncomfortable, sneaking around the outer edges of town, in an old abandoned house. Grace thought it was the sort of vampyric thing that didn't look human so it probably wasn't hiding out as some unassuming truck driver or rodeo clown.

The *thing* that was all teeth and claws and launched at him hissing about two seconds after they've walked through the door wasn't really comforting. He was glad to know Grace could handle this, almost as much as he was to be reminded he didn't panic and freeze when he was in danger. He got out of its way, and slammed the door shut while he was at it because he didn't think they wanted it wondering out there into the night for another snack.

At which point it shrieked and ran up the stairs.

Nate cursed, pulling out a wicked looking knife. "Sam, stay here and don't let it out the front door."

Grace grabbed the small crossbow. "I'll take the back, Sam and I should have a clear sight-line."

Jamie watches the way Sam eases suddenly, when Grace takes her place and he can still see her easily.

"Jameson should stay here," Sam said, voice low.

Nate huffed. "He should stay here in the middle because if it gets past me on the stairs and breaks one side or the other you'll need help keeping it in." He held a knife out to Jamie, smiling darkly. "Don't let it bite you."

"Hadn't planned on it." He moved, so he was about halfway between the doors, and compulsively looked to make sure there wasn't a heating vent or something like that over him. Which was probably not something he needed to be doing, but just because Jamie was standing there ready didn't mean he was exactly okay with the situation.

The thing that scrambled down the stairs in front of Nate wasn't anything he was prepared for, and he'd seen it before. He hadn't gotten a good look before, just teeth and an instinctual desire to avoid. The joints were…wrong, and it moved in odd jerky spasms, right past him and straight for Sam.

Jamie suspected that Sam could have snapped his fingers and gotten rid of it, but there was a line there somewhere he wasn't keen to cross. Still, Sam didn't look afraid of it, at all, and it knew that. It turned and scuttled for Grace, which Nate had obviously anticipated because he was right there between them, knife at the ready.

Until it knocked it out of his hand, anyway.

Sam was moving away from the door, and Grace was braced to try to help, and Jamie wasn't all that keen on waiting for either of them, before he crashed into its side, knocking it against the wall.

CHAPTER 10

It was like no other fight Jamie'd ever been in in his life. The way it skittered when it screamed at him, the sharp nails, and needle like teeth are nothing compared to the sheer *evil* pouring off it.

He was a rough kid, he learned to throw a punch early and his mother never put him up for martial arts stuff—there wasn't a lot of that in their hometown anyway—because he was always trouble on his own. Kids can be cruel, and long before people decided his best friend was unusually strange Jamie was a kid from the wrong side of the tracks with a mother that pretty much everybody in town assigned some level of reputation to.

Jamie'd been in fights, and he'd been in fights with people who weren't trying to teach him anything, who just genuinely hated him. More than he'd care to admit.

He didn't have trouble with the way it moved, and the fact the thing didn't seem to have internal organs for him to poke at. He had a little trouble with the propensity to bite. And the fact the damn thing kept lunging for his throat. Jamie didn't have all that much trouble keeping one step ahead of it, but he didn't feel like he was getting anywhere.

"Pin it so I can cut its head off," Nate said darkly, hitting it with something that splintered and nearly turned to dust, trying to draw its attention away. "You're never going to beat it into submission."

Jamie deftly, barely gets out of the way of the fangs. "Any suggestions for how I do that?" Because he's already worked in nearly every pin he knows.

"Stop trying to go backwards," Grace barked at him, annoyed.

Later he's going to have a solid laugh about the fact Grace figured out he was having trouble with the backwards before he did. Once he had it pinned on the floor and Nate could separate it from its head—he wasn't sure if it was creepier that it didn't make noise, or that it didn't bleed—he could see where he'd gone wrong with that. He'd been trying to flip it and pin it on its back, just like you would a human.

Only human joints went the other way.

Jamie panted, checking the split in his lip and the long scratch on his arm. It looked clean, and he was relatively sure he'd actually gotten it off the wall, not off the thing on the floor. He was also relatively sure it was the situation that was keeping Grace from giving him shit for whining about getting a tetanus shot earlier in the year. He nearly suppressed his jump when Nate moved next to him.

Nate clapped him on the shoulder, cocking a brow. "You good?"

"Yeah. You?"

"I'm good." He pulled a slightly ratted, old blue tarp out of the stuff Grace was holding, separating it from a canister of salt and a pile of metal coins he didn't recognize, handing the other stuff back to Grace. "Thanks for the assist."

Jamie waved him off. It hadn't really been intentional. He'd taught self-defense for years, and he'd done a certain level of fighting in his life. It'd been lined up on Nate and he needed help, and Jamie wasn't exactly the sort of person to walk away from that, even when the thing attacking wasn't anywhere near human.

Sam stood over the body, face dark and unsettled. Jamie had already figured out this wasn't their normal sort of job. He'd recognized Grace's look of confusion when it lunged at him originally, and given the fact she hadn't asked Nate what it was, he was going to guess he'd tipped her off somehow to the fact he didn't know.

"Something wrong, Sam?" Grace stopped next to him, looking down.

Sam glanced at Grace quickly, obviously cataloguing, just in case Grace was somehow injured and any of the rest of them had missed it. Jamie withheld a smile, because he'd seen Nate check her the instant he'd cut the things' head off. Not to mention it'd taken Jamie about half a second to watch the way Grace moved, the way she held her shoulders, and instantly know she wasn't injured. He'd learned to watch for that. Even the general stiffness that came from sleeping somewhere other than her bed.

"I have not seen a lefintas in…" Sam frowned, uncomfortable. "It has been a very long time."

"There can't be many of them," Jamie offered. "Pretty sure the locals would notice that." Although how many of them needed to be around before the general human population noticed?

"They are very adept at hiding, until they either have no other choice or until they find a lone…meal," Sam offered, still staring at it in concern.

"I've heard the name before, but I've never seen one." Nate sighed. "But there's been a distressing amount of that lately."

"Of what?" Jamie said, looking up.

"Shit nobodies seen in generations just…popping back up," Grace offered, as she and Nate snapped the tarp out next to it and started rolling it on. "Where are we burning this at?"

Nate sighed, stretching. "We're going to the factory, where no one will notice the smoke." He glanced up at Sam, frowning. "These things don't egg or anything, do they?"

"They do not." Sam frowned. "Nor do they travel in numbers greater than the singular."

Jamie took Grace's spot at the tarp, when it was time to drag it out to the car, wincing at how heavy the body was, how strangely weighted it felt. "So this is probably a stupid question…"

Nate snorted. "First job, there's no such thing." He flicked a glance at Jamie, walking backwards toward the Charger. "Since you know pretty much nothing."

"That." Jamie nodded, swallowing and working really hard not to think about what it was he was actually doing right that moment. "How did it get here? I can't imagine it just popped up here, and if it was…eating its way across the state wouldn't you have heard about it before now?"

Nate hefted his side into the trunk first, sighing. "Probably has been and no-one noticed. Most of the shit that uses us for food hangs around on the out-skirts. Also, most of them will take a cow or a sheep or whatever just as happily." He looked out at the gray Wyoming sky. "Probably a lot of farmers blaming wolves or mountain lions or something for stealing their stock." He shrugged, as Jamie placed his side in. "Missing hitchhikers. People go missing on hiking trails all the time, everyone figures they wondered somewhere or got eaten by a bear. Winter comes, eventually it slinks out of the mountains looking for a meal."

"Remind me never to go hiking again," Jamie muttered, dusting his hands off.

Grace slammed the trunk shut once they had it inside, and it was a short quiet ride to the factory—glass was Jamie's bet—across town. A blisteringly cold twenty minutes later they were standing in front of a non-descript pile of ash. Grace and Nate weren't easy. They were still watchful. Still very clearly 'on' and paying attention to the world around them. Even with that, it was strangely comfortable, watching them. They moved with an easy synchronicity, aware of each other and in tune.

He still got a fairly ridiculous kick out of watching them together.

The fire finally guttered, a pail of dirt spread over it, Nate sighed and leaned against Grace's shoulder. "Bar?"

"Bar," Grace repeated, nodding. "Warm. And probably the best place to get food that's not the diner."

~*~***~*~

Jamie hadn't stayed in Evansville long enough to do a lot of drinking.

Well. He hadn't been around long enough for a lot of the sort of drinking you did indoors. Legally.

Actually, once he thought about it, he wasn't sure he'd ever drank legally there. He'd followed Grace to college and he'd gone home once, before his mother moved away.

Still, he'd spent most of high-school hanging around outside the bowling alley with the community college kids, acting cool and old for his years so they'd toss him a beer or two. Watched the steady stream of sixteen-year-old girls who came by looking for the same thing.

Very nearly broke his hand on a guy who'd been a little too interested in Grace.

Sitting in the Route 66 Roadhouse—for the record they were so bloody far from Route 66 here they might have named it after the coastal highway or Nantucket Island—it was a little hard not to remember that. They weren't all bad memories, but it damn skippy wasn't anywhere he wanted to go back to.

He'd stopped going to bars at about twenty-six. Mostly because he *was* old for his years, and in a college town he got tired of being tilted at by drunk twenty-two-year olds.

The blond girl—he wasn't being dismissive, she was maybe twenty-one, and equally as likely to be seventeen—sitting next to him at the bar while he waited for their drinks probably hadn't ever heard the word subtle. If she had, it'd never sunk in.

She was brave, too. Not even a little concerned about the fact he was a stranger, and older, and had probably six or seven inches and at least fifty if not a hundred pounds on her. He rather spectacularly avoided her touching him, while he waited for the drinks, and once he'd had them he'd equally spectacularly managed to get away before she gave him her phone number. Or room key.

It was a crowded Friday and the rodeo was going on in town. Which meant as the only real drinking establishment for a while it was full to the brim with loud cowboys just as drunk on life as they were on cheap beer. More than a few of them were attractive, and the twenty-first century had apparently landed in Wyoming the same way it had everywhere else because he'd noticed more than one watching him walk across the bar.

He sat the bottles on the table carefully, glancing over his shoulder just to make sure she was still at the bar and not following him. "We're leaving in the morning, right?"

"We are." Nate looked up at him, frowning.

Jamie sat down and less than subtly scooted his chair closer to Sam's. He draped his arm over the back of Sam's chair and leaned into his space and a 'friendly' manner.

Grace choked down her laughter. "Get in over your head, did you?"

"She's goddamn *twelve*," Jamie muttered. "And the cowboy contingent would end badly, thanks."

Sam looked around them, brows settled in a fairly adorable frown, before turning his gaze on Jamie. "What makes you think I would willingly be your beard either?"

It took a considerable amount of self-control not to flinch at that. He didn't really need a reminder that Sam'd been around for a while when they hadn't see him. Sometime after Jamie'd come to terms with his sexuality there'd been more than a few 'professional' outings he'd taken Grace to because it wasn't as if he was dating anyone and even if he was there was a fifty-fifty chance...

The one time he'd tried to take Grace, while he was dating a guy, she'd flatly refused.

Jamie bopped him on the nose, smiling charmingly. "They're obviously together. You're stuck with me."

Nate snorted. "Just play it quiet enough you don't get us kicked out, please. I'd like to finish my beer and eat, and not find out exactly how backward people around here are."

By the time their food arrived Jamie decided the only reason it worked was because Sam looked perfectly fine with him being inside his personal space. With the fact they mirrored Grace and Nate across the table, perfectly fine in each other's pockets and just relaxing.

Jamie knocked their legs together under the table, not looking up. "You've got a couple of admirers yourself."

Sam huffed. "It would unsettle you if I changed my appearance to garner less attention, so I imagine I do."

He snorted. "What, landed a little more perfect than you were looking to?"

Jamie was completely and utterly imaging the fact he'd just made Sam blush.

"If I am not reminded of it, I forget that human beings are never truly symmetrical, though your standard of beauty lies there."

Jamie laughed softly, finishing his meal and wiping his hands. "I'm pretty sure you could look a little less symmetrical and you'd still get noticed."

Sam frowned, brows drawing low.

"It's a small town and we're not from here." Jamie shrugged negligently. "And you're hanging out in the town watering-hole."

Grace cleared her throat knowingly.

Jamie flinched. "Yes, I'd know. Moving on."

Nate laughed softly. "Did they have a road-house in Evansville?"

"No, all the local degenerates hung out at the bowling alley and picked up high school girls." She snorted, and pointed at Jamie. "Except that one, who hung out at the bowling alley and picked up JuCo girls and practiced honing his skills as a pool shark."

"Hey, I had a plan."

Sam looked at him, brow cocked and waiting.

"What, you were there."

"I was not there frequently enough to recognize that you had a plan," he replied, deadpan. "You didn't allow Grace to accompany you."

"Allow?" Grace input darkly.

Jamie pointed at Sam. "His words, not mine."

"Thank you," Sam said primly.

"Dude, you said it, you get to own it," Jamie answered. "I know better."

Nate laughed, kissing Grace on the cheek. "Did you get in trouble?"

"Jamie very nearly got himself arrested," Grace answered. "Because one of his friends—"

"Was absolutely *never* a friend of mine," Jamie insisted, glaring at her. "Bastard was creepy and overly interested in *young* girls."

Grace waited for him to finish, and snorted. "Anyway. He apparently said something about wanting to get me alone and Jamie over-reacted."

"How would that be an overreaction?" Sam asked, clearly in the dark. "He intended to harm you."

Grace glared, huffing.

"I was perfectly correct in informing him he needed to keep his hands to himself and to stay away from my best friend." Jamie winced. "Probably could have done it without somebody else's windshield."

Grace snorted.

Jamie glared at her, huffing. "And I was totally the only one who got protective, was I?"

She frowned. "That is not even remotely the same thing. She was gearing up for some insane complicated plan to ruin your life."

Nate coughed, almost choking. "What?"

Jamie rubbed his forehead, sighing. "When I...came out, whatever, my ex-girlfriend sort of..."

"I believe your Aunt Rhoda referred to it as 'losing the farm'," Sam offered.

He nodded. "She had all these plans and she was starting to spread rumors that I assaulted this girl at a party I wasn't even at and something about a tutoring position I did for a while and..." Jamie swallowed. "Anyway, would have been...messy except she wasn't as quiet about things as she should have been if she wanted it to work." Jamie cocked a brow at Grace. "And I'm still not entirely sure that was all about her going after me. You were pretty upset about the faked assault complaint."

"Yeah, I'd think." Nate blinked. "Cause that shit doesn't get swept under the rug often enough as it stands." He nudged Grace. "So what did you do to her?"

"Nothing." Grace rolled her eyes at Jamie and Sam's equally affronted look. "Alright, I might have...intimated to her that I realized she'd cheated on a test and that I wouldn't actually need proof to get her up in front of the Disciplinary committee and she should think about the danger of spreading rumors."

Nate laughed, shaking his head. "Dose of her own medicine?"

"No." Grace shrugged. "She bragged to her roommate that she'd cheated on an exam. My hear-say was enough to get her before the board, just because I hadn't reported it..." She sighed. "She was hurt, and it was a crappy situation. That doesn't make her behavior okay."

Jamie snorted. "I was a pretty horrible boyfriend, but yes it was excessive."

~*~***~*~

They didn't close out the roadhouse. The day had been entirely too long for that. After finishing their food and a couple of beers, they loaded back up and headed back for the hotel and their beds.

Jamie cracked the fact Bazel didn't get shot up to Grace's ridiculous reflexes. Nate pulled his gun out, got it leveled because obviously anyone or any thing skulking around their dark hotel room was some kind of threat.

Jamie hit the light on their way in, and someone stood up from the table, and Nate pulled his gun, and Sam jumped in front of him and Grace grabbed the barrel, pulling it high.

Nate relaxed, huffing silently. "I hope you appreciate the fact Grace just kept you from fishing for a bullet."

Bazel watched them, and Jamie didn't think he was imagining the way he seemed hung up on Sam. Of course, Sam was still standing between him and Bazel, so that might have been part of it.

Might have been a large part of it actually.

"Did you need something, or were you just trying to freak me out for funsies?" Nate asked, dropping his stuff on one of the beds.

"I have news." Bazel cleared his throat. "I apologize, I did not mean to discomfit you."

Nate snorted, then caught Grace's raised brow— because he wasn't helping—and pulled a face. But he did stop.

"What have you heard?" Sam managed, still rather tense.

"Not as much as I would like." Bazel frowned. "Malek and I are now relatively sure Tanik is innocent." He frowned suddenly. "Well, assured he wasn't involved in what happened to you. I wouldn't consider that innocent. Malek believes he is uninvolved."

"And you?" Grace asked, dropping to sit next to Nate. "You don't agree?"

Bazel frowned, shifting. Something about Grace made him uncomfortable, and Jamie had an entire life of reading the way people had issue with Grace. Of cataloging what was causing them problems and how they were going to reacting to that.

On the face of things it would have been Grace's relationship with Sam that was the issue. Whatever other issues Bazel was having, his devotion to his little brother was pretty obvious.

Or Jamie was telegraphing, which was theoretically possible.

"Tanik and I have..." Bazel paused. "We have never gotten along. There is no one incident. No point where either of us... We've simply disliked each other from the moment we met."

"And you think that means he's behind this?" Nate asked.

Bazel frowned. "No. No, all things being equal something this back-handed seems out of character."

"I was in his hart," Sam said.

"You were, but until this we haven't exactly been...quiet. Malek thinks it likely whomever is actually behind this realized you were going to be there and took advantage of events."

"I still don't understand exactly what happened here." Jamie frowned. "I thought you guys were immortal."

"It is difficult to harm us, in our...natural state." Bazel said dryly. "Not impossible."

"Right. Harm you." Jamie cocked a brow. "Because I've gotten the impression, from pretty much everyone, Sam should be dead."

Sam flushed.

"Sam," Grace waited, almost patiently. "Were you hurt that badly?"

"He was very much hurt that badly," Bazel said tensely.

Sam almost glared at him. "Do not scare her."

"Grace does not scare that easily," Bazel spit back. "Obviously, because she's held up better than the rest of us through all this, and you told me I wasn't allowed to lie to her."

"That was not in reference to..." Sam flushed. "That conversation has no bearing on this."

"Which is, I'm guessing, all sort of secondary to the fact you're still standing here," Jamie interrupted, trying to steer them back on topic.

He was absolutely going to get tired of that. Soon. Because somehow he kept winding up smashed between Sam and his brother.

Sam watched him for a moment, and then deflated. "Malek taught me—long ago now—to wrap myself into a manifestation if I was injured."

Bazel huffed. "That should not have worked. The amount of…power left behind—"

"I spent rather a lot of time in this form."

"Well obviously, now that you can speak to Grace—"

"Even before."

Jamie watched them pass a sort of uncomfortable glance, like there was some level of emotional connection there the rest of them were missing.

"And this is all fascinating," Nate interrupted. "I can't imagine you've found us here just to tell us it's not what's-his-face."

"Tanik." Bazel frowned. "No, I haven't." He paused, thinking. "Have you heard from the cambion lately?"

"Lee?" Nate blinked.

"I talked to him last week." Grace frowned. "Did you talk to Willy? They were talking pretty frequently. Even more than he talks to Deke."

"I was aware of that," Bazel said, jaw tense.

"And you're asking us because?" Grace cocked a brow at him, waiting.

Bazel let it stretch for a long moment, staring at the window across from them.

"Ba—"

"There are…reports." He looked back at Grace. 'It looks as if he's…fallen off the wagon. I know Willow believes in him. If I ask her…" He died off, swallowing.

"Then it's not just him you're questioning," Nate offered, voice soft and understanding.

Bazel nodded jerkily.

"They are false," Sam said, voice still and strong.

"How can you be sure?"

"Because I have looked him in the eye when self-preservation would have allowed him to blur a line. They were all solid. Willow put her trust in him, just has Deacon has for years. He would not forsake that." Sam frowned. "But the cambion makes a ready scapegoat."

"Which is the less disturbing option," Grace said.

Sam huffed. "In what way is that less disturbing?"

"Less disturbing than their being true, and just not Lee," Nate offered softly.

Bazel blinked at them, horrified. "Another cambion."

"There are no others," Sam assured.

"According to the council," Bazel breathed, tense and uneasy.

Jamie could nearly see Sam itching to grab a hold of Grace and wrap her in cotton wool. He blinked slowly, the horror of whatever this thing was leaching into his face.

"Well, that is something to look into," Bazel admitted. "I'll speak with Malek. You're going back to Curt's when you are finished here?"

"We are finished here," Sam assured. "But yes, in the morning."

Bazel nodded, looking around.

And it clicked then for Jamie. The quiet uneasiness on Bazel's face. He wanted to talk to his brother.

"Well, you seem to be done with us." Jamie grabbed Grace and Nate, and bustled them toward the door.

"What..." Nate sputtered, digging his heels in.

"They need to talk, obviously."

"They can go *anywhere*," Nate whinged. "Why are we leaving?"

"Because. Sam's not going to leave us," Grace offered.

CHAPTER 11

Bazel watched him, gaze flickering to the closing door. "That was not subtle."

"Subtle is not generally Jameson's concern."

"What is?" Bazel frowned, watching him expectantly. "I was under the impression he didn't like you."

"It was not that simple." Sam huffed. "He wants people to be happy."

"We are not 'people' though," Bazel countered.

"We are to him. Whatever else, it is Jamie's way."

"You like him."

"I…" Sam bit his lip. "You wanted to talk to me?"

Bazel watched him uneasily, clearly not sure where to start.

"Jamie clearly thought we needed a moment."

"Do you remember your…panic when Grace could actually see you?"

"Of course." Sam frowned. "I would not forget it." Not that he wanted to dwell on that, or that he appreciated having to admit it out loud.

"You are my brother, and you always have been." Bazel paused, watching him. "To me. And Father is constantly sure that you are nearly as unusual as I am." He shifted, uncomfortable. "You may not…"

Sam frowned. "I may not what?"

"You may not feel the same. I think you are generally fond of me. But it does always seem to be within acceptable levels."

Sam frowned. "I don't know how I...I feel about our being brothers. I have always trusted you more than anyone, possibly even more than Malek, with the exception of Grace."

"Father doesn't seem to mind." Bazel pushed a hand through his hair. "And that isn't to say that I do."

"But you do." Sam swallowed, and moved forward. He thought about the way Grace and Jamie had always been, about how he'd started to want that. Family that loved him honestly. Only clearly he'd already had it. He grabbed Bazel, pulling him into a hug. It was different. The only person Sam had ever actually initiated a hug with, before now, was Grace.

Sam felt awkward, and was about to step back when Bazel hugged him back and let out a shuddering breath.

"Grace would say it is my luck, I realize I want a family, and I already have one."

Bazel chuckled softly. "You do."

They pulled back, and Sam blinked at him. 'Willow is my niece."

His brother laughed softly, nodding.

"I suppose Deacon is deserving of her."

~*~***~*~

Sam hadn't spent as much time riding around in the back of the Charger, invisible, as one would think. It'd taken him very little time at all to realize Grace didn't need him there. Nate was relatively trustworthy, even in the beginning, and certainly at highway speed with nothing to worry about could be trusted to keep Grace safe.

So Sam had swallowed, and watched Grace crawl into the car all those times, and contented himself with popping to where she was going, and not being in the car with her.

That wasn't to say he'd never spent the afternoon in the car. It was different now. Grace and Nate had a rhythm to the way they traveled. The way Nate drove endless long stretches of road, Grace talking when she wanted to talk, and sleeping when she needed to sleep, and fiddling with radio stations or tapes or whatever else they had to come up with, to make the hours go by before they fell apart. It was relaxed and easy and comfortable, and from what Sam could tell it'd been strangely relaxed and easy and comfortable from the moment they'd met. He'd checked back in with Grace, while they were driving to Curt's from her little house in Graysville. There'd been no discontent, no tension between them.

It was probably telling, that lack of issue in the air. Nate and Grace weren't either one of them, that he'd seen, comfortable in the presence of other people. But they'd always been okay with each other.

At least half of what made this trip different to all those other ones was Jamie.

Not just the weight of him, taking up the other half of the back seat. Not just the way he shifted around sometimes and unselfconsciously stretched one leg into Sam's seat-well, took up more than his fair share of space for a moment because he needed it. Jamie took up space. Took up oxygen and light and made everything around him bend.

Jamie asked questions. For being the person in the car with more to hide, in the way of a normal life, he was less afraid of his past, less afraid of people trying to understand what he was saying than any of the rest of them appeared to be.

Jamie wasn't afraid of poking them with questions. Wasn't afraid to voice any little thought that went through his head.

"So I'm confused." Jamie turned to his side, looking at Sam across the car.

Sam looked at him, pretending he hadn't spent the last hundred miles pretending to stare out the window and silently cataloging every move the other man made. "Yes?"

"You said something about Malek showing you how to wrap yourself into a manifestation so if something bad happened to you, you were protected." Jamie frowned. "What do you look like without that?"

"What do I look like without a manifestation?"

"Yeah." Jamie nodded. "You have to look like something, don't you? And I promise I won't be creeped out if it's something strange. All tentacles and extra eyes and crap."

Sam frowned. "I am an...energy being. I don't look like anything to you."

"Really?"

"Well, I doubt your eyes could handle seeing what a Maeleket actually looks like." Sam frowned. "Why?"

"Just trying to piece things together." Jamie shrugged. "So why does the manifestation help that?"

"Because the purpose of skin is to keep your internal organs inside, and protect your body." Sam looked back out the window, watching the scrubby grass world flow past him. "Without that..." He swallowed. "Wrapping into a physical form can give you a certain level of protection, if you can hold it through the sudden understanding of actual pain."

"So it doesn't hurt if they do something to you when you're like that."

"It hurts." Sam frowned. "But I don't have nerves or a body so the pain is different. You would think it would hurt less, if there was nothing to convey that pain, but it doesn't. It just hurts differently."

"And when you manifest?" Jamie asked softly, completely focused on him.

"The pain is much nearer."

Sam was standing on the porch, in the dark night, feeling like everything about him that actually mattered was steadily leaking out of his side, pooling on the porch at his feet while he waited for Jamie to answer the door, wondering if he was going to. If he was going to let Sam in even if he did.

"It feels more immediate," Sam continued, still watching the landscape. "I can't explain it more than that."

Jamie seemed done with him, leaned his head back and watched his own side of the car. Grace leaned back and asked him a question, something Sam didn't catch about his understanding of the thing they'd seen before, and Grace and Nate bickered for a few miles about what radio station to listen to and Jamie laughed softly from the back until Grace threw something at him and pecked Nate on the cheek.

"Oi, I'm driving."

Sam wondered how hard it would be, for him to pretend it wasn't happening. This was just...life. He was traveling with them now, right where he wanted to be with his Grace and—

"So what do the Maeleket that aren't watchers do?"

"Do?" Sam blinked at him.

"Right." Jamie cocked a brow at him. "They have to do something, don't they? I mean they can't just...float around as wavelengths of light all the time. There has to be something they do."

"I don't know that there is." Sam frowned. "I suppose now that I think about it you're right. There must be something they're doing. I don't know that it works in that way."

Jamie frowned at him. "What do you mean?"

"I believe they do as they please, in ways that don't impact the humans. They live the way they choose to live, within the parameters."

"Is there some difference between the females and the males? Do you have...might you have a sister somewhere?"

Sam swallowed, and reminded himself Jamie was just curious. Wanted to know more about someone in his life. "I suppose anything is possible."

Jamie cocked a brow at him, waiting.

"I doubt it though. Female Maeleket are few and far between. There are only two on the council."

"Wow." Grace sighed. "That makes me feel warm and—"

"It is not a sign of disrespect," Sam contested, before she'd even finished. "I can only think of maybe five females that I know of in any case. As I said, they are rare."

"I'd say something about them being precious," Nate joked. "But Grace is up here with me."

"You'd rather I was in the back?"

"Not when you put it like that."

~*~***~*~

"Sam," Grace glanced at him under her arm, hands wrapped around a strainer. "Can you hand me that can of peas?"

Sam froze, one foot inside the door, and swallowed. He had options. He could pretend Curt needed him for something, or Nate. He could come up with some reason why he couldn't be in the kitchen with Grace. "Of course."

It didn't matter how likely this was to end badly, he wasn't capable of telling Grace he couldn't or wouldn't help her when that wasn't true. There were going to be enough times, over the course of her life, that he wouldn't be able to. That she'd need something from him he couldn't give for whatever reason.

Sam handed her the can of peas, trying to come up with some sort of normal facial expression—and he wasn't particularly good at those on the best of days so there was that to think about—so that she'd understand everything was fine. Because it was.

Except for where it wasn't at all.

Grace reached over and grabbed his hand, tugging him closer to her at the sink. "Can you stir this for a second, while I check on the meat?"

Sam nodded, and took the spoon from her fingers.

"Thanks, Sam."

"Of course."

I don't know how to fix this Grace, he thought. *I don't think I can.*

He did little chores for her. Stirred the vegetables, or helped with the pasta. Waited while she checked the meat and then helped her set the table. The kitchen was small, and Sam was constantly in her personal space, hips brushing while she went to the counter, shoulders bumping over the oven and the fridge, Grace leaning against him for a moment while she pulled something out of the pantry. Was this why she didn't like people around when she cooked? Because it was too intimate?

Sam knew, before this—before Nate and Curt and Grace learning to come to terms with more people than just Jamie loving her—domestic would have been the very last descriptor he picked. There was an entire house, in some strange state of half-built, on the back of Curt's property, but it wasn't there because of Grace.

Well, strictly speaking it was because of Grace. It was because something settled and domestic was what Nate wanted. He wanted a happily ever after, even if he couldn't articulate it. Which wasn't to say Grace didn't want that. She'd never have asked for it, even if she knew how. Wasn't generally in her to ask for much of anything, and it never had been that Sam had seen.

He was suddenly incredibly tempted to ask Jamie if that had always been true.

Sam stopped, grabbing Grace, wrapping her up in his arms and just standing there for a moment.

"Sam?"

"I am well," he tried.

"Don't lie to me Sam," Grace whispered, hugging him back tightly. "You're bad at it."

"There is nothing new," Sam whispered, hand smoothing over her hair.

Grace nodded, stepping back from him. "Alright."

The timer for the oven went off and Grace turned to open the door right as Nate came stomping through the back door. "I think we might get snow."

"Yay," Grace muttered, going back to what they'd been doing in the kitchen.

Sam didn't wonder about Grace's father. He knew the man was still alive. Somewhere, out in the world at that particular moment Grace had family. Real, blood family. Sam could have found them, it wouldn't have taken him much of anything. Particularly as even though the Cleary's had opted out of a watcher, the council still kept tabs on them.

The council held a policy of non-interference, generally if a line went dark they lost their watcher, absolutely, but the council didn't hunt them to the last man or anything extreme. That was reserved for a level of behavior that was altogether more disturbing.

If Grace's father had ever been trained, if he'd ever done anything more with his life that search for new and inventive ways to become intoxicated maybe things would have been different. In the beginning Sam had tried to convince himself it would have made a better person. He'd held on to that for as long as he could, mostly because Sam couldn't take Grace away from him, much as he'd wanted to. He'd needed to believe there was something good there.

Then one night he'd stupidly, drunkenly set the house on fire and Grace had nearly died, trying to drag him out before the fire-department showed up and saved them both. That was the closest he'd ever come to having to interfere before she was eighteen.

So yes, Grace's Dad was still alive out there somewhere, but Sam didn't have concern for him. Didn't wonder when he was going to try and worm his way back into Grace's life. He'd already tried more than once, and Jamie always stopped him. Because however little Sam appreciated Grace's father, it was nothing to the bone deep loathing Jamie experienced.

Grace patted Sam on the shoulder, forcing a smile. The month after Grace's thirteenth birthday Jamie had broken his ankle. It hadn't been stupid kid playing, he'd been trying to shovel in front of his house so he could go get some groceries that his mother hadn't bothered to get before, like she'd promised to. She hadn't come home the night before. Jamie hadn't asked for her, hadn't called her. He'd called Grace and Grace had gotten him a taxi to the hospital. Who'd called a social worker because Jamie wouldn't tell them where his mother was.

There'd been visits. Grace—and by extension, Sam—was around for a couple of them. Visits where the social worker was nearly certain Jamie's mother was unfit. Visits where everyone figured out they weren't going to do anything about that. Jamie put on a show for them, like they were a normal family and it'd just been a one-time thing because of the weather. Because no matter how Jamie felt about his mother, or social services, he hadn't wanted to be taken away from Grace. Sam remembered the quiet panic in his face, the way he'd clung to Grace sometimes.

She'd let him, because that was the only way Grace knew to say everything was going to be alright.

Because it probably wasn't, but that didn't change anything.

"You're eating tonight, right?" Grace asked, looking up at him. "I know you don't need to, but—"

"Yes." Sam nodded. Before Sam's brush with death Curt had taken him aside and explained that meal times weren't just about food, and just because Grace wasn't insisting didn't mean she didn't need him to stay.

They weren't talking about Monday. About the fact they'd finished the hunt, and technically Jamie was supposed to be back teaching classes by Tuesday. Deacon and Willow were back at the shop where they belonged and the rest of them were going back to that too.

Sam was swift beginning to accept this feeling—toes poised over the precipice, making decisions he had no experienced with at all—as the price for being part of Grace's life. He didn't wonder why Maeleket left the humans be any longer, if he ever had. They were emotionally exhausting.

"Alright, another twenty minutes for the meal and then we'll be ready to—"

Sam grabbed Grace at the first flash of light, pulled her behind him and released as much power as he dared to protect her. Watched warily as Tanik stumbled against the table across from them. Blood poured from his chest in a sickly steady rush, staining his lips as he coughed.

"Samriel."

Sam moved away carefully, aware Nate and Jamie were standing in the hallway, they'd started to move forward before Sam waved them back.

"Y venet se…" *I tried to…* he managed in the language they spoke. "Easeth d'na elep…" *Need to warn you…*

His knees buckled, and Sam barely caught him before he collapsed on the floor.

"Tanik…" He looked up at Nate. "First-aid kit, now."

"Betraying us…" Tanik choked. "With them, unclean."

"Who?" Sam nearly shook him, feeling at his wound, chest constricting. Tanik didn't know how to properly manifest, he wasn't concentrating enough.

His eyes glowed an unearthly white, voice cracking like an over-powered microphone. "I do not understand…"

"Focus on your shell and close it," Sam insisted.

"Thought Bazel was untrustworthy…see now it was the wrong one."

"Which one?" Sam swallowed. "Who is untrustworthy?"

"All of them," Tanik gasped, before he erupted into flashing, hot-white light.

CHAPTER 12

Jamie closed his eyes by instinct. Covered his face because something about the white crackle in the air said he didn't want to see that.

He had a bare second, when he opened his eyes, to see Sam poised to run, face focused and dark. To take that last two steps and wrap his fingers around Sam's wrist.

"Don't."

Sam looked at him, alien and dark.

A couple of weeks ago his reaction to that might have been different. He might have felt a curl of unease being stared at through hard gray eyes. But that was weeks ago, and now he got that. Got the spark of anger and the desire to do something—anything—even if it was something stupid, and barely healed from the last time would have been stupid.

"Let me—"

"I will absolutely let you go," Jamie swallowed, voice low and private. "Just as soon as you have some plan that's not just...going."

Sam was strung tight, and staring at the blood on his clothes, and Jamie didn't need to be a mind reader. The only real lessons Sam had gotten on being human had come from Grace. Grace didn't do the right thing because she liked you, she did it because it was the right thing.

Sam huffed softly, eyes still locked on the floor.

"Bazel," Grace said softly.

She said the name, and for a second Jamie thought it was a suggestion. Until the other Maeleket appeared between them. His eyes widened and his nostrils flared and Jamie was intensely glad he wasn't responsible for that look.

"What happened?" He frowned, looking around them. "Tanik?"

The name echoed in the silence around them.

"Showed up here bleeding," Nate offered, when Sam didn't answer and no one else could find anything to say, apparently. "He muttered something to Sam and then…poof."

Poof.

He hadn't been stable. Jamie understood that. Could hold it up in his head against Sam, pounding on his door, bloody and half unconscious. Tanik hadn't been stable. From what Sam had said he hadn't wrapped into his manifestation enough. He'd seen the certainty in Sam's eyes when he'd asked for the first-aid kit. The honest understanding it was already too late.

Maybe if they'd had more warning. If Sam hadn't been—rightfully—suspicious at first things might have been different.

He doubted it.

But that wasn't going to help Sam any.

Jamie'd had a boyfriend in college. It was actually the only romantic relationship he'd ever had that was 'okay' with Grace. His name was Tom, and if they'd had anything but sexual attraction to ground them they might have gone the distance. They still talked sometimes, traded Christmas cards and emails. Tom had been pre-law, and had the loosest morals of anyone Jamie'd ever met. Even when he was a kid making stupid choices. Well…*stupider*.

He'd told Jamie once, shortly before they broke up, that Grace had taken all the cold, useful characteristics, and left him with all the rest and between the two of them they made one sort of emotionally healthy human being.

Tom hadn't had a problem with Grace, that didn't mean he understood her.

Somehow the shoe had wound up on the opposite foot, with him and Sam. He was always the voice of reason. How did that even happen? Jamie wasn't good at reason.

Maybe that was their problem.

"I am...fine."

"If you charge off there alone we're just going to wind up right back where we were last week and...no. Please."

Because Bazel was there, but Sam was still about ready to disappear on them.

"Stay here." Bazel swallowed. "There's every chance they're trying to lure you away from Grace."

Sam blinked, looking around him. "Where are you going?"

"I know where Father is. I'll tell him and we'll go...investigate."

Sam nodded, tense and slow. "He said no one was trustworthy. Be careful."

"You too." Bazel swallowed. "Grace, could you please call Willow?"

"Of course." Grace cleared her throat. "How much am I telling her?"

"Everything." Bazel nodded, like he was convincing himself. "If they were somehow monitoring you that closely we would be in a great deal more trouble."

Grace nodded. "Tell Malek to be careful too."

Bazel nodded, and left.

The loud beep on the kitchen timer started them, and Grace reached back and slapped it, cursing darkly. "Bloody thing..."

Nate slipped through the room, grabbing her in a hug, holding tight.

Jamie watched them. Watched the line of tension in Grace's shoulder, the way she relaxed into the embrace and settled, clung to Nate and huffed out a breath.

He still hadn't let go of Sam's wrist.

Jamie half expected him to twist away. To be upset because Jamie had basically given him an order. Even if it was one he'd needed for the best.

Sam moved his arm, shifting to squeeze Jamie's hand for a second as he moved away. "You need to eat."

"We need to…" Curt muttered darkly. "Boy, one of your people just…"

"He is no longer here, and…" *Standing here in the quiet is not helping*, he didn't need to say.

"Yeah." Jamie cleared his throat.

They all moved around the kitchen, and Grace nudged Sam softly. "Go change your clothes."

~*~***~*~

There wasn't a frame of reference, for how long it was going to take to hear back from Bazel and Malek. Jamie knew that, just like the rest of them did, so he had absolutely no reason at all to be agitatedly pacing back and forth in the basement, between the chair to the books back to the chair, wondering if that conversation with Sam had only been a couple of days ago, and when this whole speed of life had become second nature to him.

No matter how adult he tried to be he always got dragged into Grace's life and he never could manage much of a resistance to it.

He was supposed to go back to work in two days. Obviously he'd already decided he wasn't. There was no possible way he was going to be able to leg off back to his life tomorrow and not worry freaking constantly about Sam.

And Grace.

Jamie stopped, staring at the shelves of books in front of him and just had to breathe. He wasn't replacing his ridiculous worry about Grace. He didn't worry about Grace any less just because he was worried about Sam now.

He worried a little less about Grace now because she had Nate, because there was someone else to shoulder that particular burden. In theory the same was true with Sam. Because Grace loved him, cared about him just as much as anyone would and she'd do her best to keep him in one piece. Grace was never going to jump between Sam and someone he was arguing with, was never going to reach out and grab him and physically make him stay because he was about to do something stupid.

Grace didn't get involved in other people's decisions. Because Grace managed rational, at base, every day. Rational was Grace's coping mechanism and had been since they were children. Jamie knew himself well enough to know his coping mechanism was worrying about other people. Was trying to take care of them and make sure they were happy.

Finding the line between that and stupidly co-dependent was probably a large part of why he was single. He didn't know how to behave normally in an adult relationship, he'd never had a father and his mother hadn't ever dated anything resembling healthily. He thought it was entirely possible his Aunt Rhoda had a successful relationship once. There was an old picture of a man in full military get-up in her bedroom but she'd never said who he was or told them anything about him.

Footsteps creaked on the stairs, and he froze, looking up at the bare wood.

Nate leaned his head down, brow cocked. "Can I come down? It's just me."

Jamie frowned. "Where's..."

"Grace is on the phone with Willy letting her vent about stocking so she can pretend she's not seriously worried." Nate forced a smile. "And Sam's sitting next to her because he is."

He smiled, nodding.

"And I'm coming downstairs to see why you're pacing and generally freaking the shit out." Nate blinked. "Other than the obvious answers?"

He snorted. "No, that about covers it."

Nate watched him for a long moment. "Not going back to work tomorrow?"

"No."

They stood there in silence for a long moment, and Jamie was about to tell him to just spit it out because...

"Okay Dude, I'm not...I'm bad at this whole...tap-dance around shit until we figure each other out thing you do with Grace and..." He swallowed.

Jamie cocked a brow at him.

"How much is it gonna mess your life up?"

He sighed. "It's not going to. I'm taking a sabbatical until the end of the semester. And they're understanding."

Nate snorted. "What did you tell them?"

"There was a death in Grace's family."

He blinked. "And that worked?"

Jamie flushed. "The dean's met Grace before. And honestly, she was the only family other than my Aunt Rhoda I could say anything about. It's also...as things are about Grace--sort of--it works better."

"Sure." Nate nodded. "I can see that. So that's...it's not going to end your professional life. That doesn't mean you're great."

Jamie laughed softly, rubbing the back of his neck. "I...I should be angry about this, or conflicted or something, shouldn't I? That'd be the normal response."

"Probably." Nate winced.

"It would be." Jamie sighed. "Grace and I have obviously never been normal. That's not...I wouldn't change that because it wasn't always her being a freaking mess obviously. An equal amount of that... possibly more than it was my making stupid decisions and being a mess. We wouldn't be what we are if either of us were normal."

Nate laughed.

"Worried I'm gonna freak out?"

"A little."

"Why?"

Nate winced, rubbing a hand through his hair. "Because Grace is a little...preoccupied right now with Sam and whatever the heck is going on...when that's done she's going to have a sudden moment where she realizes things might not be great with you."

"I'm fine." He clapped Nate on the back. "How are you?"

"Freaked out." He cocked a brow. "Sam's not-friend just bought it in the kitchen and they're supposed to be the hearty ones here." He swallowed. "Is that what Sam looked like when he showed up at your house?"

"No." Jamie swallowed, sight flashing behind his eyes. "No, because he knew what he was doing and he'd wrapped himself tight enough."

"Still." Nate swallowed. "He must have been bleeding pretty badly."

"It was a little excessive." Jamie pushed out a tired breath. "And he was basically unconscious for a couple of days." he snorted. "And then he forgot to eat and passed out again."

Nate cursed.

Jamie sighed. "Yeah. So...we can not do that again with pretty much anybody."

"Sounds good to me." He smiled. "So—"

"Nate, Jamie?" Grace softly called down the stairs.

"Yeah?" Nate answered, giving him a worried look.

"Bazel and Malek are here."

Jamie headed for the stairs right away, without even thinking about it. "We're coming up."

Curt was hanging out in the kitchen, and Nate froze for a second because Deke and Willy were standing in the kitchen, looking uneasy.

"Hey." Nate clasped hands with Deke, and kissed Willy on the cheek. "Fancy seeing you here."

"You're not funny." Willy whispered, because Grace wasn't in the room yet. "Why is Grace freaking out?"

Nate smiled wryly. "Because she's Grace and it's Sam."

"She called me for Dad and I thought she was actually gonna snap."

"Yeah." Nate swallowed. "It'll be..." He shrugged, dying off when Grace came in with Sam.

"Father."

"Samriel." Malek sighed. "Bazel and I looked where we could. We don't know anything. What exactly did he say to you?"

"That he thought it was Bazel that was untrustworthy and he was wrong."

"And he didn't say who?" Bazel asked, voice dark.

"Everyone." Jamie answered. "He said everyone was untrustworthy. Which I thought meant that you shouldn't trust anyone you weren't absolutely sure of."

"Most likely." Malek nodded. "Samriel, I need you to agree to stay here."

"Why?"

"Because your brother's range of movement as a member of the council is much higher than your own, and someone needs to be here keeping an eye on the people they would most likely attempt to use to get to you."

"People?"

"Grace and Jameson. To a lesser extent Nate. Willow is still a well kept secret, in general." Malek looked at Jamie then, all clear eyes and easiness.

Jamie didn't know what to do with Malek. On the face of things he seemed...kindhearted and helpful. He seemed to defer a lot to Grace, like she was important to him as well. But he wasn't sure how he felt about those eyes looking at him.

"Are you going back to work tomorrow?"

"No."

"Jamie—" Grace started.

"He cannot go back to work because I cannot be there and here both," Sam interrupted.

Grace glowered. "That's..."

"How about he can't go back because his focus would be shit right now?" Jamie insisted, speaking over them.

"And also he's in the room." He looked between Grace and Sam, brow cocked.

Sam apologized softly. Grace rolled her eyes and huffed, but didn't say a word.

Malek smiled, nodding. "All the better for us, but if there is a problem, please don't be quiet about it."

Curt snorted. "House ain't exactly quiet ever."

"So you're...going to work on figuring out who this is and we're just sitting still?" Nate made a face, clearly not pleased with the plan.

"For the moment." Malek sighed. "We'll try and get through things as quickly as we can."

Grace sighed. "We'll make do. Good luck."

~*~***~*~

Sam had never been good at sitting still when there was a problem. He didn't doubt in the slightest he needed to be there. Grace and Jamie were in danger and if he was gone someone could pop in and they'd need his protection and not have it.

He'd attached a quiet trace spell to Jamie last week.

He was very good at ignoring his own motives for things. Avoidance. He suspected Bazel and Malek would lay that at Grace's feet. That she'd taught him all those little human foibles. She hadn't. Sam had millennia of ignoring his own motives or actions if he could get away with it.

He wasn't comfortable. Twitchy and agitated and the longer he stayed in the house like that, the more he agitated Grace. She didn't call him on it, they weren't in any real danger of getting in an argument, but he could tell exactly how uncomfortable he was making her. He'd spent the better part of the day before hiding in the library in the basement. But Curt had been trying to work down there that morning, and he hadn't been willing to have Sam hanging over his shoulder all day.

Sam understood, he wasn't particularly more interested in spending those hours in the older man's company.

He'd escaped out to the *project*. Most of the major work he wanted to leave for Nate, since it was his idea, and he felt as if the vast majority of the magical warding and things Deacon and Nate should both be present for.

He knew occasionally Nate had a moment of self-doubt. A moment where he struggled with his awareness that as much as he was surprising Grace with the house, it was Nate that wanted it. Grace didn't want a house because Grace, generally, didn't *want*. Sam had done his best, in the stilted conversation he could manage with Nate when the other man was being emotionally guarded, to explain that it might have been Nate that wanted the house, Sam had no doubts at all Grace needed it.

He could have installed the big picture windows in the front by himself, but Nate had been somewhat reluctant to have him start magicking things into place. That wasn't the point of all this. So instead he was installing the smaller, narrow windows next to the front door--that wasn't on yet—and contenting himself with picturing the house.

It calmed him, standing in the cold morning and working. It'd snowed the night before after all, but the day had been windy and dry so there wasn't more around than the occasional pile of flakes bermed up against the wood Nate stacked to finish an interior wall, or the forms for the dyed concrete path that was going to wind from the little clutch of trees, along the path they walked to get from Curt's to here. He checked the shims again before he started screwing it into the frame, and stood back to smooth a hand over the edge and see how it looked.

"Well that's interesting."

He turned suddenly, taking in Jamie coming up the walk, hands sunk deep in his pockets, broad shoulders hunched against the cold and cheeks slightly pink. "Jamie."

"Sam." He pulled a face, probably alluding to the redundancy of his greeting. "It's coming along nice."

Sam turned and ran a hand over the window again, nodding. "It is."

Jamie puffed out a breath. "Do you want me to go away?"

He frowned, cocking his head to the side and watching the other man. Jamie was generally a great deal easier to read than most humans. He still said things and did things Sam wasn't entirely sure of, but he was so open—at least when they were alone—he rarely had a hard time understanding where things stood. He was fond of that, because with the exception of Grace he never knew what was going on with the rest of these beings. Also, Jamie seemed to understand better than any of the rest of them but Grace, and possibly Nate, that sometimes Sam came across as cold and disconnected because he didn't know what he was doing.

"No," Sam swallowed. "Why would you think that I did?"

Jamie plopped himself down on the picnic table, rubbing his hands on his thighs. "I didn't think it was anything personal. Nate said you were out here, I thought I'd come see how you were doing." He shrugged. "But I thought it was possible you didn't want company, so if you'd like to be alone…"

"No."

Jamie nodded, and let it go at that. "How long's Nate think it'll take to finish the house?"

"If things settle down and he has time to work on it, not more than two months." Sam started setting up the other window.

"Here, let me help." Jamie stood, and took the weight of the window, holding it over its spot until Sam had everything in place.

Sam finished the set-up and swallowed. "Now shift it—"

"I can't see where you want me to go with it," Jamie interrupted. "Just move me where you need it."

Sam tentatively reached out and grasped Jamie's forearms, steering him into place, so he could rest the window in the frame. The muscles moved, tension shifting to hold where he wanted it, and Sam let go and started screwing in the window. "There. Finished."

Jamie stepped back, pushing a hand through his hair. "Looks good."

Sam nodded.

"Sam, you know if you do wanna talk about this you can." Jamie swallowed, watching him. "You're allowed to be freaked out, at least a bit."

He blinked. "I am not human and as such—"

"Don't give me the 'I am an all-powerful celestial being' crap." Jamie huffed, crossing his arms over his chest.

"I am." Sam frowned, desperately trying not to mirror the posture. He wasn't defensive, he wasn't.

"Sam." Jamie forced himself to relax suddenly, and scrubbed at the back of his head. "I'm worried about you, okay?"

"I will be fine."

"Really?" He looked Sam dead in the eyes, expression hard. "Because you've seen one of you die before?"

His jaw tensed. Suddenly he was standing in Curt's kitchen, and the smell was in his nostrils again and his human heart was pounding in his ears while he tried to focus around it, and he wanted to run away, run anywhere he didn't have to wear this human shell that caught things like that and *couldn't let them go*. And didn't, all at the same time, because when a Maeleket died it didn't matter. Not like it mattered to the humans.

"Hey." Jamie's voice was soft and tense.

Something warm squeezed his shoulder, fingers almost digging in to get his attention.

Humans gave off a signature, a certain buzz that caught in his skin and rumbled. Grace felt like a quiet buzz, like potential and power leashed by will. Nate was the soft rumble of a large machine, never-changing and never-ending. He catalogued these things and...left them. They didn't matter, and he wasn't sure they said anything about the person and when he'd mentioned this to Bazel he'd gotten an odd look.

Jamie was still. Not still in that he was lacking that buzz. Still in that at most it was the rustle of leaves in the wind or the beat of your own heart. Hard to notice until it was gone, but felt keenly once it left.

Sam opened his eyes and looked at the other man, cheeks pink from the cold, eyes expressive and worried, straight white teeth tugging at his bottom lip.

"Sam?"

Sam reached forward, hand wrapping around the back of Jamie's neck, and pulled him into a kiss.

CHAPTER 13

Jamie had his sexual identity crisis late.

Or at least late compared to when he'd always thought people had those. In his head that was always something people dealt with at sixteen. Once they reached the age to start questioning the future, and there was some catalyst for that.

To be fair, Jamie had gotten the catalyst. It was his junior year in college and he'd gone to a frat party, he didn't remember why at all. It was rush week and he'd gotten excessively drunk, and apparently decided it was better to crash with somebody than call Grace at two in the morning. The somebody was named Burke, and he was a senior in the Architecture program who'd apparently spent the last three years living down that particular stereotype and wasn't particularly happy about flushing all that down the drain because he and Jamie happened to wake up wrapped around each other and hovering somewhere around second base.

For about a week he'd tried to act like it wasn't...anything. Another drinking story, nothing more or less. Gay wasn't a thing people were, where they grew up, and at twenty-one he'd been stupidly macho. In hindsight he was always a little surprised Grace hadn't belted him harder for that than she had.

So he'd quietly obsessed about it for a week, and then nearly drank himself into the ground for two, and then started picking up random guys at the different clubs in town. The epic fight that happened with Grace because he missed a study-date—he was sleeping it off on some guys couch, he'd never known his name—was probably the best way that could have ended.

By the end of the month he'd picked himself up and dusted himself off, and come to terms with the fact he was bi-sexual.

Obviously, Sam knew all that, so his having the guts to just grab Jamie and kiss him wasn't all that surprising. At least he knew he wasn't going to get hit for it. Not that there was any sort of guarantee Sam had thought his actions through that well. He was a little unsteady at the moment.

And *warm.* And halfway through giving Jamie what was probably the best kiss he'd ever had before he got with the program and kissed back. Wrapped his hand over Sam's shoulder and turned the kiss around on him, sliding their lips together.

They wound down after a long moment, Sam pulling back cautiously, their breath fogging in the air between them.

Jamie licked his lips, pulling in an unsteady breath. "Not that I'm complaining…" He smiled slightly, watching Sam's eyes flick around them, cheeks turning steadily more red. He wasn't sure the other man realized he blushed, but he wasn't about to tell him, it was adorable.

Sam stepped back hastily, hand pressed to his mouth, eyes wide and panicked.

"Sam?"

"I shouldn't have…" He cleared his throat, a certain distance leeching into his eyes. "I apologize. I will go back to the house, I…"

Jamie reached out and grabbed his arm, towing him a half-step closer before he scuttled off. "Put the brakes on the back-pedal, I'm not upset." He watched him, those expressive silver eyes panicked and shifty. "I'm just confused."

He could see how badly Sam wanted to run in every single line in his body, but his wrist was still lax and unresisting in Jamie's hand. If he wanted away that badly he'd have just gone, Jamie knew, so he didn't feel any reason not to hold on.

Also, Jamie didn't like to avoid problems. If there was an issue you fixed it, because if you didn't it just hung out in the back of your head and festered until it was…more than it had been.

"I should not have done that."

"Yeah, you said that part." Jamie cocked a brow at him. "If you don't give me some kind of reason here soon I'm going to feel slighted."

"Slighted?" Sam cocked his head to the side.

"As in you don't really like me, I was just here and you were…out of sorts."

Sam swallowed, blinking at him. "I should not have done that because you have a life, and you are human and I am…not and—"

Jamie grabbed him by the face and kissed him again, stopping the flow of words. He didn't hold it for as long, and consciously kept it light and easy because he wasn't entirely sure Sam had *hugged* more people than himself and Grace.

They stopped, and Sam blinked at him, confused.

"Sometimes you think too much." Jamie smiled at him, shrugging. "The way things are right now I'm not sure we need to be worried that far into the future."

~*~***~*~

By the time they get back to the house they're pink and frozen, Jamie stomping his feet in the hallway to get the circulation back in his legs, huffing. Nate paused, looking them over and cocking a brow, and Jamie was ready for…something. Some sort of shit because the other man wasn't stupid.

"Lee's coming by, apparently."

Sam froze, looking at Nate. "Here?"

Nate nodded.

"Is that an issue?" Jamie frowned. "And Lee's the...what's it called?"

"Cambion," Nate offered.

"It is an issue because Curt had made it quite clear he did not want the...man in his house." Sam said, eyes wide. "Where is Grace?"

"She's downstairs looking something up," Nate said softly. "And Curt's been a little..." He huffed. "So I'd suggest give her a bit. Curt decided of the options he preferred to have everyone here where he could keep an eye on us." He forced a smile. "Anyway, he and Deke and Willy will be here after they close the shop up for the day."

"Well, that makes for a full house," Jamie offered.

Nate snorted. "Yeah. Hey, can I get your help with something?"

"Sure." He clapped Sam on the shoulder softly, following Nate into the other room. "What did you need?"

"I need to move this desk and—"

"Nate!"

Nate paused, and moved next to the stairs. "Yeah?"

"Are Sam and Jamie back?"

"They are, but I'm stealing Jamie." Nate smiled at him. "You need something sugar-plum?"

"You to stop calling me sugar-plum," Grace muttered. "Sam, ovestum is the proper past participle of egg, right?"

Sam huffed. "Yes." He started down the stairs. "Why do you need to know? I have mentioned how uncomfortable your interest in those spell books makes me. Those are not your sort of magic and you could seriously—"

"I'm not doing it—"

Nate rolled his eyes and grabbed Jamie by the arm. "You don't want to hear that conversation again."

Jamie allowed himself to be pulled along, but frowned. "I haven't heard it the first time."

"Lucky you."

"That bad?" They trumped up the stairs into the bedroom Grace and Nate shared. Jamie was actually sort of stupidly attached to the room. It was…both of them. Grace's hap-hazard way of leaving books on every available surface, and Nate's ever-growing collection of water-glasses. Sometimes they were so goddamn cute he didn't know what to do with it.

Nate snorted. "They're probably both right, about the best I can figure is just stay out of the middle of it. Sam's a little…um…"

"A little." Jamie grinned at him. "In his defense Grace is good at getting into shit."

"She is." He sighed. "You're not so noticeable."

"I've had my moments." He sighed. "So what are we moving, and if you tell me we're moving it down the stairs I'm asking why you didn't ask Sam."

Nate laughed, rubbing the back of his neck. "We're not, but I didn't ask Sam because he needs advanced directions for this shit and if he just…zaps it somewhere it'll set the wards off more than we really want." He started picking up books and piling them on the bed. "I swear to god they're taking us over one book at a time."

Jamie laughed, shaking his head. "I actually thought it wasn't so bad."

Nate looked around him and let out a low whistle. "Alright then. Well, we're only moving the desk across the room, because the chest is going downstairs because Curt thinks he can turn it into a strong-box."

"I don't know what that is, but sure."

"Do you want to?"

"Not unless I need to."

They worked in silence for a few minutes, before Nate cleared his throat. "So you and Sam…?"

"Dude, hell if I know." Jamie snorted. "Things are a little messy right now."

"Yeah." Nate glanced up at him. "I'm totally not getting in your business."

"Yes you are." Jamie grinned at him. "But that's okay, you've got a vested interest."

"Do I?"

He snorted. "Well, if something goes south that'd be uncomfortable."

"Meh." Nate shrugged. "You're both adults, and stupidly attached to Grace."

"So the non-questions?"

"She'd be upset." Nate stopped, looking at a large book he'd just pulled of the desk. "She's not gonna get there before you do, probably not even for a while still. But I know she'd like you both to be happy, and she'd like you both to have some sort of personal life you clearly don't." He sighed. "She worries about you both."

Jamie blinked at him. "Worries?"

"Yeah." Nate snorted. "Dude, she worries about you *a lot*. It's just…Grace-worry. It's subtle."

"It is occasionally incredibly disturbing you know more about her than I do." Jamie pushed a hand through his hair.

Nate watched him for a long moment. "I'm pretty sure there are vast tracks of past shit I don't know anything about at all." He held his hands up at Jamie's dawning horror. "And I'm not asking, because I'd freaking suck at pretending I still didn't know so let's just…not."

"Yeah." Jamie blew out a tense breath. "That sounds like a plan."

"I'm not saying you need to…change anything." Nate swallowed. "She's worried the same way anybody worries about their friends and wants them to be happy. She's just got even less skill at expressing it than most people, so I thought you might not realize." He frowned. "She also said something about you being angsty over stuff sometimes and I thought maybe if I told you she'd be okay with it before we got there things would go easier."

"Pretty sure I'm not gonna be the angsty one."

"Yeah well, I can't do anything about Sam," Nate said wryly. "Sam has a sort of weekly freak-out because Grace is a really bad pattern card for humanity apparently. Also they're really not supposed to be involved with humans."

Jamie froze, blinking at him. "Like at all?"

"There is a whole list of seriously scary shit that came about because a Maeleket had babies with a human or something else. The Cambion, though that's a bad example. Whatever the hell Willy is—we're still not real sure about that—and all kinds of objectionable stuff. And I think the only actual rule is that you're not allowed to 'experiment' with humans. I know his relationship with Grace being what it is, is some kind of concern."

Jamie blew out a tense breath. "Wonderful."

"Sorry." Nate winced. "Didn't mean to make it worse, just thought you'd like to know."

"Yeah." He swallowed. "Thanks."

~*~***~*~

Jamie wasn't unduly worried about their next visitor. He trusted Nate to keep track of things, to tell him if Grace was in danger, if there was a problem. Nate wasn't as protective as he was, and neither of them were as bad as Sam was, so he generally figured the thing with Lee coming to Curt's house was Curt. Was the fact Lee wasn't human.

He was allowed to put the wrong emphasis on that because *Sam* wasn't human, and Willy was very much not human and Jamie was decently fond of both of them, though he didn't know Willy all that well yet. They didn't tell him why Lee is different, so he didn't assume he was.

Which was wrong, obviously.

Whatever the fuck Lee was, he was not bloody okay. He was dark and wrong and he walked in the room and Jamie honestly felt like he wanted to either kick him in the face or run away.

He did neither because Grace was all calm smiles and asking him how his business was.

"It's good." Lee rubbed a hand through his hair, unearthly dark eyes falling on Jamie. "Who's this one?"

Sam shifted slightly, blocking him.

"Easy, pinfeathers," Lee snorted. "I'm not messing with your toys, just curious."

Sam opened his mouth, eyes narrowing.

"If I have to separate you two it's going to make this take much longer than it should." Bazel said suddenly, appearing in the room. "Lee, stop poking at Sam and making eyes at the humans."

"Sam, is it?" Lee snorted. "Well, I'm here and I've kept my end of the deal, just like always, so why exactly—"

"What is your end of the deal?" Curt asked. "I'm a little unclear on why you're—"

"Not hanging from a spike in some Medieval castle?" Lee finished. "I was," he smiled devilishly. "It didn't work."

Willy huffed. "Stop joking. They're trying to make it look like you're...breaking parole. This isn't funny."

"Thanks for the vote of confidence, but—"

"We're not doubting you," Nate offered. "We're just trying to figure out what's going on."

"Aren't you?" Lee snorted. "What about him?" He pointed to Sam.

Sam was a giant ball of tension, standing there in front of him. All hard lines and dark eyes and now was absolutely not the time to be thinking about what Jamie'd like to do with that. Maybe if he thought they were in some kind of immediate danger he wouldn't have been, but under all of that, he didn't feel like Sam expected Lee to do anything.

Jamie sighed, and held a hand out. "Jay Williams."

Sam muttered darkly, and Nate grabbed his wrist, pulling his hand away.

"Rule number one, Jay?" Nate muttered. "Don't let it touch you until you know what it is."

Lee frowned at him. "Jay Williams...Professor Jay Williams from UIC?"

"Yes." Jamie blinked.

He snorted. "My bartender was in your sociology lecture last semester." His eyes darted over Jamie's form, and he smiled. "Had a giant crush on you, which makes sense now."

Sam tensed, and Bazel opened his mouth, but Grace beat them to it.

"Lee...Jamie's been my best friend since we were babies." She forced a smile. "You flirt with him and I'll kick your ass."

Lee swallowed, and backed down immediately. "Sure. Sorry Grace."

She forced a smile. "Have you eaten yet..." She paused, frowning. "Do you eat food, I suppose I should have asked that. I think I did ask Sam that once, but he wouldn't answer me."

Lee choked out a laugh. "You don't want to know about me, Grace."

"You really don't." Willy paled. "I talked Dad into explaining it to me and it's...icky. Just walk away."

Grace smiled slightly, squeezing Willy on the shoulder, and leaned back against the counter.

Deke sighed. "So, now that we've done the awkward greetings, can we get to the point?"

"There isn't a point," Lee huffed. "I haven't started snacking on the locals, and I'm not going to. I haven't made any under-world deals, I'm still abiding the terms of my parole."

"It's not really parole," Deke muttered.

Lee cocked a brow at him. "It's the most apt description."

"They've been keeping tabs on you for how long now? No one's going to jump to the conclusion you've crossed to the dark side."

"Crossed?" Lee muttered.

Willy slapped him on the shoulder. "Stop that."

Jamie bit back a laugh, at the way he shrank back from her, like he didn't know what to do with that. Like he was in over his head with these people. "Do we have to stand around here like we're waiting for the other shoe to drop?"

"No." Deke pushed Lee toward the table. "Why don't we all sit down."

"Because that's going to make things way less uncomfortable," Nate muttered.

Grace shot him a look, that clearly told him to shut up and sit down, and he did without another word. They pulled up chairs and stools and squished in around the small worn farm table. All of them. Grace and Nate, Willy and Deke, Bazek, Curt, Lee, he and Sam. Nine people at a table made for four--probably made for two, but it could have about handled four--made for a veritable sea of elbows.

Curt dropped a six-pack of beer in the middle of the table, and smiled at Willy. "Can I get you something to drink, Sugar?"

"No thanks," Willy smiled at him. "I'm good Curt, thanks."

Lee pulled a face, but stopped when Willy gave him a dark look. "What? You're both freaking scary beyond reason and he treats you like you're all sunshine and marshmallows."

"Both?" Nate frowned. "What?"

"He's afraid of Grace," Sam intoned darkly.

"He has a brain, of course he's afraid of Grace." Lee swallowed. "Not that I think Grace is going to do anything to me unprovoked."

"Why?"

"Witches are scary." Lee looked at him, shrugging. "Super powerful witches who do magic without meaning to are even scarier than normal. Frankly I'd rather take Sam there. I'd have better chance of surviving."

"Thought you lot couldn't be killed," Curt offered.

"She'd find a way," Lee muttered.

Grace frowned. "I don't know whether that's a compliment or not."

"If it's a compliment can I not be in your debt anymore?"

"We're getting off topic here," Bazel interjected, clearing his throat.

Jamie looked at Grace, cocking a brow at her, but she folded her fingers into an L and R, their sign for 'later' and looked back at Bazel.

The long and short of it was they weren't sure who was trying to spread rumors about Lee, Lee certainly didn't have any ideas. Once the conversation turned to other issues--whether Lee's contacts had heard anything unusual on the underground front, and if Deke had heard anything from his contacts—everyone calmed down considerably. They were still tense, because no one was stupid and the fact everything was quiet meant very bad things.

"Hell, from what I can tell nobody's even had a job lately that was more involved than some random monster." Curt sighed. "Some strange ones too. That thing you lot had last week," he nodded to Nate and Grace.

Deke snorted. "Yeah, that ranks right up there with our tree-nymph in the middle of the botanical garden."

"I didn't hear about that," Nate said, frowning. "As in an honest to god dryad?"

"Yeah." Deke snorted. "Tried to just move in and take up residence."

"So is that to distract you, or because you're distracted?" Jamie asked, looking around them.

"Even odds." Nate sighed. "It's possible its whoever's up to this trying to keep us off kilter." He smiled. "Or the stuff the council doesn't publicize that they do to take care of some of these things isn't getting done because..."

"Theoretically it's still happening just as it should." Bazel frowned. "But larger things would have to fall through the cracks before that sort of failure became apparent so it is difficult to tell."

"Yeah, let's hope that doesn't happen," Nate muttered.

"Lazy bum," Jamie teased.

"Dude, would you want to deal with the thing from last week more often?" Nate said dryly. "Not that you didn't handle it pretty well."

"Even if we were equal to dealing with more," Sam said darkly. "You don't find out about them until they've already incurred a death toll."

Curt snorted. "Let's save the discussion of an early-weird-shit warning system for later, shall we? How do we keep them from making an example out of Lee?"

"He's not a pet, Curt." Grace said darkly. "We all know he's not doing anything he shouldn't be. If he's willing to keep in touch more than normal for the next couple of weeks..." She paused, watching him.

Lee nodded. "Yeah. That's probably for the best."

"Don't want to get in trouble?" Curt muttered.

"I don't want you all paying attention to what I'm doing and missing something big."

Bazel cocked a brow at him. "Being altruistic are you?"

"Not entirely." Lee cocked a brow. "I have a vested interest in staying on your good side, collectively. Paying attention to me and someone dies…"

The table fell silent then, all of them quiet and concerned. That was the thing nobody wanted to talk about. Something this big, how did you come out the other side with everyone breathing?

CHAPTER 14

Jamie didn't spend a lot of time in the shop area of Deke's place. The one time he'd been there was about Grace and he'd sort of raced through to get to her. He knew it was camping supplies and things like that, along with under the counter 'hunting' stuff. He knew, through things Grace and Nate and Curt had said there was a spectacular, ridiculous storage room where Deke kept things he hadn't found a way to get rid of yet.

He hadn't had any desire to see that.

But apparently Curt had a big delivery in, and Grace was going to pick it up which meant someone was going with her. Nate was busy with a couple of commission car jobs—he had to pay somehow for the driving around the country hunting monsters—which meant Grace was driving her car.

He didn't know how she'd talked Sam into going to look into something with Bazel, he hadn't asked. He was relatively sure it'd required some supreme emotional wrangling. And a promise to call if she even half-heartedly suspected something was out of place.

Which left them climbing out of the jeep in front of the shop, stretching in the cold Chicago air. "Do you need to run by your house, while we're within half an hour?" Grace asked, looking up at him.

Jamie shrugged. "I probably could. I think Sam's nabbed nearly everything I could possibly need."

Grace pulled open the door to the shop, and stepped inside, smiling at Willy behind the counter. "Hey," she said quietly, because Willy was busy with an older man. "We'll just slip in the back."

"Go ahead," Willy nodded to him, and went back to the old man. "I don't know, Deke didn't say which one it was. Do you want me to call them and ask?"

Jamie followed Grace through the racks of camping and outdoor equipment, until she paused at the door from the main shop.

"Grace?"

She forced a smile at him, shaking her head. "I have to stop for a second..." She pushed the door open, and Jamie looked over her shoulder, swallowing.

When they'd said 'room full of' he'd thought they meant like a closet. Like shelves on the wall and maybe six or eight feet square, because that was goddamn scary enough. It wasn't a gray cement room about thirteen by twenty with a whole bunch of metal freestanding shelves all crammed with different...stuff. There were rune paintings all over the walls. He recognized a couple of them, some of the larger ones, because they were the same ones Deke and Sam had worked into the interior walls on the surprise.

"Holy..."

Deke came out of the office then, looking around before glancing at them, and snorted. "Hardly that."

Grace laughed softly. "How long have you been saving that one?"

"I don't know what you're talking about." Deke flushed though, and shifted, before he moved forward and gave Grace a quick hug. "Call Nate and tell him you're here? He's texted twice in like the last ten minutes."

"You could stop enabling him."

"Ha." Deke pulled a face. "Enabling him in the legitimate concern for his girlfriend? Yeah, I'll get right on that."

Grace rolled her eyes, and started back toward the dolly hanging out next to the office.

"Did you tell him not to touch anything?"

"Didn't think I needed to." Grace didn't turn, just knelt down the check the tires. "Jamie's human."

Deke looked him over, then glanced back at Grace. "Jamie spends a lot of time around Sam. It's possible there's enough residual—"

She stood, sighing. "Jamie, don't touch anything and try not to let anything touch you."

"Especially the tupelaq." Deke looked down at the clip-board in his hand. "That things a monster...literally..." He looked up and forced a smile. "It also likes to jump people."

"Jump how?"

"Literally." Deke looked up at him. "It's an ivory statue, about the size of a bank canister?"

Jamie nodded.

"Grace gets too close it'll leap off the shelf at her. Willy looks at it, it starts doing stuff." He pointed behind him. "It's two rows over. Look but don't touch."

"Nah, I'm good." Jamie forced a smile.

"We'll have to trail a few loads right past it," Grace offered, shifting a bag of salt onto the dolly. Jamie moved over quickly, helping her with the next one.

"What exactly is the point of bringing me with you if you're not going to let me help?"

"Company?" She flashed him a smile. "The fact Nate stayed at the house?"

He snorted. "And you didn't want to be my beard."

"Whatever." Grace rolled her eyes at him. "You're totally disappointed to not be sitting around in Curt's basement for the day trying to talk Sam out of a corner."

Jamie flushed, but didn't comment. Things with Sam had been weird, and there was so much of that in his life right then, he could have done with a little less. Not that it was a surprise.

Grace led him down the center row, not the one they'd walked through before, but the one he'd have taken if he hadn't been following Grace. They were halfway down when Grace just...stopped.

"Grace?"

She frowned, and moved back a little.

"Hello?" Jamie frowned. "You're freaking me out here Grace."

She stopped before a white stone and ivory thing, carved to look like some sort of animal totem, he wasn't very good at seeing whatever the original artist saw with those things. Grace reached a hand out, waving it next to it.

"Is that what I think it is?" Jamie took a step back, swallowing.

Grace swallowed, hand hovering just an inch or two from it. "Deke."

He was tempted to reach out and grab her by the back of the shirt and haul her back. Because Jamie knew Grace, and damn hell knew her well enough to tell when she was worried or honestly scared. She was both right then.

"What?" Deke stepped into the room, frowning at her.

Grace looked over at him, and experimentally waved her hand over the figure. Deke paled, like all the blood in his body had just left. "It doesn't like me anymore."

Deke came forward, grabbing Grace by the wrist and towing her away from it. "It's weird enough without you constantly checking it."

Grace huffed at him.

"Willy!"

"Yeah?"

"Are we alone?"

Willy's head peeked around the open door, frowning. "Yes."

Deke looked at her, nodding. "Flip the sign around. There's something wrong with the tupelaq."

"The tupelaq is something wrong," Willy muttered, before she disappeared for a moment.

Deke reached out, fingers just shy of it, look of intense concentration on his face.

"How sure are you it's not just lulling you into a false sense of security?" Jamie asked, grabbing Grace by the arm and pulling her back a bit.

He sighed. "It doesn't think that much." He reached out until his fingers were almost touching it, the rest of them standing stock still and waiting. "What the…"

~*~***~*~

Nate touched the ivory and alabaster shell, fingers sliding on the outside edge.

Curt swallowed. "So someone—"

"Has to be a Maeleket," Bazel countered, voice low. "No one else could have either tracked its original creator or managed the switch."

Curt sighed. "So some Maeleket snuck into Deke's strong room and just…stole this thing." He looked up at them, frowning. "Why?"

"You know what a tupelaq is," Grace said tiredly.

"Yeah, but if the person who made it and their original victim are both long gone."

"Deke speculated without a focus it'll just be…wanton destruction." Grace looked up, shrugging. "It'll just keep ripping things apart until it runs out of magic."

"And that'll take how long again?" Jamie asked, looking over at Grace, aware Sam was hovering somewhere between them looking nervous. "I sort of blanked out there for a minute while Deke was having a panic attack because someone got through his wards."

Grace almost smiled at him, sighing. "Conservatively? If it was going at something hammer and tongs with just humans or witches or whatever going at it, probably a week. Sam and Bazel and everything else we could possibly throw at it, eight or ten hours."

"It is unlikely the thing would seriously damage Bazel or I," Sam offered. "But short term we have a hard time protecting the humans, and if it got past us it would generally lay a swath of destruction across the city. For probably a week.

"Well that's just…" Curt swallowed. "Chipper."

"Also, there's really no way to know how big it is without it being out, so it could either be ten feet or thirty, and what characteristics it's got depend on what animals and—"

Nate clapped a hand over her mouth. "Hearing that isn't gonna help any of us. It's a scary giant bag of mystery shit. Got it."

Grace bit his hand, huffing at him.

Bazel cocked a brow at them, before looking at Jamie. Like he wanted to speak with someone normal. "Deacon?"

"He and Willy stayed at the shop." Jamie sighed, pushing a hand through his hair. "They wanted to come talk about the latest rendition of unhelpful and scary, but Deke was a little freaked out about leaving his wards since clearly someone could be breaking in and we wouldn't notice."

Bazel nodded. "I'll stop by this evening and see if there's anything I can do to…strengthen that."

"Why haven't you before?" Curt asked, agitated.

"Because breaking into a human's world without consent is a rather large breach."

"Whomever it is, they are breaking all the lines imaginable for a Maeleket dealing with humans." Sam defended. "At that point there isn't much point in protection."

Bazel nodded. "Anything serious Sam or I would do, it would just force them into the light."

Nate frowned at him. "Isn't that where we want them?"

"No!" Sam nearly shouted it, chest heaving.

Bazel winced. "It's…in the light the body count is likely to be a bit high." He huffed. "And not only in reference to those of you who are directly involved."

"Fun." Grace sighed.

"So why did that come home with you?" Curt asked, pointing at the statue on the table.

"Because it's a giant freaking hole through the middle of Deke's wards." Grace looked up at him, face pale. "Anyone who knew it was there could use it to slide right in."

"And here is a better idea?" Nate asked, voice wary. Jamie could understand that, he wasn't a hundred percent about this plan either.

Grace wrinkled her nose. "Better is relative." She looked around them. "They can certainly follow it here. Here isn't much of a secret, obviously. Here isn't in the middle of Deke's strong room with a plethora of other randomly scary crap."

There was something else there, something Deke and Grace had discussed softly, while Willy was otherwise occupied. He could tell by the look on Grace's face after that particular conversation they were just going to pretend it hadn't happened. That she had a plan and she needed him to pretend there was nothing to worry about.

He wasn't one hundred percent about that, but given the available options he was willing to give it a shot.

Eventually they stopped standing around staring at the statue. Grace slipped it back into the bag she'd brought it in, and they went about the rest of the evening. Sam was tense and quiet, which Jamie more or less expected. Not only were they in a strange place themselves, Sam was obviously more than a little worried about Grace right at the moment. Worried about keeping them safe in the face of something he'd never had to deal with before.

Dude was immortal, Jamie couldn't imagine that didn't equate to 'new' being freaking scary.

He slipped outside, mind set on the picnic table just off from the house. He wasn't going to go far. He wouldn't even go all the way to Grace's surprise. The house was feeling a little cloying at the moment and he needed some time and space to think.

Sam'd kissed him, and it wasn't that he wasn't flattered or wasn't interested. It was more that Grace and Sam had some serious sort of bond, and Jamie wasn't entirely sure he wanted to wind up in the middle of that. His relationship history wasn't exactly stellar.

Jamie boosted himself onto the picnic table and sucked in a lungful of cold air.

Mostly he was just running around in stupid circles in his head. He knew what he was going to do.

Something jerked around his middle suddenly, Jamie bending forward, because it felt like there was a rope there suddenly constricting.

He felt a mighty pull, and closed his eyes at the horrible whorl of light and sound around him, before he landed on his knees on rough stones.

"Haha," Someone cackled, grinning and swimming before him as he opened his eyes. "I suspected it would be the human."

CHAPTER 15

Sam felt the pull like someone reached through his abdomen and yanked on his internal organs. If Grace hadn't been right there he'd have had to waste a few precious seconds trying to figure out who'd just been moved.

But when he bent forward and nearly pitched face-first into the desk he already knew.

"Sam!" Grace grabbed his shoulders, pushing him back before he hurt himself.

Not that it would precisely hurt right then, but the sentiment was there at least.

Sam swallowed, gulping. "They took Jamie." He stood, straightening. "Call Bazel, he'll be able to find me."

Grace nodded, and stepped back, and Sam closed his eyes and followed the trail they'd left.

They hadn't meant to leave him an open door. The way they'd grabbed Jamie it should have taken hours, at best, for them to figure out where they'd taken him. Without the slightly over-the-line tracker Sam had slapped on him. He wasn't apologetic about that. He wouldn't have been apologetic about that even if they hadn't taken Jamie.

The fact was, Jamie was a risk. On a level most of them didn't realize. Jamie was important to Grace, and more or less incapable of protecting himself.

Granted, Grace's protective magic wasn't really…she didn't know what she was doing, it just happened. Much as that was the sort of thing the council was concerned with. There wasn't anything they would do, unless a practitioner started crossing into the sort of things Richards had been doing. No, someone in Grace's position was much more likely to have random, emotional magical outburst. And even that was uncommon. Usually. Grace had obviously tripped over the 'uncommon' line.

Only an idiot backed that into a corner until he or she figured out where all the lines were, as to what Grace was actually capable of.

But Jamie was easy.

Sam didn't think they were stupid enough to seriously injure Jamie. He was worth more to them as bait, alive, and the aforementioned magical explosion was a strong deterrent for anyone with a brain intentionally angering Grace.

If whomever was behind this were likely to make that sort of mistake they'd have stood much better chances of finishing this well.

That didn't mean Sam was willing to wait for back-up.

Sam followed the string, and found himself standing next to a kneeling Jamie in some dirty old warehouse—again—in Chicago this time.

He knew how they'd pulled him, and he knew it was a bumpy sort of ride. The fact they hadn't taken him far didn't make Sam any more inclined to be grateful.

It was a dark, dirty little place—again—that smelled like some ridiculous mix of vomit and dead fish, and given the distance to the nearest water source Sam didn't really want to even contemplate why that was. He looked around them quickly, verifying it was only the one henchman before them. Sam turned back, eyes fixing on the figure before him, muscles tensing.

"Don't vaporize him," Jamie said wryly, standing and dusting himself off.

Sam huffed, feeling the anger claw at his insides. Jamie was standing, and well, but he was pale, and Sam could smell blood. Shifting a person without proper control was dangerous.

"You are injured." He didn't look away from the rather panicked looking lackey standing before them.

"Skinned my knee when I landed." Jamie put a hand on his upper arm, not pulling, just steady pressure. "And if you burn him into little bits we won't be able to find out who his master is."

"I have no master, *human*." The lackey sneered, greasy black hair hanging in his face, looking around them, licking his lips. He'd found his spine again apparently. His skin seemed to shiver strangely, rippling.

Jamie swallowed audibly, and Sam could feel him wanting to pull back. He wouldn't, because it'd never been Jamie's way to show fear. He was good, because at that moment Sam knew Jamie well enough he could tell he was afraid but even the air was devoid of that odd tang of human fear. "What the hell are you?"

"An abaonwai." Sam frowned. "In North America they're called Awa-hon-do by the Abenaki. Shape-shifters who can assume the form of a swarm of insects for short periods of time." Sam closed his mouth suddenly. Jamie didn't need to know the rest of that, particularly right this moment.

It hissed at them, an odd skittering quality to the sound.

Jamie snorted. "That's…fun. Are they venomous?"

"No." Sam shifted his stance slightly. If the creature decided to form its alternate option, Sam was going to have a harder time controlling him. Without killing him, in any case.

Also, he was relatively sure the one standing across from him was some sort of half-breed, probably capable of doing something difficult with the wand hiding in his pocket, or whatever he was holding in the bag slung over his shoulder.

"Well, strange creepy insect guy, do you have a name?"

Sam almost closed his eyes in exasperation. "Jamie…" There was a limit to where that basic fear-less-ness would get him.

"As if I would tell you."

"Alright, Creep it is then." Jamie huffed. "Whatever it was you thought you were going to manage here, it's clearly busted because he showed up sooner than you were expecting." He pointed to Sam then.

He laughed, smiling unctuously. "You think because I am alone I am unprotected."

There was as stuttered flash behind them, and Sam didn't have to look to know who it was. He'd never have mistaken either Grace or Bazel for anyone else. He could feel the distortion in the room, the hum of Willow's presence. The reverb of Deke and Grace, the call and response of their wavelength.

"You assume it matters whether you are or not," Sam countered darkly.

Bazel stepped up next to Sam, frowning. "He's still breathing."

"My fault," Jamie offered. "I thought maybe if he was still capable of speech he might tell us something useful."

The creepy insect guy cackled, pulling something out of a bag slung over his shoulder. "That was your first mistake." He grinned at them, a softly edged white statue in his hand. "Tupelaq tupaksimayok!"

"Shit." Deke cursed behind him, voice fraught. "Bad…"

He smashed the canister on the ground, and Sam grabbed Jamie and jumped back several steps, getting him behind the only available cover with the rest of them as it grew quickly, magic crackling in the air.

"*That's* what he stole from Deke's strong-room?" Jamie panted, eyes wide.

Sam could see Jamie's face out of the corner of his eye, eyes pointed significantly toward the ceiling.

"Holy Crap that's big," Willow breathed. "What do we do with that again?"

Bazel's jaw firmed. "If we can wear its magic down enough it's possible Samriel and I can...deconstruct it."

Nate craned his neck around, edged against the side of the office structure, eyes flicked back into the window behind him with the pathological need of a seasoned hunter. "Do you have a plan for doing that that keeps anyone from being—"

"Torn limb from limb?" Curt asked lowly. "Also, why is it stuck to the ground?"

Bazel lazily flicked something over his shoulder. "What is it humans say?"

"I could tell you but I'd have to kill you," Jamie offered. "So can you answer Nate's question then?"

Sam added his own blend of intent to the spell—it wasn't what they were doing, but he wasn't in any position to start cataloguing the differences at the moment—Bazel was using to keep it stuck to the ground. "Bazel and I will focus on the tupelaq."

"And me," Willow interrupted.

"Willow—"

"Dad, take what you can get," Willy said darkly. "Anyway, we'll work on gigantor there, while..."

Sam glanced back over his shoulder, watching as the abaonwai tried to unstick his new pet from the floor. "We three will concentrate on the tupelaq, the rest of you try and deal with the abaonwai." He looked at Nate, frowning. "You know how to deal with that, right?"

"I know if I shoot him he'll fragment for a minute and he can't hurt us while he's a mass of insects. Otherwise pretty sure somebody has to take his head off."

"And he's a half-breed capable of magic, obviously," Deke offered, dryly.

An ominous cracking echoed through the space, the floor shuddering.

"What was that?" Nate asked.

"It's breaking." Bazel leaned around the corner. "You are swiftly running out of planning time."

Sam looked around them, swallowing. "Do *not* let the tupelaq get a hold of you it is—"

"Bad," Grace interrupted softly. "Got it. I think we're as good as we're going to get. Let's not let it have a full range of movement."

Bazel stepped out, nodding to them. "I will take the corner." He pointed Willow across the room. "Watch yourself."

Sam stepped out, and narrowly avoided a rather grotesque fist aimed at his head. It had a larger reach than he'd expected, but given the thing contained bits of multiple different animals and some things that weren't animals that wasn't a surprise. Even if one had seen a tupilaq before there was no gauge. They were all different, a product of the intent that fueled the original spell and the base materials chosen to create it.

Nate tossed a gun and a knife to Jamie out of his stash and while Bazel taunted the tupelaq Sam looked to make sure they were all out of the corner. Not that he wouldn't have rather they all stayed someplace safe.

Without the extra distraction for the tupelaq they had even less chance of this than normal.

Nate was clearly intending to swing around the stack of disused pallets and come up behind the abaonwai. But it noticed him and ran forward, obviously understanding the tupelaq wasn't in its control, and being trapped between it and Nate wasn't a good idea.

Jamie stood by Grace, gun at the ready, clearly intent on trying to keep her safe, and Curt was moving forward slowly to help Nate.

A blast of icy air pushed Bazel back into the corner and the tupelaq turned, large spindly hand grabbing the pallets and throwing them wildly.

Sam followed the trajectory, and opened his mouth to tell Grace to duck, before it hit her in the head—

Jamie grabbed her by the shoulder and forcefully hauled her out of the way, nearly tumbling them both over.

The pallet splintered and crunched as it hit the ground, breaking glass raining down across the room as another sailed through the high, small windows along the side of the warehouse. Deke moved forward, trying to avoid the broken glass and other things, and Sam checked to make sure Grace and Jamie were still on their feet.

He turned back and nearly cursed, dodging the tupelaq as it clawed out randomly for him and managed to get one foot completely off the floor.

Bazel blasted it, nearly reeling it around on it's one foot. "Deacon, MOVE!"

Sam looked over, heart stopping because Deke had somehow gotten between the tupelaq and the henchman.

Sam mentally reached out for one of the pallets on the floor and threw it at the monster's head, hoping to pull its attention away for a moment. Unsuccessfully, it shook its head once and turned toward Deacon.

At the same time the henchman leveled his wand at him, lips forming around some sort of spell. Before he finished a shot rang out, and the abaonwai managed to shift to a dizzying cloud of insects a nanosecond before the bullet connected.

Grace pulled a crystal out of her pocket, and pointed the end at the tupelaq, voice sturdy and calm as she shouted, and astral force of magic slammed against its head. It wouldn't hurt the thing, but it did disorient it long enough for Deke to run, getting away from them.

"Grace!" Deke huffed, grabbing her by the shoulder.

"You're welcome."

The tupelaq bellowed, angrily throwing the pallet across the room as Willow hit it with a rather spectacular blast of water.

She'd apparently inherited more from her mother than they'd ever discussed.

Deke pushed Grace out of the way, which was really more pushing her toward the half-breed practitioner and away from the giant nightmare, diving back between Willy and Bazel himself.

"Can you two focus?" Willy yelled. "You can bitch about her casting later."

Deke whipped around, eyes narrowing and throwing something small at the insect guy that caused him to almost trip. "I can do two things at once."

The tupelaq swung wildly, and Nate shot it. Likely just to annoy it, not that that was any more evolved than what the rest of them were doing at the moment.

Sam felt the wall behind him, and mentally tallied all the ways he could get out of that position without forcing the tupelaq closer to any of the rest of them. Losing his room to maneuver was not ideal.

Willy managed to freeze its feet to the floor, but it was less permanent than what he and Bazel had done, and less elegant. She shrugged at him. "Ten seconds is better than nothing."

"Conserve, Willow," Bazel yelled. "It's got a lot more to expend than we do."

Sam watched under its arm as the henchman pointed his wand at the fallen pallet closest to them and flicked his wrist. Sam screamed out a warning even though he knew it was too late, anger making him forget he was supposed to be focusing his fire on the tupelaq. He lashed out and hit the henchman with enough force he had to revert to his pile of insects. Jamie was laid out and still on the floor.

Sam stepped forward, and nearly growled when Bazel pushed him back to the wall.

"Don't be an idiot," he huffed, passing close, trading places while it was still pinned to the floor. "Grace has got him."

She did, throwing the pallet off him and over into a corner while she started dragging him back toward the unused space by the boxes and crates. Curt was standing with his back to the tupelaq, and when it took one giant sudden step forward Sam leashed it and pulled back as hard as he could, feet planted in the ground below him, feeling the cement floor of the warehouse crack under the strain.

He couldn't hold it back though. It was going to throw him off any second.

Willy hit it with the equivalent of a ten-pound ice-ball in the face, screaming at Curt to get out of the way, and then had to scuttle and duck off to the side herself when it tried to turn on her. Deke threw something at the henchman, to get his awareness off of Willow, that he countered back at Deke. He ducked out of the way and it smashed harmlessly against the back corner, another tinkle of breaking glass as those windows gave, too.

If the abaonwai hadn't turned right then Nate might have managed to sneak up on him, the way he'd somehow slipped around the back of the room and behind the tupelaq and the rest of them. He had to feint back, but unfortunately he was already against the wall and there was no-where to go. The henchman threw Nate's gun off to the side and wrapped his hands around Nate's neck.

Sam shifted to his side, because he knew better than to take his eyes off the tupelaq. It had a—probably intentional—ability to tell when they weren't paying attention to it. To sense any weakness and look for a way to exploit it. It was probably a large part of the reason it kept concerning itself with the humans and Willy.

As soon as he shifted to the side even a little it turned to him, ignoring another ice-ball from Willy and a charge from Bazel.

The other problem with a magical construct was that eventually its connection to the magic around it meant it grew immune to the same attacks. They kept having to come up with new things to throw at it, and trying to reserve their hardest options for when there was no other choice.

Sam was about to do that, to give it a good solid smack so he could blast the bastard off of Nate's throat because he wasn't thinking about what Grace was doing instead of watching her boyfriend. Jamie was fine.

Curt was lined up with a shot he couldn't take because if the abaonwai realized he was being shot he'd shift and the bullet would just keep travelling until it hit the next convenient thing, which happened to be Nate.

Sam raised his hand, words on his lips, and Nate managed to push off the wall—despite the hands around his throat—and kick the abaonwai someplace uncomfortable enough he let go. Curt flashed forward while it was incapacitated and pulled Nate back around toward the front of the building. Sam turned and intercepted another slam of something magical pointed at Willy, before trading her places and skirting along the front of the office. He slipped past Deke, keeping his eyes on the tupelaq.

"Grace…"

"We're good."

He watched out of the corner of his eye as Jamie came out, Grace already checking Nate's throat. "Made me wait while she tested my eyes," Jamie muttered, before he turned and threw his knife, unerringly slicing the henchman's arm, the noise alerting Grace he was close. "Watch what you're doing, Grace."

Bazel threw a large wave of energy at the tupelaq, trying to drain some of its defenses, and for a moment all of them froze, the sound and shudder of tearing metal and raining glass making them hold still.

"You do realize there's a limit to how badly this building can be hurt and stay standing," Deke said, eyes flicking away from the giant construct he was entirely too close to, and toward the gaping hole the ricochet had just torn in the corner of the building.

Bazel brushed himself off, panting quietly. "Have to drain it somehow."

The abaonwai moved forward, trying to back Grace into a corner. Sam reached out with a tether, pulling him back away forcefully, before trying to throw him into the tupelaq that chose that precise moment to get Willy effectively backed into the wall and—

"TAHAME," Deke shouted, wand erupting in purple fire that hit with enough force to nearly lift the building off the foundations.

Bazel and Sam both froze, shocked as the construct stumbled drunkenly and fell against the office structure, Willy scooting across the front of it and grabbing Deke, pulling him back away from the thing because after that much expenditure he should collapse.

He was still mobile, and Grace managed to get out of the corner, scooting around behind him, past the shocked, still henchman. The tupelaq stumbled to its feet, furious roar echoing off the walls loud enough Sam almost checked to make sure Jamie and Grace were alright. He was aware the henchman was behind him, and he almost turned to just to make sure he wasn't going to do something inconvenient—like stab him—when the tupelaq managed to get a hand on Bazel, throwing him against what was left of the office.

Sam reached out with everything he had and hauled the construct back, before it could get to Bazel again, stumbling back with it, trying to hold it into the chains.

"DAD!" Willy ran over, Deke on her heels.

"I'm fine." Bazel shook his head, crawling up. "Just a bloody nose."

Sam swung with the tupelaq, trying to pull it away from Curt without actively throwing it at Bazel, arms straining in the chains.

"Sam!" Grace screamed.

He ducked, loosening the chains and swinging to the side, a spell from the abaonwai narrowly missing his face. He turned, hand flashed out at him when Willy screamed, and he watched her catch the edge of the spell and tumble back against Bazel, rolling to the floor as he tried to take her weight.

The abaonwai edged toward the door, and Jamie got between them.

"I don't know where you think you're going."

"No!" Nate started running for him, because Jamie wasn't in any position to protect himself and he had a gun but that wasn't enough.

Sam watched the tupelaq turn, less than a full arm's length from Jamie, and narrow in on him, reaching out. Sam flashed across the room, knocking Jamie out of the way. He didn't let himself worry about the speed, or the force he hit Jamie with because at best he would bruise a rib. The tupelaq would have killed him.

A large, gangly clawed hand wrapped around Sam's chest and he threw all his focus into maintaining his form. He heard the sickening crunch of his ribs, felt something pierce a lung. It shook him, nearly jarring his teeth loose, and repositioned it's fingers to grip again.

Sam managed not to scream, but seriously started to reconsider the idea it couldn't kill him. Given what'd happened to him before *should* have killed him and it hadn't hurt as badly as being squeezed in half.

He saw Grace, behind the tupelaq, watched in slowed time as she reached into the bag she still had on her and pulled out the white statue they'd brought back from Deacon's. The fake. The tracer whoever was behind this had used to slip through Deacon's wards.

"NO!" Sam almost couldn't get enough air to scream, felt the sickening certainty in his stomach that he wasn't going to stop her.

Grace looked him in the eye, and he watched the magic glow in her fingers as she cracked it open and blew across it, her magic nearly crackling in the air around her as she poured everything she could into it.

The tupelaq dropped him, wheeling around, and lashed out for Grace magically. What was left of the electrics in the building crackled and sparked, the rest of the windows shattering, the smell of lightening and unimagined plasma heavy on the air.

Grace held the fake out in front of her, open side front, and took the wave.

CHAPTER 16

The warehouse was ten minutes from Deacon's shop.

Sam had passed millennia that were shorter than that ten minutes.

Grace was still breathing, but she was dangerously weak. Abraded in so many places he couldn't see them all, and possibly broken in a couple more because once the wave had hit the fake—or more appropriately, the bone of the creator the caster had used to create the fake—the tupelaq had just...

Well, it hadn't precisely just disappeared. They'd been lucky to get out of there before the fire-department showed up after the explosion. Bazel had managed a decent protection bubble around the rest of them, but he hadn't been able to do anything about Grace.

Deke kept assuring him they didn't need to take her to the hospital. That there wasn't anything wrong with her he couldn't fix with a couple of supplies he kept at his place and five minutes.

Jamie squeezed his shoulder, gentle because Sam wasn't in particularly good shape himself.

"You need to rest," Bazel said. Again. He'd said it three times before they made it to Deke's, and once while they were all getting through the door.

"Not until—"

"I need her to sleep to heal," Deke muttered. "She's not going to wake up for hours and there's *nothing I can do with you.*" He huffed. "And you look like hell, Sam, it's gotta hurt."

He looked at Deke, itching with the desire to back him against the wall and vent some of his frustration. "You and your designs about her casting are going to—"

"Fuck you," Deke snapped at him, without even looking. "I didn't tell her to do that. You know damn well I'm not going to do anything to get Grace hurt. Even if she wasn't attached to my best friend, and my girlfriend wouldn't tan my hide for that, my goddamn magic's tied itself to her." He pressed a gentle bandage to Grace's head, muttering for a moment, before he looked back at Sam. "And you know that, not that I don't understand why you're pissed. I'm pissed. If she'd made the connection she could have damn well *told me.*"

Nate laughed, short and amused. "Sorry, I thought you two were talking about Grace there for a minute."

Sam looked at him, blinking at the sight before him. Nate was bleeding from the corner of his forehead, and he had giant bruises blooming across his neck. Another bruise blooming on his cheek, and he was moving like he'd hurt a rib at some point.

Willy was steadily attempting to get her father to hold still long enough to clean the blood off his face, ignoring the scrape on her arm and the cut across her cheek.

Curt was holding himself unusually stiffly, standing at the coffee pot.

He looked at Jamie suddenly, eyes casting around. "Your head."

"I'm fine." He smiled weakly. "Ears might be ringing for a while, but I'm hard-headed." He frowned. "I'm a little more worried about you, given the fact you were coughing up blood for a minute there."

Sam looked back at Grace carefully and forced himself to settle into the chair. If he relaxed he would heal faster, and he knew that, but that didn't make it any easier. "Punctured lung."

Deke froze.

"It has healed itself already." Sam closed his eyes for a moment, twitching and starting to open them again.

"Rest," Jamie said softly, warm hand wrapping over his wrist. "Come on, I'm right here and I'm not supposed to close my eyes for a while. I'll keep an eye on Grace."

"You can't do that while you're staring at me," Sam muttered, trying to even his breathing and lose some of his tension.

"I'm multi-talented."

~*~***~*~

Sam didn't want to go to the council meeting area. Aside from the fact he wasn't entirely healed, and neither was Grace, and life was more than a bit concerning at the moment, he didn't feel like his mask was all that well connected. Like the instant one of them said something unhelpful to him he was going to just—

Do what Bazel had started to do several times now, and just lay into them.

They both knew better, not that that seemed to be doing either of them much good lately.

He didn't have a choice. The council had called him and ignoring that was tantamount to declaring himself turned. Certainly would have eroded whatever standing he had left with the council. He really should have been much more upset about how little of that there was left. For a very long time the only thing he'd had was his standing with the council.

Sam wouldn't say he'd thrown that away in the last year. Not just because that made it sound like Grace's fault. Arguably it had been happening since the day he found her. The first year, the time the council had officially assigned him to follow her every move hadn't injured him at all. It was after that, after they let him keep doing it but started to whisper Sam was overly attached. As time went on those voices got more and more prevalent.

Then Grace had turned eighteen and technically he hadn't needed to watch her any more. The council had more or less reassigned him and there hadn't been any way for him to buck that. But her family was still his, technically, and there wasn't any way for them to keep him from watching her as much as he was able given his other duties.

The rumors had started coming thick and fast then, and until he'd actually spoken to Grace there'd been a subtlety to it. That'd all gone, because as soon as a choice had to be made Sam had whole-heartedly chosen Grace. He wasn't going to regret that. He couldn't even feel particularly sorry about it. It might have alienated him from the council, but Bazel was still…whatever they were and if anything he'd grown closer to Malek.

Knowing he wouldn't change anything didn't make him feel any better about this summons before the council.

Bazel appeared, touching his shoulder carefully. At the moment they were the only two there, and Sam wasn't sure how badly this was about to go, but he was thankful for his brother's presence. "Malek is coming, though I believe he's waiting for once the meeting is technically in session."

"Do you know why I'm here?"

"We're discussing Tanik, and Azazel and what could possibly be going on. Losing two of our number in close succession is worrying. Even if Tanik was somewhat low ranking and Azazel was disgraced, the fact still remains."

"And I'm here because I was involved with both of those."

"Not…actively," Bazel said carefully.

"Though the fact remains," a still female voice joined them, before it's owner melted in. "These things do appear to be happening around you frequently."

Penemue commanded a level of respect out of Bazel that Sam had never really understood. All the female Maeleket were somewhat unique. Well, she presented herself as a female, in a human form, when it was convenient. When she'd been known by humans they had seen her as a male. For a very long, long time she had been revered as a being of nearly unattainable wisdom, revered as the one to teach humanity the art of writing.

Sam hadn't ever mustered the courage to ask if that was actually true. He, like any other Maeleket with a brain, gave Penemue a wide berth.

Her manifestation was beautiful, dressed in a traditional Sari. Nearly every time Sam had seen her it'd been draped in a different fashion. She was one of the only Maeleket he'd known who actually committed to a culture. Once, she'd been in charge of one of the most influential lines to ever have existed, one of the first lines to organize themselves as anything more than a group of humans. She'd accepted a certain level of their culture and apparently never left it behind.

"One cannot escape the fact you have at the very least been present during these occurrences."

Sam swallowed, and nodded deferentially. Scary as they all tended to find Penemue, he didn't at all equate that to her being untrustworthy. If anything, everything he'd ever heard of her led him to believe she was one of the few Maeleket other than Bazel and Malek he could actually hope for anything from.

He just wasn't keen to use that until he absolutely had no other options.

Before he had to come up with anything else to say, either in response to their current issues or any other kind of greeting, the others started to arrive. It was a small meeting today. Bazel, Penemue, Locif, Zerel, Josa, and Ananl. He didn't know any of them but Bazel well. Sam was relatively sure they were all so much older than he was it actually made *him* slightly uncomfortable. Bazel was, to the best of his knowledge, the youngest of them.

Malek arrived last, melting into the back and just pulling up a bit of cloud.

"Hello, Malek." Penemue frowned at him. "I wasn't aware you were joining us today." She cocked one regal brow high, dark brown eyes steady and direct.

"Penemue," Malek nodded deferentially to her. "You know I have a special interest in Samriel, and my distance from the council isn't out of lack of care for the rest of you."

"Eloquent as always." Penemue forced a smile. "We should begin."

Sam tried not to shift uncomfortably. The conversation wasn't going to be easy or pleasant, and he doubted he would enjoy it. But there wasn't anything to do about that. He was still a Watcher, and as long as that held true the council still had some sort of say in his life.

"What of his involvement with this human?" Ananl said, face tense and drawn. "Are we to be concerned?"

"I doubt it is a problem for us." Penemue frowned at him, looking down her nose at them. "The intent behind our concern was to discourage Maeleket from creating children with humans, because of the resultant issues." She lifted one brow again. "Not an issue Samriel and his human male are going to have."

Sam nearly bristled at the reminder that if Jamie had been female the council might have input some sort of control on their relationship. Not that they had a relationship, or that he had any real intention of them having a relationship.

"Yes, Maeleket having children is deeply troubling," Locif rumbled quietly.

"Maeleket having children for some sort of experiment should be concerning," Penemue huffed at him. "We have long discussed that the simple creation of a child through connection is not the same."

"To you," Locif supplied. "The rest of us feel this to be—"

"I know what you feel it to be." Penemue glared at him. "Tread carefully, Locif. Even among the humans my sex is not always considered a detriment to my ability to reason."

"Among your humans it certainly is."

"They are all my humans." She frowned. "I hold them all equally dear, not simply the ones I patterned myself after."

"Well stated," Malek smiled genuinely. "And I believe the concern of Samriel's relationship status is unnecessary."

"In that they are not in a relationship?" Penemue offered.

"In that it is none of our concern whether they are or not." Malek smiled. "We have greater issues to debate."

"I see no such debate," Josa said. "Samriel is not directly involved with these issues, or as such he is but he has not misbehaved. That was our only concern."

They talked themselves out of that quickly.

"The fact that these things are still occurring remains an issue," Penemue insisted. "Tanik was still killed. Samriel was seriously injured. Azazel, despite his issues with this body, was also killed. If there is some rogue Maeleket or whatever else operating in our environ it is definitely cause for concern."

Locif frowned. "Other than allowing Bazel and Samriel to continue their…investigation I do not see what else we could do about that."

"Assign them some level of help?" Josa offered dryly.

"I cannot imagine they would trust anyone the council suggests," Locif replied.

"I trust all of the council's suggestions," Bazel said carefully.

Malek beat Samriel to the skeptical huff there. "I do not."

"But you are helping them," Penemue asked, looking directly at Malek.

It amazed Samriel how comfortable and willing to push against Malek Penemue was. He knew they had dealt with each other. According to rumor Penemue was nearly as old as Malek was.

"To this point I've aided more with securing their own safety."

Several of the others in the room looked uncomfortable, as if the concept of Malek becoming more involved in their day to day running made them wary. Sam did understand where they were coming from. Even before the situation with himself and Bazel he'd understood Malek was one of those more prone to a certain level of experimentation. Both with the other Maeleket and with the humans. To the best of anyone's knowledge that hadn't ever crossed a line it shouldn't have—well, in full disclosure *creating his own Maeleket* might have been crossing a line—that didn't make anyone less concerned with what would happen if he slipped.

Also, Sam had always understood that Malek was stronger than the rest of them were, and clearly the council still worried about their ability to ride reign on him if they felt like they needed to.

"Then I suppose there isn't much for us to do at this time, but leave it in your capable hands." Locif smiled easily, and stood.

One by one the council members took their leave, some more warmly than others, until it was only he, Bazel, Malek, and Penemue.

"I do hope you know what you are doing," Penemue said quietly, arms crossing over her chest.

Malek smiled, standing next to Bazel. "You used to have such faith in me."

"I was younger then," she answered wryly. She looked between he and Bazel, and sighed. "Do let me know if you need anything."

Malek nodded, and she disappeared as well.

Bazel sighed, voice tired. "Why is it I always feel like she sees through every word that comes out of my mouth?"

Malek chuckled, slapping Bazel on the shoulder. "Because she does."

"You trust her," Bazel said, bald and serious.

"Absolutely."

"Why?" Sam asked, aware he was leaping into a conversation he wouldn't have gone near before. If Bazel was his brother and Malek was his father then he should be just as capable of holding a conversation with them as he was with Grace.

Malek looked at him, and for a second he expected a brush-off. Something wry and pithy before they went back to what they were supposed to be doing. But then Malek looked back in the direction Penemue had started walking, before she'd faded away, and sighed. "I have known her a very long time, even for us." He smiled at Sam. "Penemue is quiet about her motivations. Unless she is angry with you. If she has a problem, she tells you. It got her in a fair amount of trouble, when she was younger and she's learned to temper it. It's still there." Malek shrugged. "If she was involved in this, suddenly plotting against the council or...she would never do that in either case, but she would be much less quiet about it if she was."

~*~***~*~

"I would have thought you'd be..." Jamie died off, not mentioning Grace's house out loud, and sliding up onto the hood of the rusty old car parked next to the house.

Sam felt his muscles tighten, felt himself lock down because he didn't know how to do this. They weren't in a relationship and beginning one was a horrible idea. He knew that. Intellectually knew he shouldn't be there.

"Or not," Jamie muttered.

He didn't know what to say, which meant they just sat there on the cold vehicle and watched the steely gray clouds move over-head while they day got steadily colder and colder.

"I'm supposed to be giving finals week after next," Jamie said suddenly.

Sam glanced over at him, out of the corner of his eye. He sounded strange. Not forlorn, but distant. "Do you miss it?"

Jamie blinked at him. "Teaching, or having a normal life?"

"Either." Sam swallowed.

His nose wrinkled, looking off in the distance and thinking. "I don't know. I wouldn't be anywhere else. Even if you and Grace don't need me exactly." He shrugged, smiling at Sam. "I'm not signing up for what she and Nate do. I told Nate, I can't stand car trips, and the small-town America thing isn't my favorite either."

Sam swallowed. "We need you." He frowned. "Why would you ever think we didn't need you?"

"You don't need me for this," Jamie said drolly. "It's fine Sam, I understand that. I'm not much against even the general stuff and definitely not against—"

"No." Sam huffed. "It isn't about whether you are an able fighter. The nature of magic means Grace needs you here, because you are her closest tie and her ability to access that is affected by contact with you."

"But Nate and—"

"It isn't as cemented." Sam looked away, breathing. "I wouldn't presume to try and decide whom she cared more about, she has cared for you so much longer than anyone else."

"It's not about more, I don't think," Jamie said softly. "I don't think it works that way. That whole saying about how the human heart is boundless. I think you've always got more space for love."

Sam nodded, because that was definitely something he'd take Jamie's word on. He didn't really understand the 'human heart' because quantifying something like that wasn't one of his better skills.

"What about you?"

Sam blinked at him. "Me?"

"You." Jamie's brows knit together. "I said I was here for both of you and you told me Grace needed me." He swallowed. "But there was a 'we' up in there somewhere. Which makes me think you're not tap-dancing around you *not* needing me."

"Tap-dancing?"

"Sam," Jamie huffed, unimpressed. "I'm not asking for…anything. Other than that I'd like to know what you're thinking. You said you shouldn't have kissed me, and you look—"

"The council said they were not watching us because you are male." Sam frowned, looking up at the sky. "And that makes me feel…wrong."

"Okay, my brain goes to the 'homosexuality is wrong' connotation there, but I don't think that's what you mean."

"No." Sam looked at him, biting his lip. "It means the opposite. It means as long as a Maeleket is attempting a relationship with a human male everything is fine."

"Ah." Jamie winced. "But if I'd been female and we could possibly have children then…" He wrinkled his nose. "Yeah, that's actually kind of shitty." He shifted, frowning. "What about if you were female?"

Sam blinked at him. "There are very few female Maeleket." He flushed. "As I said before. It's…complicated. They are not unheard of."

Jamie cocked his head to the side. "Is that because you don't naturally have sexualities but you all went male because of the human power dynamic?"

Sam shifted uncomfortably. "I do not actually know any female Maeleket. I have met several, but I do not know them well enough I would begin asking questions about them."

"I would imagine they're attractive, given what the rest of you look like."

"How would I gauge that? I have only ever…" Sam flushed, brain catching up with his mouth. Because something like that wasn't something he wanted to share thank you.

But of course Jamie realized what he'd been about to say. He smiled, looking away, shoulders tense. "Sam…"

"Jamie?" Grace peaked her head out of the house, breath fogging in the cold air. "Oh…sorry…"

Jamie rolled his eyes at her. "What's up? Did you need something?"

She bit her lip. "Nate was looking for you. Something about you offering to help him with something."

"Oh." Jamie slid off the hood of the car. "Yeah, I did." He shot a look at Sam, eyes full of promise, because apparently they weren't finished with that conversation.

Sam nodded, because he didn't have anything else to do and clearly he wasn't going to be allowed to avoid it, and watched Jamie walk into the house, shutting the door behind him.

He was debating going back in the house. The cold wasn't a problem for him. Obviously he felt it, because as he'd said before it would be a rather giant marker of how abnormal he was, if he didn't. The door opened again, and he looked up as Grace slipped out into the cold evening, hooded sweater unzipped, hands sunk deep in the pockets. She picked her way across the cold ground, before taking Jamie's spot on the car.

"Well, at least he kept it warm." She huddled down against Sam's side, brushing her nose against his shoulder. "What's up?"

Sam looked down at her, words trembling on his lips. *For the first time in my life I do not know what to do with a personal problem. Jamie is…here and he obviously cares for me and my feelings for him are not insubstantial but there is no way for us to have a human relationship. I have seen the human conceptualization of creating a relationship with an immortal being and I cannot make him immortal or myself mortal and that leaves us at an impasse I am not going to successfully ignore for the entirety of your lifespan.* "Nothing."

Grace cocked a brow at him, unimpressed. "Sam…"

He looked away from her, staring at the dry brittle ground in front of the car. They would have to go in soon, it was too cold for her to be outside. The last thing he needed right at the moment was for her to come down with a cold or something similar.

"Come on. Give me a little credit." Grace knocked their shoulders together. "I can tell when you're lying."

Sam wasn't particularly surprised by that. He'd never gotten the hang of lying. Never seen the point in his previous encounters with humans. Clearly his own people lied just as frequently as humans did. Or they were capable of it. Someone was lying about their involvement in the current issues, and Malek had lied by omission for years about his relationship with Sam, as had Bazel.

Clearly that was one of those things just he was unskilled at.

"Just because…" She paused, swallowing. "Just because it's about Jamie doesn't mean you can't tell me."

"I wouldn't want to put you in the middle."

"I know." Grace looped her arm through his, squeezing him tight. "But you can tell me what you're thinking without doing that."

Sam frowned, watching her. "Did he tell you?"

"Tell me what?" Grace sighed. "You're both being really quiet. I can tell there's something there because I'm not completely blind, and I know what Jamie's like when he's…" She stopped suddenly, forcing a smile. "But he hasn't told me anything. He won't, because the concept of his asking me for relationship advice is a bit laughable."

"But you know that is what he would be asking for."

"No." Grace watched him, steady and quiet. "No, we just covered I don't know anything. I'm guessing." She frowned suddenly. "You know I'm not gonna be disapproving or anything, right?"

"No, I know you are understanding of Jamie's sexuality."

"Yeah, that," Grace muttered. "And also I love you and I want you to be happy."

Sam looked away, chest squeezing. He was beginning to think it wasn't the excess time in his manifestation making his reactions more severe than he was used to.

"Is it the council?"

"No." Sam shook his head. "Jamie is male, they have no issues."

"Alright." Grace nodded. "There's totally a story there that's secondary to this present conversation so I'll just roll right on past that." She forced a smile. "I can't imagine Malek or Bazel have an issue."

"They do not."

"Nate and I are cool, and you wouldn't care about anybody else's opinion." Grace frowned. "If you thought Jamie was going to hurt you you'd be much more actively attempting to avoid having this conversation with me."

Sam choked out a laugh. He knew Grace had an internal misconception, that she was bad at reading people. In his experience that applied more to their reactions to her, than it did in the general. All the analytical reasons behind a person's actions tended to make sense to her, as long as they weren't about her. Which meant he didn't have much chance of extricating himself from this moment.

"So I'm a bit blank on where that leaves us."

He stared at his feet for a long second, wind whipping through the trees around them, night steadily closing in. Grace waited, patiently allowing him to marshal his thoughts.

"It is more complicated than..." Sam pushed a hand through his hair. "I cannot make him immortal, nor do I think he would take it even if I could offer. I can...twist myself into appearing to age with the rest of you, and I would happily take whatever years he could give me."

Grace blinked back tears, eyes wide and earnest. "Okay."

"There are things I could never tell him, because he is human and..." Sam's voice dropped low.

"And normal people get upset by that?" Grace finished for him.

"One thing I have learned from generations of watching humanity?" Sam forced a smile, shrugging. "A romantic relationship is no place for secrets."

She frowned, settling in next to him, brows drawn in concentration. "I don't think that's true."

Sam cocked a brow at her.

"Sure, you have to...share all the things you're supposed to share. But there are things..." Her nose wrinkled. "Secrets you keep from...everyone." She looked at him then. "I think if someone loves you they understand that. At least in my experience they do."

"Nate."

Grace nodded, smiling slightly. "Thing is, sometimes he's curious. Half that time I can see him forming the question before he just...stops."

"Why?"

"Because he loves me, and he trusts that I'll tell him when I can, if I can. That poking at certain things isn't helpful." She sighed. "And a lot of that is just Nate. He's always been that way, more apt to make concessions for something he thinks is there than make me talk about it." She zeroed back in on him, cheeks pinking a bit. "The point to all that is, maybe with people without so much to conceal that's true, that they feel slighted and it becomes a problem."

"Not us?"

Grace bit her lip. "I've known Jamie since I was basically a baby, and he knows a hell of a lot more about me than even *you* do," she said softly. "I'm not going to pretend there aren't things I've never told even him. And he knows that, but he doesn't push. And he's never, that I can think of, thought that meant that I didn't trust him, or didn't care about him." She knocked his shoulder suddenly. "And maybe you and I haven't been speaking as long..."

Sam scoffed, smiling.

"I don't insist on knowing all your secrets." She frowned suddenly. "Though this conversation sort of makes that a lie."

"You're concerned and I'm obviously struggling, it doesn't count."

She laughed softly. "Something like that. I trust you. If I can handle it, and Nate can handle it, and whoever else you'd tell things to. You shouldn't assume Jamie can't just because you'd like to…"

"*Please* do not finish that," Sam said, clapping a hand over her mouth. "Grace Cleary, there is absolutely nothing I want to hear out of you that even *alludes* to sexual behavior."

She smiled, all pixie fire. "I was *going* to say 'be with him' but it's nice to know where your mind is."

His cheeks heated, and he huffed.

"Alright," Grace rolled her eyes. "I was going to change it to 'be with you' before it left my mouth. Better?"

Sam laughed, folding her into a hug. "You are spectacularly impossible."

"I do my poor best." Grace squeezed him, sighing. "Just…maybe now's not the time, because we're up to our ears in…junk. I still think—"

The particular guitar chord that heralded Grace's phone echoed around them, and she instantly stopped and looked at it.

"Isn't that Deacon's ring?" Sam said, freezing.

"Yes." Grace swiped her thumb across the screen, holding the phone up to her ear. "Deke, you're freaking me out here. You never call."

CHAPTER 17

Jamie tried very hard not to stare at their newest addition. When Sam had said the female Maeleket were different he'd never pushed for a better explanation than that.

But she felt different. Just standing in the room across from him she felt different. And maybe a little of that was that she did a better job of looking freaking terrifying than Sam or Bazel ever had. Or that she was staring at Grace like she was some strange little thing.

"I will not harm her," Penemue said stoically, watching Jamie.

"I didn't think you would." Not really.

She cocked a brow at him. "You were shifting nearer, to protect her."

He frowned, and looked at the distance between he and Grace, and he had subtly shifted closer, apparently. "Sorry. Subconscious."

Penemue frowned, cocking her head to the side. "I do not understand. You know what I am. What do you imagine you could accomplish?"

"Probably nothing," Jamie shrugged slightly. "It's instinctual."

"Because she is your First." Penemue nodded.

Malek appeared suddenly, eating up half the left-over space in the kitchen. "Because she is Grace and Jameson is devoted to her." He smiled, and kissed Grace on the cheek. "Willow and Deacon are coming, and Bazel."

"But she is sleeping with the hunter," Penemue said, eyes transferring to Nate. She sighed. "Even after all this time human interactions make very little sense to me."

Grace choked out a laugh. "Join the club."

The others popped in then, and Willow glanced around them. "What club is that?"

"The 'people don't make sense' club," Grace said, hugging her in hello. "You look chipper today."

"It's raining in Chicago." Willy shrugged.

"So, this is the girl-child," Penemue watched her for a long, uncomfortable moment, before melting into a smile. "I'm quite pleased to meet you, dear. Your grandfather has told me everything of course." She nudged Bazel slightly. "She's wonderful. Lucky you."

"Th...thank you." Willy swallowed, shoulders tense. "Dad said you'd been...working together a long time."

"I've been on the council longer than he has, yes." Penemue nodded. "And of course there was that whole distressing incident when he was a child."

Bazel froze for a moment, everything locking down.

Jamie knew exactly what that was. He'd seen a lot of that in his life. Child-hood trauma that wasn't as adequately dealt with as you thought it was.

"What incident?" Sam insisted, looking at the other Maeleket.

"It is not important," Bazel countered darkly.

"Of course it is important," Sam snapped. "If you have a weakness whomever this is will exploit it, obviously. And you already have Willow—"

"My daughter is not a weakness!"

"Yes she is," Sam didn't back down, didn't let it go. "Just as Grace and Jamie are mine, and you've forced me to deal with that, as you should have."

"Deal with that?" Grace questioned, dangerously.

"Admit it," Sam back-pedaled. "Take what precautions I can to protect you."

"Your brother is right, Bazel." Penemue watched him, eyes warm. "In theory no one, but myself and your father, are aware. But it would be best to tell them, I think. So there are no nasty surprises later. Do you think they will think less of you?"

Bazel froze for a long moment, hands wrapping over the back of one of the chairs, and drew a deep breath. "There was an incident before Samriel was born. Somehow, I don't know how, I lost control over my manifestation. Possibly because I never had it to begin with, because I was...young."

"Equate young to human years," Grace prompted softly.

"Six?" He glanced up at her. "Eight maybe. I completely and utterly lost control. Luckily Penemue found me before any of the rest of them did, and managed to help me...control until Malek came. At the time they thought it'd been intentional. That someone had issue with me and they'd realized I was wrapped into my form differently than normal, and decided to pull at things."

"But it didn't work, and they didn't try again," Grace offered.

"Penemue and I kept an eye on him nearly constantly until it was no longer an issue," Malek said easily. "It was traumatic, it would be suddenly and completely losing control over one-self."

"And the worst someone is going to do with that is taunt me with it," Bazel stood, shoulders settling.

Sam grumbled. "I'd like to see any of them deal with having their manifestation ripped out from under them, at any age. It is not pleasant."

Jamie cocked a brow at him, because there was something under that.

"Yes," Malek winced. "I never doubted you would understand, Samriel. Just because you weren't a child at the time."

"So." Jamie coughed into the silence. "Not that this isn't a fascinating conversation. I'm relatively sure we're all here for another reason."

Penemue watched him, before nodding slightly. But it didn't feel like agreement, it felt like approval, and Jamie didn't know what to make of that.

"I trust Penemue completely," Malek said easily. "And as such I've told her what we know so far. And she's come up with a plan." He grinned, eyes sparkling.

"As I've always been rather careful about throwing my lot in with Malek, I believe if I spread a rumor we may be able to draw this into the light in a way that dealing with it will not create a giant death-toll."

"How?" Bazel asked, frowning.

"Do you know what a touchstone is?"

Deke blinked, leaning back away from her. "It's a magical construct, that you bind a group of people's...essence into to cement their magical bonds."

"Construct as in the giant bits of animal thing?" Jamie asked.

"Not like that." Deke shook his head. "It's an actual stone, not a bunch of animal parts. A lot of families have one floating around somewhere, and every generation they...reconnect with it."

"Why?" Willy asked, frowning. "Wouldn't their first basically be that?"

"Because you don't always live in the same house or the same town even as your first, the way they would have hundreds of years ago, so that bond isn't as strong," he answered.

Penemue nodded. "Which is what makes it logical that you would be looking into the creation of one. Clearly you have been adopted into Grace's line, but I doubt they know that."

"How would they not, if you do?" Deke asked carefully.

Penemue smiled. "It is not the reverberation that passes between you while you are charged—when you are in danger and likely to need to cast—that tells me how attached you are. Any two people with ability chosen to ally in a fight will create that subconsciously, wherever their other ties lie."

"Because they need it to keep themselves alive," Willy offered.

Penemue nodded. "Conversely, the instant the danger has passed their bonds will go back where they belong." She cocked a brow. "You are not in clear and extreme danger at the moment, and yet you're tied so closely together you're practically glowing. Never mind how deep your secondary bonds go. I know you do not need a touchstone, and it would at best do minimal good." She shrugged. "I doubt very seriously they've seen you all in calm surrounds. Perhaps they've seen Samriel, or Bazel but separated only the strongest tie appears."

"Sam appears attached to Grace, and Bazel to Willy, but that doesn't say anything about the rest of us," Jamie clarified.

"Something like that, yes. So, I will tell someone in confidence that Samriel has informed me his First is going to create a touchstone with people she is not related to by blood—not something we normally encourage—and I've assured him it is no problem."

"Why?" Bazel frowned. "We don't encourage them to do that because it's generally a prelude to inappropriate things."

"Simply put, Grace has no other family and we think the extra connections will better ground her. Get her magic under control a bit."

"Which makes her less of a risk," Deke said seriously. "I can see the point there."

"Yes well, you've all managed to do this instinctively so as to remove it from the problem category. I know that, and Malek knows that. The rest of them don't. Yet."

"Deke." Grace sighed. "Did I adopt you without your permission?"

He flushed. "Um…it wasn't…" He rubbed the back of his neck. "My family magic is more or less worthless for anything other than healing. I realized what was happening but then we were sort of up to our eyeballs and that connection was making it so I could actually manage decent combat spells. And the more I let that go because it was useful the less...cut-off I felt. It's pretty hard to resist when you don't actually want to. You're my first now, even if my family pieced itself back together."

"You are a rather unusual clan." Penemue looked intrigued. "Two Nephete, two and a half Maeleket, and a handful of humans." She frowned at Malek. "Well...for now in any case."

"I'm rather excited to see what you all get up to." Malek grinned. "So. Penemue will tell them you are going to create a touchstone, and we will set the stage. It needs to be done someplace decently removed from people anyway so that will be helpful."

"Outside or in?" Grace asked, eyes distant.

"Oh lovely, Grace already has an idea. Outside is preferable." Malek clapped his hands together. "I do so love Grace's ideas."

Jamie nearly groaned. "You haven't been around for as many of them as I have."

Grace elbowed him. "Relax, at least nobody's going to get backed into a corner this time."

~*~***~*~

Jamie was down in the basement to get a book for Grace, and any second he was going to get on that.

He'd known Sam was in the house, helping Nate and Curt resupply. The humans weren't a whole lot of good against the Maeleket—weren't any good at all against them actually—but Malek had assured them he had a plan for getting their rogue Maeleket dealt with once it was out in the open. No, what they needed to be prepared for was anything else their new friend decided to bring along. Because 'out in the open' was a relative term, and however it finally removed them from the equation it wasn't going to show itself quietly. There was nearly guaranteed to be at least one more henchman hiding in a corner somewhere.

He'd tripped down to the basement to grab a book and he was going back to help Grace finish faking a touchstone. Except Sam was hanging out alone in the basement, elbows planted on his knees, just staring at the floor between his feet.

"So I'm a weakness then?"

Sam looked up at him suddenly, eyes zeroing in on him by the stairs, shoulders tensing.

He really hadn't meant to start there, but now that it was done.

"You're human."

That was supposed to be an answer to why he was a weakness, but he actually sort of thought that was most of their problem. Jamie was human and Sam was still panicking. "I am. Imperfect and flawed as I am, I realized that."

Sam frowned. "I have never implied that you were—"

"No." Jamie moved forward, pushing a hand through his hair. "No. Sorry. I know you haven't." He huffed, frustrated. "You also haven't actually *talked* to me in ages."

"Jamie…"

He waited, thinking maybe Sam was going to marshal something to say there. Tell him what he was thinking. He got that Sam wasn't experienced with any sort of relationship, really. And he absolutely wasn't wondering about what that mean about…other areas of his experience because this, right here, was complicated enough without chucking extra shit on.

But Sam didn't say anything. Just went back to staring at the floor.

"I'm pretty sure I've already said, at least once, that I can't read your mind."

"It would break—"

"Sam." Jamie clenched his hands, struggling for some sort of control. "Don't…don't be pithy with me. I'm trying here. Because I care about you and I thought we were going somewhere. If I was wrong, that's fine. Just tell me you don't want a relationship."

"I never said that."

Jamie dropped his head into his hands, huffing out a sigh. "You've never said anything. I'm getting a little tired of trying to bridge the gap blind."

"Then why are you?"

"Because I care about you, you *ass*." Jamie took the last couple of steps toward Sam and hauled him up out of the chair, reeled him in close and kissed him. "Because even if it's not enough, if I'm not enough I still—"

Sam kissed him hard, almost angry. "Do not *ever* even imply you are not 'enough' to me."

Jamie felt his back hit the bookcase, Sam pressed down his front, eyes stormy and dark. "Well then tell me what the hell's going on, Sam. You kissed me, and damn near vaporized some asshole for giving me a skinned knee, and... Is it really that hard to just tell me what you're thinking?"

"I don't know what I'm thinking!"

Jamie grabbed the hands fisted in his shirt, about to push him off.

"No." Sam closed his eyes, head dropping forward. "Just..." He swallowed. "I don't know what to do. I have no clue what the right step is and..."

"Sam?" Grace called from the top of the stairs.

Jamie dropped his head back against the case, and nearly groaned.

"Yes?" Sam instantly let go of him, and stepped back.

"I think I'm inventing words here," she sighed. "Can you come help please?"

"Yes." Sam turned, and started for the stairs. He glanced back at Jamie, eyes dark and unreadable, but in the end he headed for the stairs without another word.

Jamie thunked his head back against the bookcase, blowing out a breath and closing his eyes. There was a point he was going to have to stop this. No matter how

much of a mess Sam was, constantly throwing himself at
the other man because maybe they'd get it right this time
was pretty damn unhealthy, and likely going to cause all
kinds of other problems.

"Don't bang your head against the bookcase too
much." Malek said, startling him.

Jamie grabbed a hand on the bookcase, willing his
heart to steady. "Jesus Christ."

"I apologize." He smiled, eyes warm and sad. "I didn't
mean to startle you. I forget you aren't as accustomed to
the unusual as the rest of them."

"Sure." Jamie swallowed. "Did you…need
something?"

"No." Malek settled himself into the chair Sam had
been sitting in, comfortable and easy. "Have a seat,
Jamie."

If he'd thought 'no' was really an option he'd have
legged the fuck off. But aside from the fact Malek was
ancient and faintly scary and capable of popping his head
like a grape without much more than a passing thought,
he was Sam's dad.

Jamie dropped himself into the other chair. "Did you
hear that?"

Malek shook his head. "I'm going to tell you
something my children don't actually know."

His blood froze, heart stopping.

"I can feel when they are hurt or emotionally
charged." Malek glanced at him. "I didn't have to hear it,
to know Sam is…conflicted."

"And you're here to set it straight for him?"

"No." Malek gave him a quiet, fatherly smile. "No,
you're both adults. You deserve to work things out on
your own."

Except they weren't. They were chasing around in
goddamn circles.

"And I know you understand how…scary this is for
him."

"That's not an excuse."

"It's not," Malek agreed.

"So?"

He smiled. "I've known Samriel his entire life, obviously. I'm his father. Emotion has never come as easy for him as it has for Bazel, no matter how hard he reaches for it. His relationship with Grace is no sort of card for that."

"Because she's the same way."

Malek nodded. "And your relationship with Grace took years to forge, to grow into each other and find your corners." He cocked a brow. "Even by a human timeline you and Sam—"

"We've barely known each other, really, for two months. I'm not asking him to *marry me*. I'm not asking him for anything, except to tell me what he's thinking."

"Which is the hardest thing for him to give," Malek offered quietly. "Especially right now, when everything is sideways and he's rather consistently worried about getting yourself and Grace out of this alive. All of you actually, I don't blame him for that."

"Because they're so closely bonded he'll have to feel her grief."

"Because you're all so bonded poking a hole in that is going to be hard on all of you. Most especially on Grace, because as First she's taking responsibility for protecting all of you. Even Sam and Bazel and Willy." Malek laughed softly. "I must give the girl credit, she doesn't do things by halves."

"And if that does happen?" Jamie asked softly, because he wasn't stupid. Of course he was afraid of the answer.

"The responsibility Grace takes as First is nothing to the responsibility Sam has as her Warder, or Bazel has as Willy's father," Malek said softly. "They will both jump through faintly ridiculous hoops to uphold that, and I will do everything I can to protect them, and the rest of you."

Which wasn't any sort of promise of success. Knowing they were all going to try their best didn't really make him feel better, it felt a bit like mutually assured destruction.

Still, Jamie nodded and let it drop because there was only so much of this that wasn't just talking around in circles.

"Don't give up on him, or yourself," Malek offered softly. "Faith is a curious thing."

Jamie looked up at the ancient being across from him, and frowned. "I have a question."

"I most likely have an answer."

He snorted. "Why are you so much better at human interaction than the rest of them are?"

Malek smiled, eyes going distant. "That, Jamie me lad, is a story for another day. Grace is looking for you."

He frowned, about to say he wasn't stupid enough to believe that, when her voice echoed through the house, calling his name.

"That's just…creepy, so you know."

Malek laughed, shaking his head. "It fun being a bit creepy sometimes. Go on, I'll find that book for you."

~*~***~*~

Before Jamie met Grace he didn't really believe in things like ghosts. Actually, to be fair, even after he met her he didn't really *believe*. He believed Grace, because he'd promised to, and when you made a promise you should keep it.

But standing in some old field, crumbling chimney off to his left, gnarled dead trees surrounding him, he might have re-scripted that anyway. Place was seriously freaking creepy. "So…you've started a list of strange, freaky places to hold rituals then?"

Grace stuck her tongue out at him. "So what if I have? I'm a witch."

"Remind me to buy you a broom next Christmas," Jamie muttered.

"Oi, let's leave the late-Christian prejudices at the door, please," Deke huffed.

"Sure, tell me where it is."

Nate snorted, finishing the chalk painting he was doing on the large stone in the middle of the clearing. "It's like they're surprised we're mouthy."

"They?" Grace muttered. "I'm never surprised when you're mouthy."

"You're never surprised," Deke said darkly. "That's not the same thing."

"Oh, I don't know." Grace looked up at him. "I'm standing in some old field pretending to do a ritual so I can lure a malicious not-angel out into the open and do…nothing about that actually…Not really any of that that's predictable." She shrugged. "Maybe I'm surprised a lot and I just hide it well?"

Jamie laughed, shaking his head, because he'd seen Grace really and truly surprised *once* and she hadn't hid it well at all.

"Shut up." Grace muttered. "You don't count. Whatever you've just remembered—"

"Jane." Jamie grinned at her. "I remembered Jane, and pretty much anything she did."

"Jesus…" Grace shuddered. "The stolen snake, or the somehow managing to out-drink half the freshman class, or still managing to post a 4.0 and transfer to Harvard on scholarship?"

"That." Jamie laughed. "And that night we came back from the library and she was…entertaining the star of the football team."

Grace laughed softly. "God, he didn't know what hit him. I haven't thought about Jane in ages."

"College roommates are fun," Deke muttered.

"Jane was alright, minus being absolutely insane." Grace shrugged. "She was pretty constantly shocking though, it probably desensitized me."

"She stole a snake?" Nate asked, voice low.

"Yeah." She snorted. "From the biology department. She gave it back eventually; it kept escaping and trying to eat the neighbor's chinchilla." She stood up, stepping back from the stone. "Alright, that's done."

"Ready to start this?" Curt moved their supplies to the outer edge of the circle they'd made. "I'm not sure there's much point in pretending we're not prepared. Once they're here they're going to realize it's a front."

Grace nodded. "Probably. And I'm ready."

They took their places, all of them ranged around the circle. Grace was closest to the stone, and there was an order this had to happen in, apparently. He didn't really understand this, even though they'd explained it. Presumably his part wouldn't matter. Since he was the closest tied to Grace—not really a surprise, given how long they'd been close—he would be the last one to deal with the stone. As they were only faking it until whomever their bad guy was showed up, it was doubtful they'd get to him.

He felt the spark when Grace started the spell, and it made his skin crawl. Once when they were in high school the science teacher had let them play around with a Van de Graaff generator. The other kids had enjoyed themselves, shocking each other and making their hair stand up. Every time Jamie touched it he felt like his back teeth were vibrating. Felt wrong and…disconnected. He'd decided right then and there he never wanted to get anywhere near electrocution. The concept of any sort of open power source was seriously uncomfortable.

The fact the open power-source was Grace was the only thing that kept his feet planted where they were supposed to be. He could feel it building, as she started the chant. Jamie was happy to be just your garden variety human. Theoretically he could do some of these spells—sometimes the objects one used were what made the stuff work, not so much the person doing it. Curt explained it as the same way Curt could run an exorcism—on low level things the fact he didn't have a magical bone in his body didn't matter if he had the will to pull it off.

In comparison Grace could manage something serious with the wrong spell, if she was well grounded enough for it.

She'd spent most of the last two days trying to make sure she wasn't accidentally going to start something while they were waiting for their little friend. He seriously hoped she'd gotten it right. It certainly felt like she was starting something.

Except it needed to. How else were they supposed to get attention?

"My, my, my." A soft, sinisterly urbane voice floated across the clearing, its owner appearing off to his left. He was tall, and thin with almost white blond hair and ice blue eyes, and utterly, achingly perfect to look at. Down to the immaculate light gray pinstripe suit and matching silk tie.

"Locif." Bazel, standing next to him, growled and shifted to face their new friend. "I should have known."

"Tisk tisk," Locif waved a negligent hand. "As if you could have."

An eerie skittering sounded, and Jamie turned back to the center of their clearing, a woman he'd never seen before zeroing in on Grace. Sam gently pushed Jamie closer to Grace, before edging toward Locif.

"Grace dear, you've never met Malerice, I suppose in some way you two would be cousins."

Malerice hissed, baring sharpened teeth. A soft wind made the tattered and threadbare black cape she was wearing bustle around her like a living thing.

"Distant cousins, of course." Locif smiled brightly. "Now, now girls, do play nice."

There was a flash, and a strange pop, and Deke took a giant step back, staring horrified at the creature that'd just sprung into being was. Jamie didn't know what the seven feet of evil and ugly was across the clearing from them, but he was betting it wasn't good. Malerice looked like she'd like to forgo the magic and just rip Grace's throat out with her teeth.

Whatever Malek's plan was, he hoped it was a good one.

"You know, I do have to give your little Grace credit. I really thought that tupelaq would do for you. Or at least her. Clearly I underestimated her." He grinned, and pulled a giant, ornate silver sword out of nothing. "And if it hadn't been for your connection to her I would never have realized we could influence their abilities. It'd never occurred to me to create a connection."

Sam growled softly. "So glad to be of help."

"Gracious." Locif shook his head. "She's even taught you how to back-talk. The things I could have done with you. Oh well. I suppose it'll be nice to finally remove you from your head."

He started to charge forward, and Jamie was a step toward...

Well, he didn't actually know what he was doing with that. Rushing to Sam's aide was about the stupidest thing he could do. If Sam couldn't protect himself about the only aide Jamie was going to give was getting himself killed as a diversion.

Grace grabbed him by the shirt and towed him further toward her, a non-verbal reminder that they all had something to do here, and if he wanted to be helpful he needed to stick with her.

"You…" Malerice pulled a wicked looking knife out from under the cape, holding it by a long wooden spindly hilt. "It's all your fault! My family was respected once, part of the Rus line, we would have been the greatest there was until your ancestor kicked us out for being too dangerous!"

"Are you kidding me?" Grace breathed. "How long ago even was that?"

Her monster straightened to its full height, hands working anxiously, chaos black eyes watching them.

"What in the hell is that?" Nate shouted, grabbing his trusty crossbow.

"Bad." Deke shouted, throwing something to Willow. "That is bad. Holy crap."

Jamie felt absurdly like someone pressed a giant red button, and everything started at once. Locif hit Sam with a mighty clang, and later he was going to ask Sam if he had just *envisioned* his hand with a sword in it, or if he'd always had one hidden somewhere, because that was what they were doing. Having a sword fight.

Malerice shouted words, things that sounded Russian and strange, and Jamie could actually see them tinging off Grace's protections, see the shield around her neck starting to glow brighter with every successive hit.

Stay with Grace, Bazel had said, finding him alone in the kitchen the night before. *The most help you can be to any of us it to stay as close to Grace as you can.*

"I've waited so long for this," Locif called out gleefully, as he and Sam passed behind them. "Do you know that, Samriel? Nearly six-hundred years. I thought I'd finally set everything in place, and everything was ready to go and then you found her again."

Sam almost stumbled. "It was you."

"Yes." Locif laughed. "Are you surprised? Azazel was my second hand from the beginning. That stupid girl didn't trick him into anything, it was always planned." He deflected another hit from Sam, huffing. "And then she was there, and you were so infatuated with her…I rather hoped that you would actually cross those particular lines as it stood, that would get you out of my way nicely. Both of you. So easy to make it look like an accident." He huffed. "But then you were so…broken I rather thought it didn't matter."

Sam screamed, charging Locif, knocking him back into a decaying stone wall, nearly knocking the sword from his hand.

"Have I hurt your feelings, little boy?"

Nate yelled, startled, and back-pedaled over the top of the touchstone, trying to get away from the night-terror that was scratching him again and again no matter what they did to it.

Jamie watched one of those clawed, wrong hands reaching for Nate, and he was about to shoot it even if it wouldn't help—it might very well piss it off and focus it on him, but on him was better than it slicing Nate's throat open—but then Bazel blasted it with something that slowed it down for a moment, long enough for Nate to get some distance between them.

Curt shouldered him out of the way of their moving sword-fight, stumbling them across the clearing, behind Grace and Nate. "Focus on what you're supposed to be doing. Sam can take care of himself."

"I'll kill you," Malerice screamed, throwing her knife at Grace, with some sort of spell.

Jamie barely caught her, hands pressing to her back, praying that shield was going to hold and protect her. It kept most of the spell out, knocked her back off her feet, and Grace ducked away from the blade of the knife, hissing at a slice on her cheek before it winged its way back to its owner.

"Sam..." Grace gasped, eyes wide.

Jamie looked over, freezing as Locif's blade sunk into Sam's shoulder, pressing him against the bole of one of the dead trees.

"I'm going to enjoy this," Locif said darkly, face bright. "If only I could tie you here so you could watch. Do you know what I'm going to do to your little pets, Samriel? Which would it hurt you more for me to kill first? Of course, you'll already be dead, but I don't mind. You can die knowing what's going to happen because you couldn't protect them."

Sam moved suddenly, planting a foot in Locif's chest and kicking out, even though it ripped the blade out of his shoulder as Locif stumbled back.

"Grace!" Deke grabbed Curt by the shoulders and moved him away from the creature, ducking away from a spell. "I need you and Willy to keep her focused on you!"

Grace shook herself, and crawled to her feet.

"If she's focused on you, she's not dumping extra energy into it," Deke said, grabbing her wrist and pulling her further away from Sam. He looked at Jamie then, eyes dark. "She needs you to watch her back, Jamie."

"Got it," He nodded, cocking his gun, watching Bazel kick Locif away from Sam before they could reconnect.

He did try, but the truth of the matter was, as long as he was standing there next to Grace she didn't need him to do much else, and Bazel and Sam fighting with Locif was like a train-wreck happening right next to him. He couldn't look away, not for any length of time.

"You!" Locif tried to blast Bazel with some sort of spell, but Bazel spun out of the way of it. "I knew you would be trouble. Did you tell them, how weak you used to be? I nearly killed you, and I didn't do anything more than take your shell away."

Bazel's eyes narrowed in fury, shoulders tensing.

"Yes, little boy, it was me." Locif grinned. "Did you cry? You were a strange, eldritch thing. I've never understood why they cared for you."

The monster reached for Willow, and Jamie and Curt both shot it, hitting it in two separate points. It hissed, and the bullet holes smoked and glowed, but really it only looked angrier.

"Why?"

"Because it should be mine!" Locif screamed, the entire clearing echoing around him. "I am tired of pretending to be a protector. These creatures don't need protection, they need an exterminator! Dirty, stupid little things, and we *serve them*."

"We protect them!" Bazel yelled back. "Because they are still children and—"

"You're as bad as Malek," Locif growled low. "I'll take care of him next, don't you worry."

Locif knocked Bazel's blade off to the side, and sunk his own into Bazel's stomach, pushing it all the way through, until he was kneeling, leaned back at the other man's feet with a hand on his shoulder. "Say goodbye, *e'haset.*"

"Bazel!" Sam screamed, body leaned to charge in.

CHAPTER 18

"Release my son!" Malek thundered, appearing at Bazel's elbow bleeding power like a super-nova.

Suddenly the clearing was full, and Penemue and several others were there as well. She spun Locif to face her, glowing ropes springing around him and binding his arms to his chest, the others following suit.

"Take care of Bazel, we have him," Penemue said as an aside.

Sam glanced back, to make sure Grace was focused where she was supposed to be, watching as she did something to lock the witch in place, watched the girl blanch and start to lose her concentration, before he turned back to Bazel. Malek gently removed the blade from Bazel's chest, and pressed his hand to the wound.

"Just like I taught you, focus on your form, you can do that," Malek whispered. "I've got you son, it's okay…"

Bazel closed his eyes and glowed brightly for a bare moment, before he was…fixed. "Sam's shoulder is hurt."

"I'm fine," Sam muttered. "I'll heal, I didn't let him stab me through the middle."

"I'm sorry, sword fighting isn't one of my better skills but you didn't seem to be doing particularly well." Bazel looked at Locif then, eyes hard. "All of…he tried to kill me, and he purposefully ruined Sam's family and… Why?"

"Because you were in his way," Malek said softly, standing and turning to watch the Council finish tying Locif up.

"No!" Locif screamed, thrashing around, eyes wide and crazed. "No, I will—"

"You will listen!" Penemue shouted, voice vibrating with fury. "I appeared here with every intention of laying the crimes at your feet and sending you away!" She forcibly calmed herself. "But clearly you have hidden them too well. We will lay the charges before you once we have them all. For now, you are banished to the Sallow Fields for the self-confessed crime of sabotaging a family under the auspice of the council." She looked at the other council members. "Do you all agree?"

"We do."

She nodded. "Very well, we will—"

She barely avoided the tree that chose that particular moment to sail past her head, and Sam spun around, heart thudding in his chest.

They were all right though. The witch's familiar was powerful and problematic, but so far Nate and Deke had stayed ahead of it while Grace and Willow tried to deal with the woman. Sam tensed, ready to jump into the fray.

"No." Malek placed a hand on Sam's arm. "I know you want to help," he whispered, "but you know what your duty is. Reserve your help for when they need it most."

Particularly when the entire council is watching you.

It was…hard. The witch skittered out behind whatever Grace had been doing, to lock her in place and sever the connection with her familiar. She cackled happily and lined up on Grace again, when Willow smacked her with something harsh.

"Grace," Willy yelled, excited. Her eyes glowed bright blue as the water from the ground crawled up around the witch's feet, toward her knees.

"Do you think you'll drown me, bitch?" She laughed, tossing her head back.

Willy snapped her wrist to the left and the water instantly turned to ice. "No, I think I'll make you stay in one place. Now Grace."

Sam couldn't help his smile of pride, as Grace, from twenty feet away, etched a protection rune in the ground underneath Malerice's feet that caused her magic to lose its connection to her familiar. She thrashed and screamed, but nothing happened.

"My." Penemue swallowed.

"Grace is clever," Malek said easily. "People forget that at their peril."

The familiar stopped, shaking its head. Without the connection it had no direction, no impetus, but it wasn't any less dangerous. Eventually it would be just like the tupelaq, and simply turn to wanton destruction. Sam opened his mouth, intent on telling them what they needed to do.

But, of course, Deke knew what he was doing.

"Cut its head off!" he shouted at Nate, panting with his hands on his knees because he'd just poured a serious amount of energy into locking it into place. "You have to release it!"

"NO!" Malerice screamed, struggling in vain.

Nate snorted, and borrowed Sam's large blade to slice its head off, wincing away from the magical explosion.

"Well. That was anti-climactic," Nate muttered, looking at the small scorch mark on the ground where it had been.

"Speak for yourself," Bazel said dryly, taking Sam's sword back. "I got run through with one of these things, Sam's got a giant hole in his shoulder."

Sam watched as one of the council members took possession of Malerice as well.

Grace let out a sigh, and collapsed onto her knees, one hand steadying her before she face-planted on the ground.

Sam rushed over, but Nate and Jamie were already there, Nate grabbing her shoulder.

"I'm fine," Grace panted, leaned forward, just breathing.

Willy collapsed next to her, just laying out on the ground. "Crap, I don't know how. I'm not fine."

Deke laughed softly, dropping next to Willy's hip. "We're all fine, just a little exhausted."

Bazel picked his way over and dropped a kiss onto Willy's head, squeezing Deke's shoulder. "Once we're finished on our end I'll come say hello." He sighed. "Would you like me to send you home, or to Curt's?"

"Home sounds good," Willy said, wincing as she stood again. "Unless you need something Grace?"

"A bed," She muttered, letting Curt haul her to her feet. She looked at Sam, eyes steady. "You better come say hello too, once you're done."

"I will." Sam nodded, and hugged her carefully, avoiding his bloody shoulder.

"And let someone fix that, it looks painful," Grace muttered.

Sam nodded. "I'll send you three back with Curt, if that's what you want."

They all nodded. Jamie was watching him, and he wasn't enough of a coward he wouldn't even look at him. Not that he had any real way to discuss anything at that moment.

"She's right, that looks like hell." Jamie frowned at him. "Sure you're okay?"

"I am." He pushed out a sigh. "Malek has very good timing."

Jamie almost smiled, nodding. "If I'm not still there when you make it back…"

"I'll find you."

Jamie nodded, and stepped back. "Alright. Good luck."

Sam nodded, and concentrated on sending them home, before he did his duty by the council.

~*~***~*~

Whatever concerns Sam had had, over the long-range effects of Locif and his plotting against the council, he hadn't been even remotely prepared for what actually happened.

"We have so many new recruits I don't know what to do with them," Ananl said with a tired sigh. "Malek, I know why you don't generally help us with this, but I honestly don't have anyone else I can ask who exists on the 'completely trustworthy' list. I'm about to start begging. Someone needs to cull out the ones that actually have any business being watchers from the ones who feel like they should be just to prove they don't agree with Locif."

"Not to mention we're having to look at everyone who's had contact with Locif during his time on the council," Penemue muttered. "He's right Malek. We're not asking you to take over. We need assistance."

Malek sighed. "Very well. I'll look into the recruits." He took the scroll with their names. "You know the humans have vast, incredible ways of storing information that aren't these stupid things."

"Then change it," Ananl answered. He rubbed the back of his neck. "We've missed a great deal. That is a separate problem, and I'm not sure it's one we can deal with at the moment."

Sam thought that might have been a case of too little too late, but he wasn't going to say it. His position with the council was precarious. He'd rather failed at 'following orders' there for quite some time. Mostly because he'd intentionally worked it around to being Bazel responsible for giving him orders and that was just as backward and unuseful as one would imagine.

Malek sighed. "Very well. And then Penemue said something about needing everyone at a council meeting."

"We're going to formally charge Locif, I think we have everything now," Penemue said darkly. "It's rather a large charge, and we may need evidence from you three." She flicked a glance at Sam. "Have you been to see your charges yet?"

"No." Sam blinked. "I haven't had the chance."

Penemue nodded. "Be swift, we'll hold for you."

Malek patted him on the shoulder. "Say hello to Grace and Jamie for me."

He nodded, and shifted himself to Curt's. Maybe he should be seeing Grace first, or Jamie, but Nate was outside and alone and less complicated than the rest of that.

"Hey." Nate grinned at him, pausing with his work on Grace's surprise.

"It's coming nicely."

"It is." Nate dropped his tool and stretched. "Wasn't sure when you'd be back."

"I'm..." He cleared his throat. "It's only to say hello. I have to go back."

Nate rubbed the back of his neck, nodding. "Yeah. Grace mentioned she thought we'd probably see a little less of you now that things weren't quite so insane."

Sam almost laughed. "Is that the word?" He shifted, looking up at the house. "I'll..." He'd what? Come as often as he could? Try harder?

"I'm pretty sure we all understand it's not by choice," Nate said softly. "No worries Sam, it'll be alright."

He nodded, swallowing. He didn't have to ask where Grace was, or Jamie. He could feel them both in the house. Grace was in the library with Curt, and he went there next because he was stalling, because he was an idiot, basically.

Grace grinned at him, hugging him tight. "You look much less bloody."

Sam leaned into the hug, feeling her presence leach into him. "I did clean off. Not just for you, Penemue said I was assaulting her senses."

Grace laughed softly. "I bet."

"I can't stay long, they're waiting for me, for a meeting." He flushed. "And I don't know..."

"Yeah." Grace forced a smile. "Don't be a stranger. You're still my Watcher, aren't you?"

"Technically." Sam nodded, and pulled her into another hug. "Even if I'm not, I'll be back as soon as I can." He kissed her forehead. "Even if they say I'm not, they can't keep me away from you even if they wanted to."

"K." Grace nodded. "Have you talked to Jamie yet?"

"No." He almost winced, aware Curt was across the room pretending not to listen. "He's packing."

"He has to be at work on Monday," Grace said wryly. "Something about improperly handled classes that wasn't his fault, but now that the crisis is over they need him, so…"

Sam nodded. "I suppose I should send his things home, since I brought most of them here."

"I'm driving him up tomorrow, I need to take some things to the shop for Willy anyway." Grace shrugged. "But you can always offer."

Or just talk to him, Grace's eyes said.

Sam nodded, and popped himself into Jamie's doorway. Except he was still being a giant coward and he wasn't actually in Jamie's doorway. He watched for a moment he didn't really have, while Jamie piled his clothes into a duffel bag, along with a couple of charms and things that had Grace's signature all over them.

"Planning on standing there long?" Jamie asked without turning around.

Sam phased the rest of the way in, frowning. "How did you even…I wasn't actually here yet."

Jamie looked back over his shoulder. "Maybe not entirely." He turned back to his stuff, cramming another sweater in the bag. "Everything okay?"

"I don't know," Sam burst out, actually agitated. He winced. "Sorry. That was…" He huffed. "I've been given a moment to check in with all of you while the council is waiting for me, for the final…wrap-up?" He rubbed the back of his neck. "I don't actually know what they're doing after that. Bazel's been…quiet, because whatever use we've been he's obviously been telling me things he's not supposed to."

Jamie turned then, almost smiling. "Just one thing after another, isn't it?"

Sam nodded, swallowing. "So. Grace said you have to go back."

"I do." He looked back at his things. "I should. She's fine and you're busy, and I feel co-dependent enough without completely ignoring my own life when no one is about to die."

Sam frowned, because most of that didn't make sense. If you cared about someone shouldn't you do everything you could for them? He'd have dropped everything in the universe if Jamie needed him.

"So, this is goodbye?" Jamie prompted quietly.

"No." Sam frowned. "I can't imagine I won't see you again. Grace—"

"For now," Jamie sighed, wincing. "I didn't mean forever. Sorry. I'm not good at this. You're still busy and I feel like I'm wasting your time."

"You're not."

Jamie cocked a brow at him.

"Well…you're not wasting it." Sam huffed. "You're taking it, but it's…fine." He flushed. "Grace said she was taking you tomorrow. Did you want me to…" He waved his hand, motioning sending Jamie's things back.

"No." Jamie shook his head, smiling sadly. "I need the time driving back, after being in each other's pockets again I'm not ready to just zap back to my life."

Sam nodded. "Of course."

"Thanks for the offer though."

Sam stepped back. "I should go. They're waiting on me."

"Sure." Jamie smiled, pawing a hand through his hair. "Good luck. You know where to find me, if you need anything."

Sam watched him, tall and proud and clearly swallowing the eight million things he wanted to say.

There were words crowding his head, things he wanted to say as well, but the council was waiting for him and it wasn't good to keep them waiting. They might have had a point, about his adopting the mortal fascination with time. It was uncomfortable and fleeting and…painful.

He wasn't sure he could give it up.

"You as well." Sam managed, voice thick, before he nodded and popped away.

~*~***~*~

The list of Locif's crimes was so long Sam lost focus in the middle of it. He could have pretended he was losing focus because he was angry. Because Locif had decided he disliked Sam, that Sam was a threat to his plans, because Sam wasn't ever going to sit back and let him take over the Maeleket and jettison the humans—because he wasn't, and he was sincerely worried that any of the rest of them would have let that happen—so he'd broken Sam's family to try and shake him loose from the council.

If he and Bazel hadn't been so close it might have worked, he supposed.

He didn't miss the main point of all Locif's plotting. To use the blood of a first and a whole host of other questionable magic to kill off Malek and the rest of the council. Every time he thought of it he shuddered. Just the fact he'd plotted it was disturbing enough, whether he could have pulled it off or not.

The general consensus among the older members of the council was that he couldn't have. That perhaps they weren't tied together the way a coven would be, but they were capable of using their talents in conjunction. More importantly, they didn't any of them have an honest accounting of what Malek was capable of.

Sam wasn't always entirely sure *Malek* had an honest accounting of what Malek was capable of.

"Locif, the council finds you guilty of all these crimes, and sentences you to indefinite imprisonment in the Sallow Fields. Several of the Council members have suggested you be punished further and taken back to the place of happening and forced back through the veil between dimensions. We have only opted not to do this because we do not yet understand what will happen to you if we do. It is possible you will not die, and simply become someone else's problem."

Locif thrashed around in his little cage, still bound into his manifestation. "Let me go! I will—"

"You will shut up or I will change my vote!" Penemue shouted, voice shuddering with power. "Guards, remove him to his punishment. We are washed clean of him." She waved a negligent wrist, and visibly collected herself while they took Locif away.

Sam watched the fuzz of power as they left the realm and sincerely hoped he never saw Locif again.

"Now then." Penemue shifted, sitting carefully on her cloud stool.

She was gaining a feel for dramatics. Or she'd always been that way and Sam had never noticed. Either was possible. She was clearly coming out of all this as a more central member of the council than she'd been before.

"We find ourselves with a rather distressing hole in the council." Penemue paused, looking over the rest of the council members. "We are short a member at a time when our work-level has increased badly, and we need to fill this post quickly."

"Is there any chance we could convince Malek?" Josa asked softly.

"No." Penemue frowned. "I didn't even bother to ask him this time. He won't, he never does." She sighed softly. "I suppose at some point we're going to have to accept that he's right not to." She looked around them. "He's helping us a great deal more than we can legitimately expect as it stands."

Malek smiled wryly, sitting off to Sam's side. "You're welcome."

Penemue shot him a friendly glare. "In any case, I believe given our time constraints and the recent issues, we should elevate Samriel into our vacant place."

Sam blinked, heart stopping. "What?"

Malek laughed at his whispered shock.

"He is old enough," Zerel said, looking at him thoughtfully. "And he has done quite well with all of this."

"There is the concern of his relationships," Ananl input, twirling a blond mustache.

Penemue frowned at them. "What concern is that of ours?"

"His connection with Grace Cleary is unavoidable." Ananl conceded. "And we've all stayed in touch with families at some point, even when they were no longer ours." He wrinkled his nose. "His connection with the human male is inappropriate for a council member. You know as well as I do Penemue we must hold the most focus for our duty to the council."

Josa sighed. "Given our possibilities I suppose it's the best option we have." He nodded. "I agree."

The others said the same, nodding to Penemue.

"What do you say, Samriel?" Penemue asked, watching him closely. "Are you ready to take a place on the Council of Watchers?"

CHAPTER 19

Jamie rinsed his glass in the sink, phone pinched between his ear and his shoulder, listening half-heartedly.

"So." Aunt Rhoda sighed. "Are you ever going to tell me what's wrong?"

"Nothing's wrong," Jamie insisted. He closed his eyes, wincing.

"Jameson Nathaniel—"

"Aunt Rhoda." He sighed, rubbing the back of his neck. "It's...nothing. All taken care of. Grace had a...personal thing and I helped her take care of it."

"And that's why you're so unhappy?" Rhoda asked darkly. "Because I don't believe that. Whatever personal thing Gracie had, that girl's the happiest I've ever heard her in her *life.*"

"She is." Jamie smiled, scrubbing his thumb at a spot on the counter.

"You're not feeling left behind, are you?"

He looked up at the spotty rain, gray light filtering through the windows. "Maybe a little. I like Nate, and he's good for Grace." He cleared his throat. "Just haven't spent that much time with her in ages."

"And you miss her, I understand that," Rhoda said easily. "You two've always been connected. You know I've never known anybody who didn't wonder when you were going to wind up together."

"It's not like that."

"I know." Rhoda sighed. "It never was. And I've never been sure if that was for the best or not. At least if you'd had each other like that you might not have felt so lonely."

"Grace isn't lonely, Rhoda. She's happy with Nate."

"I know she is." Rhoda huffed. "I meant *you* might not have felt so lonely. As in just my nephew Jamie. I don't doubt Grace is happy, and I don't doubt you're happy for her. But you're not happy."

He really wasn't.

"It's…" He swallowed, about to come up with some way to explain that he'd stupidly gotten attached to someone he shouldn't have and—

The doorbell rang, and Jamie dropped his head forward.

"Aunt Rhoda, somebody's at the door. Listen, I'm…fine. Just a little in the dull-drums today, with the rain and everything. I'll talk to you next week, okay?"

"Alright," Rhoda answered. "Take care of yourself, love."

"I will." He smiled, and hung the phone up, looking at it for a minute before he left it on the counter and walked to the door. "Coming." Jamie puffed out a breath, and unlocked the door, opening it. "Sorry I was…" Jamie stared at the form on his porch, voice strangling in his throat, heart beating erratically in his chest. "Sam."

Sam shifted tensely on the porch, worrying his lip between his teeth. Sam looked tense and uncomfortable, and just because Jamie was freaking out a little he looked to make sure Sam wasn't bleeding anywhere.

Sam cleared his throat. "Can I come in, please?"

"Yeah." Jamie stumbled back from the door. "Sorry, I just didn't expect you."

Sam moved past him, into the middle of the house, glancing around himself.

"Is everything…" Jamie rubbed the back of his neck. "I don't want to make it sound like the only reason you'd be here is if there was something wrong, but…"

Sam looked at him, eyes almost panicked. "They offered me a seat on the council."

Jamie ignored the twist in his chest and forced a smile. "Congratulations. Are you—"

"I told them no," Sam said quickly.

"You told them…" Jamie blinked at him. "You told the Council, as in the people who are…creepily scary and in charge of everything, no."

Sam nodded.

"Why?"

"Because I don't want to. Well, I suppose I don't actually have anything wrong with the concept of being a council member other than the proposed workload and their habit of being faintly obnoxious about actually doing anything," Sam said quickly, not looking at Jamie. "And they do rather need the help so it's possible they wouldn't be impossible about me and all of that I just—"

"Sam!" Jamie choked out a laugh. "Slow down, my ears don't go that fast."

Sam looked at him, eyes almost panicked. "Sorry."

"It's…fine. So you told them no even though you wouldn't mind…"

"I don't want it," Sam said softly. "I want you."

He blinked, heart stopping, and tried to convince himself he'd actually heard that.

"And I can't…You are mortal and I'm not and I cannot…change either of those things and there are things I will never be able to tell you and I'll have to keep some secrets because I *have* to and as I've told the council no I'm not sure what sort of job I have at all anymore and—"

Jamie grabbed him by the shirt, pulling him into a deep kiss. "Jesus, you think too much."

Sam blinked at him, shocked.

"I get that you can't tell me things." Jamie didn't let him go, kept him close and tight. "I just got off the phone with Aunt Rhoda and I was doing an abysmally bad job at lying about you, by the way and…I understand sometimes you don't tell people things because you're protecting them." Jamie swallowed. "And the immortality thing is a bit strange, I grant you." He smiled wryly. "If you want me I'm yours, Sam. You're the one going into this knowing there's an end-date. I don't think I'm vain enough to actually care that someday you're going to still look thirty and I'll look sixty. At least not today."

Sam relaxed, air puffing out of him and burying his face against Jamie's shoulder, just holding him tight. "Don't be stupid, I can make myself look sixty just as easily as I can make myself look thirty."

Jamie laughed softly and wrapped his arms around Sam's waist, kissing his temple. "Then we'll make the rest work."

EPILOGUE

Jamie looked up at the house, grinning. "So. Are you falling apart yet?"

"Shut up," Nate muttered, sitting next to him on the picnic table.

"She'll love it," Jamie said easily.

"She better." Deke slipped out the front door, shutting it securely behind him. "And by the way, that's literally everything we agreed to do before we showed her. If you're done panicking."

"I'm not panicking."

"You so are," Jamie said, laughing. "You're giving your girlfriend a house, you're allowed to panic."

"About that." Nate flushed. "I...did something and it didn't occur to me until now that I should have talked to you about it."

Jamie sat up, grinning. "Is this the part where you ask me for permission to marry my best friend?"

Nate glared at him. "No. It's not freaking eighteen-fifty."

Jamie snorted. "Just checking."

"How did you even know I was—"

"Dude." Jamie bent an unimpressed look on Nate. "You're giving her a surprise house."

"He has a point," Deke offered, leaning back with his elbows on the table to look up at the house. "At least the outside of one."

"I'm seriously rethinking about putting a room for either of you in there," Nate said darkly.

Deke snorted. "Too late now, you're stuck with us."

Jamie blinked at him. "You…"

"You and Sam." Nate flushed, rubbing the back of his neck. "And it's not like I expect you to live in it or…whatever." He shrugged. "It's always there."

Jamie hugged him, squeezing tight.

"Yeah, yeah, it's not that big a deal."

"God you're painful sometimes," Jamie said darkly. "You better be happy she's in love with you."

Nate smiled, soft and thoughtful, completely smitten.

Deke shot him a dark look. "They're going to be insufferable for the foreseeable future."

"Ha." Jamie snorted. "I'm the only one who's other half knows about this little thing. You're all gonna choke me with cute."

"Speaking of…" Nate frowned. "When was Sam bringing them?"

"Any minute now." Jamie stood up, dusting himself off. "He and Curt were walking the girls through the path, blindfolded obviously. What did you tell Willy?"

"That Nate did something ridiculous for Grace, and did she want in on the surprise part." Deke smiled. "And she did, because you're adorable."

Nate made a face at him.

"And then Sam'll bring the food out and we'll all freeze our asses off and eat in front of your new house," Deke said to Nate. "It's under control, just worry about your part."

Bazel popped in then, with Malek. "Oh good, we didn't miss anything."

"You didn't." Deke smiled. "Except Nate panicking."

"It's a big thing for Nate, a little panic is allowed," Malek offered easily.

"Thank you."

"Alright" Sam called. "We're coming."

Jamie stepped back at watched Sam lead Grace and Willy into the clearing before the house, and pass them over to Nate and Deke.

"So." Nate swallowed.

"You are ridiculously nervous about this," Grace said darkly.

"I am." Nate pushed out a breath. "Ready?"

"Yes?"

"Did you mean that to be a question?"

"Nate…"

He laughed softly, and pulled the blindfold off for her. "Surprise."

Jamie wrapped an arm around Sam, pulling him close, while his best friend blinked in shock at the pretty little yellow farm-house in front of her. Well. It wasn't little really. Sort of giant.

"That…" Grace swallowed, clutching onto Nate. "That's a house."

Nate winced. "Yeah, the outside of one anyway."

"The…" Grace wrinkled her nose, swallowing again. "Nate…I can feel the wards. Did you build me a house?"

"Sam and Deke and Jamie all helped," he said honestly. "Deke keyed the wards and stuff, and Jamie's pretty handy with a hammer, actually."

"You built me a house," Grace said, voice soft. "You built us a house, obviously, because the wards aren't just reacting to me, so…"

Nate rubbed the back of his neck. "What do you think of it?"

"What do I…?" Grace coughed. "Are you kidding me, it's gorgeous. I'm sorry, I'm just a little shocked by the fact you *built me a house*."

Jamie laughed softly. "She'll get over that in a minute, just give her a second."

"I'll get to you in a minute," Grace said, mock threateningly.

Sam wrapped his arms around him. "I'll protect you."

Grace drew a deep breath. "The house is…lovely and perfect, I can tell from here, and given the 'outside' comment I'm guessing the inside isn't done yet and that's

kind of a big job but it's not like I'm going to complain."
She swallowed. "Am I allowed to ask why?"

Nate linked their flingers together, looking down at
their hands. "You told me once that sometimes you have
to make your own happiness." He looked up at her, eyes
meeting. "I thought maybe it might make a decent
engagement present."

Grace blinked at him for a second, eyes wet and dark
before she tackled him in a hug, kissing him seriously.

"Is that a yes?" Nate managed, smiling brightly.

"Yes." Grace nodded seriously. "Yes, I'll marry you,
and yes I love the house."

Jamie settled himself against Sam, grinning, and
kissed his cheek. "I love you, have I mentioned that
today?"

"You have," Sam said easily. "Several times, but I
don't mind hearing it again."

"Did Nate tell you he made us a room?"

"No." Sam smiled brightly. "But it's not a surprise. It's
a family house."

"And we're family." Jamie nodded. He leaned in and
whispered in Sam's ear, grinning evilly.

"I'm absolutely not going to ask what you just said, I
don't want to know," Grace said, tackling him in a hug.
"Thank you."

"Hey, he'd already started before I showed up," Jamie
said, but hugged her tight anyway. "I'm happy for you,"
he whispered, squeezing her again.

"I know." Grace looked up at him, eyes bright and
warm. "Me too."

Jamie grinned. "Do I get to be the maid-of-honor?"

Grace rolled her eyes at him. "Don't be absurd,
somebody's got to walk me down the aisle." She kissed
Sam on the cheek then. "You two get to be the parents of
the bride."

Willy grabbed her then, begging for them to go look
at the house because she wanted to see the inside, and he

could feel Sam watching him, but he didn't have any clue what sort of expression was on his face.

"You look like you can't decide whether to be horrified or burst into tears," Sam whispered.

Jamie choked out a laugh, falling against Sam. "We are *not* the parents of the bride, she's only a year younger than I am."

Malek wandered over then, clapping him on the shoulder. "Weddings are strange things, I've always thought."

Jamie watched him wander away and had to swallow twice. "Sam…you guys don't do…marriage ceremonies, do you? Not like…I don't know, ancient rites are always like…"

"Are you afraid you'll have to trade your goats for me?" Sam asked, voice dry.

"I would, absolutely, but…"

Sam shook his head, laughing. "We don't, and even if we did…" Sam blew out a breath. "I'm not sure I want to introduce your aunt to my father. Ever."

Jamie laughed, remembering the twenty questions Rhoda had put them to when he'd finally taken Sam for supper. It'd only helped a little Grace and Nate were there. "We're going to have to tell her eventually."

"I know." Sam looked at him. "But in the same room, at a serious function?"

"They're both going to be at Grace's wedding, I'm sure."

"Grace's wedding is not *ours*."

"You have a point."

They'd get there someday, maybe. Jamie was strangely okay with exactly where his life was right then. Maybe it was short, and strange, but it was his.

ABOUT THE AUTHOR

Body and Soul is *J*.M. Beal's forth full length novel, and the last in a three-part series about modern magic and monster hunters.

J.M. grew up in a small town in the Midwest, concocting elaborate ghost stories themed around the dilapidated Victorian mansions, abandoned zoological parks, and deserted frontier forts that populated her childhood.

She insists her childhood home was *not* haunted.

Most of the people who visited disagree.